TWINKLE TWINKLE LITTLE WEASEL

By Robert H Page

FORWARD

The first volume of this trilogy, 'Bang Goes The Weasel', told the story of how, in a few short weeks, Annie Montgomery's life had transformed from her being a young, defenceless victim to an accomplished murderer; serial killer if you are being precise. Her apprenticeship had been short, but she had learned a lot from her master. And when she had the knowledge and experience she needed to embark on the next phase of her life, she turned from a caterpillar into a butterfly, consuming her master in the process.

This is the continuing story of Annie Montgomery. It shows how life goes on, whatever is thrown at you. To move upwards you need to re-invent yourself, accept new challenges, hone your skills and meet your goals. This next stage of Annie's life will see her learn new skills whilst assuming new identities. The common thread is the trail of death and destruction that follows her. But this isn't all that is following her. She must run quickly and use her guile and charm if she is to evade the bird of prey that silently swoops down. When you play with the big boys you have to accept the consequences.

If you haven't yet read 'Bang Goes The Weasel' then you really need to read that book first!

PART 1

CHAPTER 1

Ricci knew his days were numbered. There was nothing he could do to save himself, but he might be able to spare his family's lives if he did the right thing. He stopped running and hid behind a large oak tree and listened. He could hear voices around three hundred metres away, or so he reckoned. They were getting closer. He had little strength left. He was extremely tired and now running purely on adrenalin. He knew he couldn't go much further. Heading into the forest had seemed a good idea at the time; but now he knew how hard it was to hide in a place like this, not like in the movies. The ground was hard, the trees were dense, but he struggled to find somewhere large enough to conceal himself from the two guys that were hunting him down.

The worst thing was they wouldn't kill him. Not here. They'd take him back and interrogate him until they found out what he'd done with the letter. But he didn't know where the letter was. He'd given it to his contact and the very next day the contact was dead. He had no idea what had happened to the letter or even if it had also been destroyed. Whichever way he looked at it he was fucked. When they didn't get the answers they needed, they'd turn to other means. They'd probably get his wife Angeline and tie her up next to him and then rape and torture her. When she was broken, they'd cut off her fingers and toes. If she lived long enough, they'd cut off her hands.

He started to cry. Warm tears rolled down his dirty face. His gun was still clutched in his right hand. He had six bullets in the gun that morning, but he'd already fired four – was it four when they had jumped him in his car? He had no option but to jump out and run for his life. He had hidden behind a wall, which was where he had discharged his shots, then run for his life into the forest where he was temporarily concealed. Once they reached the wall and got over it, they could see him in the distance as he entered the trees. They had fired a few shots at him, he had no idea how many, as it was a blur, then he had run for what – thirty minutes? Probably a lot less but it seemed like more. He wasn't unfit but he wasn't a marathon runner either. So, now, here he was, hiding behind a big oak tree. The two guys who were tracking him were now getting closer and it was only a matter of time. He knew it was now too late to leave the sanctuary of his tree and run once again as they'd see him and shoot. From that distance professionals rarely missed. They'd get him in the back of the leg, immobilise him, then take him back to Vincenzo. This was unthinkable. He waited, listening intently with the gun pointed at the ready. If they saw him there was only one thing to do. He would use one more shot.

It was only two minutes later when the shot rang out. They had spotted the large oak, it stood out like a sore thumb. They circled either side of it. With guns outstretched they approached him with the intent of taking him alive, ideally unhurt. When Ricci saw them, tears rolling down his face, he did what he had to do. The shot rang through the forest and quickly died away. His brains were spread over the bark of the huge oak tree like a big grey and red bird poo. His body then fell back on the trunk of the tree and sat there. Blood was dripping from his face onto the branches. "We're fucked." said Nolan. Campo didn't say a word.

They both knew Vincenzo wouldn't be happy at the news that Ricci was dead. There would be hell to pay. They knew that he wouldn't have the letter on him, or he wouldn't have run. Maybe he stashed it somewhere in the forest? But why would he do that? After a brief discussion they decided to leave him there, the way he was, for some unsuspecting person to make the grim discovery; just another suicide, albeit a little unusual being up a tree.

CHAPTER 2

Where am I? What happened to me? Stephanie awoke in a daze, on the pavement beside the quiet country lane. It was the same lane she had been walking along before..... but before what? Her head spun and her hands and knees hurt as did her left hip. She'd been walking along this lane and she remembered hearing a car approaching from behind at speed and that was where her memory abruptly ended. The car must have glanced her and knocked her over and she must have hit her head. Who was driving? They obviously hadn't stopped – maybe they were drunk? Or on drugs. It must have been an accident.

Upon inspection she found a small dribble of blood on her forehead. She wriggled her fingers and moved her legs – they seemed to be working – no bones broken. Slowly she got up. Her head continued to spin but she counted herself lucky. For her this was a good day – she hadn't been killed.

Stephanie Garcia had been dealt a very poor hand. Her mother had died in childbirth and her father had blamed her for her mother's death. He remarried two years later and within another two years became a father again to twin boys. With his new family he was reborn; but the pain still remained, hidden in a dark corner where he never wished to venture. Sometimes, he just couldn't help himself; dragged in there against his will by something as simple as a friendly remark from an unwitting soul. Stephanie lived somewhere between this world, now and that dark corner.

From the age of fourteen she'd longed to leave her home in Zaragoza. She would work at the local bar washing up and later waiting on tables to save up, ostensibly for clothes and makeup, but she was frugal and put most of it by for the day she had enough to leave town, never to return. She was a hard worker, so she knew that, wherever she ended up, she could scrape a living and build a new life for herself – one that was better than this, one that didn't involve beatings and worse from her father. His new wife was lovely, but the honeymoon period was history, and her father was becoming more like his old self. Soon she wouldn't be able to take any more which would leave Stephanie looking after her stepbrothers and at the mercy of her father. Whilst she was fond of the twins, she longed for a life of her own. And she would have one, for today was the day she had chosen to take her leave.

She had taken the cheapest mode of transport, in order to conserve her savings, and landed here in Tarbes after many hours on the bus. She had studied French in school and spoke the language fairly well. She hoped that no one would be able to track her down. She doubted her father would come after her anyway and no one else cared. She doubted he really cared but she was useful to him, even with his new wife. But now she was free – it was the first day of the rest of her life and she would enjoy it! As soon as she recovered from being knocked down that was. She dusted herself off and, after proving to herself that nothing was broken, started walking on her way once again, albeit a little slower than before.

First on her list was to locate the hostel and that was where she was heading now. As she walked, she continued to dust herself off, wiping her forehead with a tissue as she walked. Her hip throbbed and the grazes on her hands were tender, but that would only last a few days. If she had a scar, which she doubted, it would serve to remind her of the first day of her new life. Despite being run over and nearly killed, she remained upbeat. Nothing that went wrong for her here could be as bad as if she had stayed there. Nothing. If she were in possession of a crystal ball at that moment, she'd have turned right round and gone back to Daddy with open arms.

She continued along the lane and after some fifteen minutes of slow walking spotted the hostel. She had found the hostel on the internet and called ahead to book her room. As a precaution she had left her old phone at home and bought a cheap new one at the station when she arrived, so it had a French SIM card fitted and no one knew the number. That was only an hour ago. She went into the hostel and at the reception Stephanie filled in the paperwork for booking in and was handed the key to her small, modest room. Except it wasn't a room, it was a bed – a bed in a dormitory. Still it was cheap. She intended looking for work in a hotel or similar that offered accommodation with the job. Hopefully she would find something quickly. She didn't like the idea of sharing, but she would keep her purse with her at all times. The only thing she had of value was her cash and credit card. Maybe, if she met the right people, she would change her identity and get a new passport. But that wouldn't be necessary for now. Back home she was always called Stephanie. From today onwards she would be known as Steph. A new start for Steph.

CHAPTER 3

After hanging her few clothes on the hanger provided, Steph took her purse and ventured into town to look around and see what potential employers were there. There was a number of hotels and restaurants, but she needed one that offered both a job and accommodation. She made a note of the ones that looked promising and wrote the names and locations down on her pad and ranked them in order of what looked the best suited to her needs. Tomorrow she would see a little more of the local area and become familiar with the local tourist spots, so that if she was asked about these in an interview, she could speak confidently with first-hand experience of visiting them. She daren't spend her hard-earned savings on booze or expensive food so she picked up a sandwich in a store and sat on a bench to eat it. French food was always tasty, and this sandwich was no exception. Tuna, egg and mayonnaise – Pan Bagnat, which according to the wrapper was a speciality sandwich from Nice. She washed it down with a diet coke. She then continued on her walk around the town noting more potential places to seek work.

She wondered if her father would be worried yet? Or indeed at all come to that. He'd need help with the twins, but he could afford to hire someone. Part of her felt bad for abandoning them, but she had to put these feelings aside, as that bond would have been the same bond that held her to her old life forever. Then she may have come to resent them as her father had resented her. Was she like her father? Not a bit she assured herself. By all accounts her mother had been a beauty – both inside and out. Long blonde hair and a really lovely personality; always the first to offer help should anyone need it. Always thinking of others and not herself, unwilling to see the bad in people. Had she seen the bad in her husband? Maybe her life had ended before that had happened – alas she would never know. Her father had rarely spoken of her mother to her. It was too painful for him. When he had a new wife, he only spoke of her once - to tell her not to mention her dead mother ever again to his new bride. That was it. Her memory expunged.

She walked past a clothes shop and admired the tops and cardigans in the window. Whilst she knew she'd need more clothes, she couldn't risk spending her money just yet, not until she found her feet. If she got a job in service, she may get a uniform and not need so many clothes after all. She continued for a further couple of hours but by then it was getting dark and her legs and hip were now aching quite badly, so she decided to return to the hostel and have an early night and to rest. She hoped it was quiet in there. There were six beds in the room she was in, but she had no way of knowing if any of the other beds would be occupied this evening. She saw no possessions or clothing earlier. She assumed most people only stayed for one night, as part of a journey or holiday or something. She was quite early to arrive – maybe there would be more girls there when she returned. It was girls on one floor, boys on another she had been informed. Never the twain shall meet. A boy was the last thing she needed right now. Maybe just a shower and an early night. Tomorrow she would be refreshed, and she could properly begin her new life.

She went back inside the hostel and decided to sort through her things for her toiletries so she could shower. As she was doing this another girl arrived in the room – she too looked young and lost. Had she run away too? Stephanie glanced at the new girl and then went back to her task at hand. "Hi" said the new girl in English. Stephanie had learned English in school as did many Europeans. She was better at English than French. "Hi, I'm Steph." She said. "I'm Annie" the new girl replied. She looked like she'd been travelling and appeared a little nervous and tired. It was a long way from England if you were travelling frugally, she thought to herself.

CHAPTER 4

Annie looked tired and badly needed a shower. She too only had a few things with her. Steph felt a certain bond with this girl that she didn't even know yet. Their paths had been thrown together by fate. She didn't know if she should try and talk to the girl or just get on with what she was doing.

Annie put her stuff on the bed next to Steph. She too started to empty her things out. Steph said "If you need a shower, I'm just about to go in there. Would you like to go first?" She then went bright red. Would the girl think she was commenting about her personal hygiene? She really wasn't very good a socialising which was probably why she had so few friends back home. "No that's fine – I can wait" Annie replied. "I'll be quick then." Steph said and took her things with her in the direction of the shower. When she got there, there were two showers. She hadn't thought of that. Still it didn't really matter. It would seem very strange if she went back and asked the girl to join her in the shower. So she hung her clothes and purse up and quickly showered. No-one else came into the shower in the ten minutes or so that she was showering. She dried off and got dressed again. Once she was done, she returned to her bed. Annie was nowhere to be seen.

Steph had brought the book she was reading with her for the journey. She was about half the way through it. She sat on the bed and started to read. Reading usually made her drowsy after a while and this helped her to sleep. But tonight she couldn't sleep. This was the first day of her new life – so much to plan – so much to think about. She was only now coming to terms with the fact that she had actually done it. She had escaped, left, departed and now she struggled to follow the story within her book as her mind wandered off. But wherever her mind went at no point did she regret leaving. Not really. She tried to focus on the book.

In the lobby Annie was flicking through a map of the area. Her day had been even more frantic than Steph's, although neither of them knew it. After leaving the hotel, in Paris, she had taken her rucksack of belongings, leaving no trace whatsoever that she'd been in the hotel. She had also taken the rucksack of money and then fled on foot. She'd returned to the TT. After deliberating the pros and cons of using the car on the way there, she decided to just take it. So far as she knew the body in the hotel room wouldn't be discovered until morning when the cleaners tried to clean the room. She decided to continue across Europe in a way that would make it very difficult for the police to track her, if indeed they even started to look for her. She doubted that anyone would look for her but the receptionist at the hotel would remember her and probably give her description to the police. But she could change her appearance once again – she was quickly becoming a master of disguise.

She'd found the TT and got in, leaving her bags in the passenger footwell where she could see them. She left the windows shut, locked the doors and hit the aircon button. She couldn't risk someone snatching her money from the car. She quickly looked around the area for anyone looking suspicious. She then drove through Bayonne and East on the A64 to Toulouse. She'd heard of Toulouse but knew very little about the place. As a precaution to the possibility of being tailed, she decided to make a few detours along the way. Each time she did so she felt sure no one was following her. But she had to be careful. She had nowhere particular to go and enough money to last her a while, so she was in no hurry. She tried to avoid cameras but, not knowing the area, it was difficult. She hoped that no one would be looking for the TT. Much as she liked the car, she couldn't keep it, it would have to go. Despite having no driving license and not being technically old enough to drive, she'd successfully managed to avoid any collisions or near misses.

Outside Toulouse she found a railway station that was quite large with no cameras on the car park. She parked the TT at the bottom of the car park and left the key in the ignition. She wiped the keys, steering wheel and door handles clean, plus the switches she'd touched, grabbed her bags and left the car unlocked. She hoped that a local thief would take it away for her, destroy the plates and sell it on or better still burn it out. She couldn't imagine joyriders in a place like this, but she suspected they were probably everywhere. It was a good choice of car for joy riding. She felt sure it would be gone in no time.

Once she left the car and went into the station, she went to the ticket office and bought tickets to get her all the way to Paris. There were several cameras in the ticket office – she kept her head bowed so her face wouldn't be picked up by the screen. She then walked back down the platform and out of the station where she didn't pass any more cameras. She proceeded out to the road and walked back the way she had come, to the bus station, which was about a kilometre away. The bags were quite heavy, but it had to be done. Now, should anyone try to trace her, they would continue to look for her in Paris. In her heart of hearts, she knew she was being overly cautious, but there was no such thing when you'd just committed a murder in a foreign country. She had to be doubly careful. And she wasn't in a hurry to get any place.

Not knowing the area well, she found out that the next bus went to Muret, so she purchased a ticket with cash. She'd brought her mobile phone with her but hadn't switched it on so that it could not be traced. She now removed the sim and stood on the phone breaking it. She broke the sim into two pieces and placed them into the bin. She could get a new mobile at some point when she was settled. As she waited for the bus to arrive, she planned her next move. Was she becoming paranoid? Buses and trains were traceable. She had decided to hitch when she got to Muret.

She departed at Muret and walked over to a café with a truck stop and car park for trucks. Sure enough, a small sized truck with a small sized trucker at the wheel had picked her up. He was going to Tarbes. This was back in the direction she had come from – perfect to put anyone off the scent. She travelled with him speaking as little as possible. His English was very poor which helped to stem their conversation.
In Tarbes she left the truck, thanking him for the ride. She had earlier decided to look for somewhere to spend the night where she could pay with cash. She had walked through the town and stumbled upon this hostel – it was perfect.

What Annie really needed now was a new identity. But how could she get one? She had no contacts. She couldn't speak the local language very well. She couldn't just ask around. And then it came to her – the ideal way to get a new identity, without involving anyone else to help her. But it wouldn't be easy and would require planning. She went back to the dormitory where Steph was sat on her bed with a towel around her blonde hair. Steph had sounded Spanish or Portuguese. Her English was OK though. She was a similar age and height to Annie and so her plan began to unfold.

CHAPTER 5

"How was the shower?" Annie asked. Steph looked up at her "OK. There are two showers and they were both free when I left." She said, blushing slightly. "Thanks – I think I'll take a shower now then." said Annie. Steph smiled then picked up her book and continued to read. Annie now faced a dilemma. Should she take the cash with her, which may look suspicious, or leave it on the bed where it may get stolen by Steph or someone else. "I'll take my bag and sort my stuff in the shower room." She said, clutching the rucksack of cash as she headed out to the shower. Problem solved. No-one trusted anyone in places like that. It paid to be careful. Everyone knew that.

She showered quickly, watching the rucksack. She needed to know more about Steph to see if she was a good fit. She dried off, dressed and then wrapped her towel over her hair and returned to the bed where Steph was still reading. No-one else had taken up residence with them. "I feel much better now." Said Annie. "I've just travelled from the UK – it's a long way. Where have you come from?" she asked. Steph looked at her and, for a minute, Annie detected a little girl lost look in her eyes – they were hiding a sad secret. She knew that she needed to know more about Steph. "I've travelled from Portugal. I'm taking a holiday. I'm thinking of settling here and finding work." Annie looked into her eyes but now Steph was a little more confident. Nevertheless, Annie knew she was lying. But shy? "Do you know this place? Have you been before?" Annie asked her. "Erm... no not really." Steph replied, her tone uncertain. Annie knew at once that she too had never been here before. "Fancy a walk around before it goes dark? We could grab a drink somewhere maybe." Annie said. She expected Steph to decline but after a few seconds to think, she replied "OK then. Let's do it". Annie wondered if Steph's English had let her down and it was easier to say OK than feign an excuse. Neither of them trusted leaving their purses and Annie even took her rucksack with her. She said it was just as easy to fit it all in a rucksack. Steph just agreed and out they went. "There is a bar around the corner, just over there." Steph said. Annie nodded and they headed in the direction of the bar. Annie offered to get the first drink. She came back to the table with two glasses of dry white wine – large ones.

Annie told Steph that she was on holiday, backpacking across Europe and today was her first day. She'd never done this before, and her parents had pleaded with her not to go but she had insisted. She said she was rebelling against them but really had no clue as to what to do or what to expect. Steph seemed to relate to this and explained that she too was on holiday. She seemed to realise this was a little at odds with their previous conversation so, after a pause, she said "Actually I've run away too. Well not run away, I'm 19 years old so free to go where I want. I chose here because I like France and there are plenty of hotels, plus my father is unlikely to find me here." She went on to explain that she didn't have many friends, her father was not a nice man and he probably wouldn't come after her. She had brought all her savings and her passport and documents, which was why she was clutching her purse. She was so glad she had found a friend, as she was really scared.
Annie told Steph that they were both in a similar position. She too was running away hence the two rucksacks. All her treasured possessions and cash were in her bag – the other just had clothes. They were soon chatting away like old friends. They decided to try and both get jobs at the same hotel, or at least two in the same town. Tomorrow they would go sightseeing to ensure they both knew the local area well enough to pull off an

interview. Lourdes seemed the obvious choice of destination for their first day together. Steph wore a cross and looked like a good Catholic girl. She seemed most pleased that she had found herself a kindred spirit. Annie was even more pleased that she had found something more.

CHAPTER 6

Both girls elected to take all their valuables with them for their day trip. Neither had many clothes and Annie had managed to fit her valuables into one rucksack leaving the other, with some clothes in, on her bed. She said the clothes were dirty and smelly so no one would think of looking in her bag!
They left at 8am. Both girls claimed to have slept well, but both of them knew this was not true. They both had a lot on their minds. No-one else had checked in so they had the small room to themselves. They hadn't spoken to anyone else there either, bar the receptionist.

The next day brought a clear blue sky. They arrived at the pickup point at around 8.15am to find a small bus waiting for them. It had around 20 seats. They sat at the rear on the right-hand side where they thought they'd have a good view on the outward journey. Annie seemed to like the scenery and the fields as she stared out intently during the journey. Steph told Annie of her father, her mother's death and how she had run away leaving only a note saying she wouldn't be back. She didn't bare all but said enough – more than she had told anyone else in fact. She had left no note and had spoken to no one even the twins. No-one knew where she was heading for – even her as it happened! She felt liberated – the start of a nice, new, long life hopefully filled with happiness.

They decided that evening they would walk around the town together, checking out the hotels and making a list of places they could apply. Hopefully they'd get to work in the same hotel – that would be cool. Annie kept correcting Steph's English – which was fine by Steph as she wanted to hone her language skills and thanked Annie every time she corrected her. Annie knew there was more to Steph's father and suspected that he had abused her in some way. But that didn't really matter. Steph had no boyfriend back home. She'd had a few casual friendships but nothing serious. She'd left home with her sole objective being, to get away. It seemed to her that no one would really miss her – not for a while, if at all. Only her father could potentially come looking for her but that seemed highly unlikely from what Steph had said. She'd considered that Steph could be lying but had decided that she was telling the truth. Annie was getting good at spotting lies and liars. Steph now had a place to stay and a plan. She was happy. Annie was happy too for she now had a plan of her own.

Steph had her new phone, but she hadn't used it yet. She had charged it up the previous evening, so it was ready to go. But neither of them had anyone to ring! But it was useful to have google. They decided to purchase some small speakers that evening, so they had music to listen to via YouTube or something. Annie suggested she leave it switched off to conserve battery for when they needed it later. After all no one would be ringing them. Steph agreed.

The bus arrived at Lourdes five minutes early and they disembarked. The tour guide led them in, then left them for two hours to do what they wanted, before meeting back at the bus. Lourdes was nice and Steph particularly liked it being Catholic. Annie seemed deep in thought. Steph told Annie that she was brought up a Catholic, but her church visits had lapsed in recent years. Her father had stopped going when her mother had died by all accounts, so he hadn't insisted that she attend. Whilst she had faith, she didn't feel the need to go to church regularly, faith was a personal thing to her. Right now, she felt sure that He was watching over her. He had guided Annie to her side to help her through this period of her life. She felt so much better than she had the day before, picking herself up from the side of the road. She told Annie of her accident the previous day. Annie seemed surprised she hadn't been more badly injured. Maybe someone was looking after her after all.

They decided it must have been a hit and run and Steph must have banged her head or something as she fell over and been out for a few seconds. The driver had left either knowing she wasn't badly injured or simply not caring. How can people be so callous Steph asked Annie. For all the driver knew she may have needed urgent medical attention to save her life. Annie didn't reply, because she didn't care either. However, this incident troubled her. Either it was an extremely rare incident and Steph was very lucky or something else was going on, something neither of them understood. Had Steph told her the full story? "What did your father do for a living Steph?" she asked. "He worked for a Spanish company, I think it was import export or something like that." She replied. This too troubled Annie. "What did they import and export?" Annie asked Steph and she simply shrugged her shoulders. "I never asked. I wasn't that interested. He made a decent living. We had a nice house and had everything we needed. He even had a nanny for the boys."

So, he had money. Maybe his business was legitimate, maybe not. Annie had been taught to be thorough and leave no stone unturned. Steph's Dad was probably a normal working guy. He wasn't rich and if his business was nefarious, he surely would have had more money, bigger house, flash car etc. They just can't help it. She crossed this one off her list. Annie was now a little happier as the obstacles to her plan were ticked off.

They decided to get off the bus a couple of stops early on the way back to town so they could have a walk through the fields and see this side of town on the way back. It was a relatively straight route and they felt sure they could find their way back. Annie fancied a walk and Steph could always call up Google Maps if they needed guidance. They passed a small shop where they both bought a sandwich and a diet coke. Annie wished for something stronger. They spotted a tree in a field about a hundred metres off the road. Annie suggested they sit by the tree and eat their sandwiches there. They walked down the track to the tree, which was only twenty metres or so from the track. They set their bags down and Annie announced she needed a pee. She went back to the path and into the trees on the other side. From there she couldn't be seen from the road or the track. That land looked undisturbed – like it was trapped in time.

A couple of minutes passed by and Annie hadn't returned. Steph began to get a little concerned. Then Annie appeared from the trees and shouted to her "Over here – you've got to see this!". Steph got up and trotted back to the lane and into the wooded area where Annie had disappeared, leaving the bags where they were – after all there was no one else around. But when she got there Annie was nowhere to be seen. She continued to a very thick tree stump around ten metres high where she could see Annie disappearing around a tree further ahead. Not wanting to be left behind, she hurried to the tree and that's when it happened. Whack. The last thing she saw was Annie, her face raging, swinging a large piece of wood at her head. She had no time to react. It hit her square across the forehead and snapped her head and neck backwards. All it took was one, clean blow to end her life. A life that had so much promise, so much unfulfilled. Steph was now a stiff.

CHAPTER 7

Nolan and Campo returned to the place Vincenzo had told them to wait for him. It was now two hours since the death of Ricci. They had searched him thoroughly and found nothing. They then dug a shallow grave and buried him there as instructed. In the time it had taken them to dispose of him, Vincenzo had battled with the London traffic to escape the city and arrive at the allotted meeting point. They explained that he had killed himself. Vincenzo knew only too well that Ricci knew what his fate would be should he be caught. He himself would have done the same thing in his shoes. But he wouldn't have ended up in his shoes. He would have been more careful as to whom he had spoken with.

Ricci had decided that he would do the right thing, get Vincenzo and Rimmer bang to rights, by going to the police with some evidence. But he couldn't trust the local police as he knew how many cops Vincenzo and Rimmer had in their pockets. So, he went to the very top. To Bernard Trainor. Trainor was about to retire in a few weeks, and he knew that by giving him the evidence needed to convict Vincenzo, it would be the icing on a fine career. He didn't take the letter directly to him but bumped into him on his way to his car outside his home. He said he had evidence that could convict Vincenzo but if he gave it to him and went through with it he'd need a new identity. He wouldn't go to court as he knew he'd be killed. He said he'd attend the trial by video.

Trainor had said all this was possible, but he needed written evidence that confirmed details of at least three crimes that

Vincenzo had committed or organised to get the ball rolling. He then told him not to meet him again ever but to pass the written evidence to a contact of his who would arrange things for him. Ricci agreed to write the details down in a letter and pass these to the contact at a specific place in London the next day, at noon.

He did this and the contact gave him a burner phone, which was untraceable. He told him to hide somewhere, ideally abroad, and wait for the call. He had to leave the phone on at all times so he could be tracked for his own safety. Ricci wasn't to know that, in his attempt to avoid corrupt police officers, he had gone to the one person that Vincenzo had the most control over. Trainor had immediately informed Vincenzo who had mobilised Nolan and Campo. They were to track Ricci down and bring the letter to him before he fled the country. That bit had worked perfectly. But now he had a problem. Ricci was dead. He had passed the details to his contact as requested but, through a twist of fate, his contact too was now dead. But where was the letter? He had people search everywhere. He decided that Ricci's contact must have had the letter on him when he was blown up. But the police can't have found it or they'd he'd know by now. The best outcome all round was that the letter must have been destroyed by the bomb. But he couldn't know for sure. This disturbed Vincenzo but there was nothing more he could do about it.

All this was now a few weeks ago but it still played on Vincenzo's mind. The contact had been eradicated in a twist of fate. But he didn't believe in fate. If someone had killed him deliberately, before the bomb had gone off, then they may have taken the letter. According to the police and the media, the contact was possibly on his way to pay a ransom demand for the release of his daughter, who was also missing. A complex state of affairs, it had to be said. Loose ends.

CHAPTER 8

Annie had selected this particular spot on their way out through the bus window. It looked secluded, away from the road and hidden well enough to do what she needed to do. She had hit Steph over the head a couple more times with all her strength to make sure she was dead. Her delicate head caved in on the third whack with an awful sound that combined splintering bone with a sloppy squelchy noise unlike anything she'd heard before. Confident that Steph was now dealt with she quickly returned to their tree and grabbed the bags leaving nothing behind for any passer-by to spot or steal. She took them back to where Steph lay in a bath of her own blood and put them by the tree. She knew her next task would be sweaty and dirty in this daytime heat, so she removed all her clothes, apart from her shoes, and set about digging a shallow grave. It needed to be deep enough to stop wildlife finding her and pulling her out. She hoped that it would remain undisturbed for some time. She removed all Steph's clothing and jewellery – just a small gold necklace with a cross on it. She also used her knife to cut her hair to shoulder length. She put the removed hair into Steph's bag along with her clothing and shoes.

It took her two hours to bury Steph. During that time, she heard many cars go past on the main road. She couldn't see them so they couldn't see her. She would have made a fine sight for sore eyes. She remained alert, scanning the area back towards the track just in case anyone should venture close by, but no one did. She'd chosen this spot well. Even if someone found the body relatively soon the police would still struggle to identify

her. They'd be looking for missing local girls with shoulder length hair. They wouldn't have a great description of her anyway, after Annie had remodelled her looks. This was the culmination of a plan quickly put together during the past twenty-four hours. She filled the hole in and covered it with twigs and leaves until it blended in with the surroundings.
She sat on the grass for some ten minutes as she cooled off and stopped sweating.

Eventually she felt a little chilly, so she took out Steph's tee shirt and used it to wipe herself down with. She then placed it back in Steph's bag and got dressed. She would dispose of Steph's bag soon, but first she checked it for anything useful. She retrieved Steph's purse and found her passport, credit card and cash. Amazingly Steph had nearly two thousand Euros in cash. She took the passport and cash and put it into her own bag. She cut the credit card up into small pieces using her knife. This took longer than she thought. Some pieces she repeatedly bent to ensure the digits and chip were destroyed. She put the pieces into her pocket. As she walked back to town, she would disperse them one at a time into the bins or river or such to ensure it could not be put back together to reveal Steph's details. She would find somewhere to dispose of Steph's bag of clothes soon.

As she neared the town, she passed a hotel with a large car park. It also had a clothes bank at the far end of the car park where there were currently no cars or people. She walked over and removed all Steph's clothing and placed them into the clothes bank. She put Steph's ruck sack into one of the bins. She knew these would be emptied regularly, and soon, judging from the fullness of some of the containers. This stuff would be long gone before Steph would be found. Hopefully Steph would never be found but she always had a contingency plan. Be thorough. Plan for every eventuality however unlikely. Don't rush. She had had a good day so far. She quickly returned to the road and continued into town. She knew Steph had left nothing behind at the hostel. She returned to collect her other bag and left. She would now leave this town, it had served its purpose, and head out to somewhere else.

CHAPTER 9

Annie kept Steph's passport to hand. She kept looking at the picture. From this day forward Annie was now Steph. She would need this passport for the next stage of her journey so when she arrived into town, she found a pharmacy. By now she had disposed of all the pieces of SIM card and smashed and disposed of the phone as well. If Steph had never switched the phone on as she had claimed, then this was unnecessary, but given the cost of a new one, it wasn't worth the risk however small.

In the pharmacy she bought makeup, false eye lashes and other products. Her hair was near enough in colour to the picture so that was one less thing to worry about. The length was similar, but passport pictures ended at the shoulders. She felt sure that she could make her appearance work using only makeup. That was the main reason for choosing Steph. She was so lucky to have found someone who fit the bill so well and so quickly. Someone somewhere was looking after her, but it wasn't God.

She had decided that Spain was her next stop. She would continue making various hops to confuse any potential followers. Or anyone following in her steps in the near future. She would avoid anywhere that required ID to ensure no one had any record of Steph having been anywhere. Steph's trail would end at the hostel or even some point prior to that. And France was a big country.

She went to the bus station and took a bus to Bilbao. There were three trips daily and the journey took around five hours. The bus had FlixBus written on it. She had to wait an hour for the bus,

so she found the ladies toilet and cleaned herself up and applied some makeup.
When she returned the bus had arrived, so she took a seat near the back of the bus and quietly observed each and every passenger that followed her onto the bus. No-one sat next to her as she had taken the window seat and left her bags on the seat by the aisle and feigned sleep as anyone approached. She knew if the bus filled up that she would need to move her bags and risk someone being in close proximity to her. Luckily the bus was only three quarters full, so her bags travelled by her side. No-one would pay her any attention, and therefore remember her. Travelling in this way also meant no passport check thanks to Shengen.

This far she had planned well. As for the next stage or stages of her journey she would need to plan at Bilbau, as she had no internet to help her. She hadn't slept much the previous evening as she had been planning todays activities. She now snoozed as the bus wound its way South and into Spain.

She had considered finding a room in a hostel at Bilbau on the off chance anyone tracked Steph to here. She decided this was unnecessary and as this mode of accommodation offered little privacy and higher chances of having her money stolen, she decided to find a hotel. The station was very close to the centre of Bilbau, only five kilometres or so. She followed a group of girls out in the direction of the buses. They got onto a bus heading for the centre. She stayed quite close to them so that anyone would think she was part of their group. After disembarking she quickly found a shop selling phones and sim cards. She purchased a pay as you go sim card loaded with lots of data. She then found a bench where she unpacked the phone and inserted the sim card. She worked out how to change the phone to English and then followed the menus to set up the phone and connect it to the internet. She then installed google maps from the Android store and set about choosing a nearby hotel in which to spend a day or two planning the next stage of her journey. Steph was Spanish and Annie spoke no Spanish. If asked she would say she was brought up in England as her mother was English. She felt sure this wouldn't cause her any problems. Still a British passport might be a better option if she found an opportunity to acquire one.

She chose the Ercilla Hotela about half a kilometre from her current location. If she spotted something better on the way she'd check it out. This hotel was a four-star hotel, nice, but not too nice as to attract attention. Her appearance was of a travelling single young woman of modest finances. The Ercilla charged from 60 Euros a night and had free Wi-Fi that required no registration. She would need to set up an email address in her new name in case she was asked for it at any point. She did this now in case she needed it to check in. She went to Hotmail and signed up with a new address comprised of Steph, Garcia, and 1995. She had to try two combinations before she found one that wasn't already taken. She looked up her phone number to add to the account. She then loaded the Outlook app to her phone, set up her email address and tested it by sending herself an email. She memorised her new email address and new phone number. She then put the phone in her back pocket, picked up her bags and headed for the hotel.

Whilst she passed several other hotels on the way, none looked more appealing or appropriate than the Ercilla. She had to check maps a couple of times to correct wrong turns but when she arrived there was no queue at reception. She went up to the desk and asked if they had any rooms available. She chose a cheaper room on the third floor. It was a tall building with a restaurant on the top. The receptionist gave her a guide with a map of the area and some of the local attractions She pointed out that the Guggenheim Museum Bilbao was only fifteen minutes' walk and the beach at Sopelana was twenty kilometres. She could organise taxis for her if she wished.

She carried her bags up to her twin room herself, entered her bedroom, dropped her bags on the bed and went over to the window and looked out at the town as the light was receding. It was quite beautiful. She decided to sort out her bags, dispose of anything she didn't need and try and get down to needing only one bag for her clothes and the cash. After emptying her things out onto the bed she decided neither bag was big enough. She elected to buy a new bag. One more suitable for hand luggage on a plane where she could keep her cash to hand. Her clothes and toiletries etc. could go in the other bag. That would mean a cabin bag and a rucksack. That would be better than two rucksacks. Having two rucksacks was a bit strange – no one carried two rucksacks. She would keep the rucksack that the cash came in – she liked it. Buying a new bag could wait until the morning. Her stomach was now growling. She hadn't had a proper meal for what seemed like days and she needed to eat. Her room had a safe, so she placed her passports and money into the safe leaving the bags on the bed. If anyone came into her room, it would look like two backpackers with nothing worth stealing.

She went downstairs and out onto the street. She followed the signs to the Bermeo restaurant. She was shown to a small table in the corner of the restaurant. She ordered a beer and water and studied the menu. The bar was black and had stools up against it. The tables were arranged in rows and the décor was largely black also. She chose the tasting menu for fifty Euros.

The service seemed quite slow and the restaurant wasn't cheap, but when her food arrived it was very nice indeed. She didn't strike a rapport with any of the staff as she was trying to remain anonymous in the corner of the restaurant. She had two more beers during her meal, she daren't drink too much as she couldn't afford to let down her guard yet. She finished her meal off with a black coffee and then returned to her room. All her stuff was exactly as she had left it. She locked the door behind her and then drew the curtains.

Her main priority was planning her new career. Maybe she would need to follow her nose a little. The thought of befriending old couples and taking money from them had seemed very appealing to her and Dom. But she couldn't really afford to ply her trade on a cruise ship as this was a captive audience with no place to hide. To do this successfully, she needed to be in a town or city, ideally a tourist place with a big turnover of people. She decided that a holiday resort by the sea would be a good choice; ideally one popular with British tourists. She could pass herself off as a tourist and then take money, by some means yet to be decided, using her good looks and guile.

She again consulted google maps and decided that she could go for coastal Spain or Portugal. She chose Portugal as it was another leg of her journey making it that bit more difficult to track. But it was quite some distance – five hundred kilometres? She couldn't risk flying and she didn't want to risk stealing a car and being stopped at any point. The bus was the safest way to travel. From a google search she found that FlixBus covered Bilbao to Albufeira, but it could take up to twenty hours to get there. She decided to try and get a ticket that evening, sleep on the bus, then take it from there.

She packed her two bags, showered, got dressed and went down to reception where she checked out and headed for the bus station. On the way she found another clothes and recycling point where she offloaded her unwanted clothes and rucksack. All that remained for disposal were her old passports. At a large bin she tore up the passport page by page and set alight to them using matches she had obtained from the restaurant the previous evening. She spread the ashes around the inside of the large bin. That should be more than enough to terminate her previous identities. She then carried on towards the bus station.
She spotted several stores selling bags. She found one, an ideal trolly dolly type bag with four large wheels. It looked fairly sturdy and was a pale pink, very girly, and befitting to the new

Steph. She also purchased a smaller bag, just big enough to hold her cash. She purchased the bags using some of Steph's cash. She also bought a hoodie in case she became cold on the overnight bus journey.

When she came to the bus station it was larger than she had envisaged. She found the ticket office and purchased her ticket to Albufeira. The bus left after lunch, so she had some time to kill. She headed for the nearby shops. She decided to purchase some sexy beach wear for Albufeira. This passed some time and she then stopped in a café and had lunch – a tuna salad washed down with a beer. She also purchased four cans of beer for the journey. When she had finished her meal and paid the bill she headed off to the toilets and went into the disabled toilet. She removed the cash from her rucksack and placed it into the recently purchased small bag and then placed this into her new trolly dolly bag along with her new clothes. She left her old stuff in the rucksack. Anything of importance was in the trolly dolly bag now.

She left the café and headed back to the bus station where she waited patiently in line for the bus to arrive. Once again, she went towards the rear of the bus, sat by the window and placed her bags on the seat beside her. This time the bus was nearly full by the time it departed but her strategy of feigning sleep worked once again.
Whilst there was light, she planned. She considered all the various options open to her. The world was her oyster. That reminded her of the old Frankie Goes To Hollywood song and the fact that she had no headphones. She also had no music on her phone. Never mind, no time for listening to music just yet. She had to draw up a list, quite a long list, of possibilities. She intended to remain in Albufeira for a while. This would be the new birthplace of Steph.

PART 2

CHAPTER 11

The bus arrived at Albufeira mid-morning. A great time for arriving at a new and as yet unknown place. Steph knew this was a place that attracted lots of British holidaymakers. Families, stag parties, hen parties, old and young. It wasn't an exclusive place for the rich, it attracted all walks of life. She could blend in here. It was big enough to hide. And close enough to other coastal resorts should she decide to move on.

The bus station was surprisingly close to the beach. But the beach was no place for a single girl with two bags. She needed to find a hotel to make her base for the first few days. She decided to book in somewhere touristy for a week – she was on holiday on her own after breaking up with her boyfriend in London. She headed towards the old town. She knew that would be a little quieter, more popular with families than stags and hens.

She walked up an alleyway from the square towards the many restaurants by the beach. She could find work in a bar; the ones by the sea seemed to be a higher class and would attract better clientele. However, it would be harder to get a job in an up-market restaurant especially when she hadn't done this type of work before. She had never waited on or cooked or done front of house. She'd done nothing. Many restaurants employed a good-looking man or woman to stand outside and pull people in to eat. She could certainly do that – her looks would get her a job anywhere. She watched some of these at work as she walked – it soon became apparent that they spoke several languages and could converse with people from almost anywhere! Hereby lay another problem for her. If she were to find the cover of a job, she would have to find something that only required English - maybe an Irish bar or the like? But she didn't like the thought of working in a bar. It wouldn't attract the right sort of person for her to exploit in some way.

Maybe she should just pose as a rich, single woman on holiday, pick up a restaurant owner or rich tourist. But she could only run this ruse for a finite amount of time before people realised, she was on a very long holiday. Still people went away for weeks, sometimes months on end. It could work for a few weeks and sounded better than the alternatives. Still she may think of something else. She wasn't in a particular rush. There must be lots of options in a place like this that she would never have considered before visiting.

She walked around until she got her bearings in the old town. She measured up the many bars and restaurants. Tomorrow she'd look for a job that only required fluent English, if she could find one. She knew some French and Spanish from school – no doubt she'd pick up some Portuguese if she stayed here long enough. It was an option but not really her preferred option. Her legs and arms were beginning to ache from carrying the bags and from the previous day's activities. She needed a place to stay so she set about choosing a hotel.

She found a hotel in middle of Albufeira old town called Hotel California. Music again – she must buy some headphones this evening. With a name like that she couldn't refuse. It wasn't full so she booked herself in for seven nights and said she may stay on or choose to go elsewhere for the remainder of her holiday. They said they offered a discounted rate for anyone staying for 4 weeks or longer. The guy on reception was English which helped a lot. She couldn't commit to four weeks, so she kept it as a week. They said if she chose to stay on, she could keep the same room. The receptionist had taken a shine to her and showed her up to her room where he gave her the key and then returned to his desk.

The room was quite small. She unpacked and reviewed her clothing situation. She was travelling light – just the stuff she'd picked up on her travels. She decided to choose a new name – a nickname if you like. To avoid being known by her real name or the dead girl's name. She liked the name Elvira but being small, blonde and not quite as curvy it probably wouldn't do. She was more the Baywatch type – how about Erika or Pammy? Casey or CJ her character was called. Shame she hadn't the skills to be a lifeguard – it always seemed an easy job. Maybe just Blondie?? She was blonde? She wanted something suitably vague just in case anyone ever came looking for her. Planning ahead again. Never be too careful. But for now, she was Steph.

Tonight, she decided to try a curry. She'd spotted an Indian restaurant, off the square by Buddies Bar. It had a roof with tables on. No doubt the food wouldn't be up to UK standard or cruise standard, but it was likely a good spot to people watch without being harassed by anyone. What to wear? The remaining cruise gear was a bit too elegant for Albufeira she decided – especially for a curry house. She wanted casual sexy. Maybe have a look at the shops? She could buy something beach tacky, but not too tacky, to blend in. She had to look the part of a holiday maker and not stand out - be unnoticed. But she knew her looks made that near impossible. Your best asset could sometimes be your downfall.

Indian Taj – cracking name for a curry house. It was still early, so she decided to look in the clothes shops nearby before eating. She decided to take the side streets where the local boutique type shops were. She noticed the people off the main drag appeared to be a little older and more sophisticated. It seemed Albufeira attracted a wide age range - good choice for her it seemed. She walked down the street observing the people. She passed a couple of bars and shops and came to a boutique on the right. A small place but with nice things. She went in and noticed a cat sat on a shelf close to the serving bar where the till was. It seemed content to sit and watch, a little like she was. It obviously lived there, and that shelf had been reserved for its use, separated from the clothes on display. She looked at the dresses and tops. Much of the wares were aimed at older people, she was only 24 according to her current passport and she could pass for that age with the right makeup and clothes.

The shop didn't sell jeans, but she chose a nice dress – somewhere between casual and dressy – suitable for dining in a curry house and scouring the bars afterwards. She tried it on in the tiny changing room. It had a mirror – she surprised herself at how good she looked in it. She looked classy and yet up for some fun as well. She'd definitely buy this one and wear it this evening. She also bought a top that would go with jeans. They weren't cheap, but she was worth it. She wouldn't be running out of cash for some time yet.

She asked the owner about any really nice, classy restaurants, who said the best ones here were on the seafront, which she'd already worked out. She mentioned A Ruina – apparently like a castle just by the beach – specialising in fish. Steph said she'd try it. The owner also mentioned one nearby - Villa Joy; Michelin starred but not in Albufeira, but eight or nine kilometres west; halfway to Praia dos Selgados and this was a beach side restaurant. This sounded a lot better than Albufeira. She'd go there over the coming days and check it out, get to know the staff and see if any regulars were suitable to strike up a friendship with. Single guy ideally – young or old she didn't care so long as he was wadded.

She thanked the owner and headed back towards town. She headed for the beach with all the other tourists to check out A Ruina. She called back into her hotel on the way and changed into her new dress. She then went back out heading back towards the beach. This hotel was indeed ideally located. On the way she passed through a small market with craft stalls and clothes shops on one side and tat shops on the other. She found some nice handmade earrings and a leather bracelet that she liked. She haggled on the prices a little. She also bought an elasticated belt to go with her new dress. She was now looking for shoe shops. She got all the way to the front and then spotted A Ruina on the right quite high up. It was elevated like a castle – it must have had fantastic views from the terrace on the top. Maybe she'd go there tomorrow evening. They had a smartly dressed man outside by the steps to pull people in – she booked for 7pm the following evening. She'd have a leisurely meal and observe. She said she wanted to sit up top with the best view looking over the beach and the restaurants below.

CHAPTER 12

It was not yet 7.30 so she headed back the way she'd come and back to the curry house. She had forgotten to book but she needn't have worried as it was quite quiet. She got a table upstairs. It wasn't quite as nicely appointed up top as she'd hoped. Inside was very traditional but the top was like a neglected roof garden. Plastic tables and chairs, ashtrays. Still she needn't stay too long – she had a good view of the bars and restaurants below and the endless people mingling and walking. She was now very thirsty, so she ordered a pint of Kingfisher and looked at the menu. She was starving. She hadn't had a proper meal in what seemed like ages. Was this the first time she'd eaten in a restaurant like this alone? She ordered poppadums and a chicken madras with pilau rice and a peshwari naan. She'd have a go at eating the lot. She failed but not by much. Between courses she observed. She finished the curry but left some of the rice and a bit of the naan that was a little burned. Still she'd done well. She finished her third pint and by now felt a little tipsy. Strangely, she was in a holiday mood. She was too full for a frozen sweet, so she asked for the bill, paid with cash, and headed back down the stairs via the toilet.

She then headed back out and across and into Bar Piccadilly Cocktail bar. The waitresses were all attractive and young and slim. A bit like Hooters but without the uniform. She'd never been in a Hooters bar just seen pictures on the internet or maybe an ad.

She went in and to the bar inside and ordered a half a lager. She didn't fancy a cocktail on her own. She was the only single person in there. The karaoke was set up for later. She'd never had a go but something deep inside her had fancied it. She'd always loved singing and thought she had a pretty good voice – her singing tutor at home said so – but then again, she would. It must have been the outgoing side of her that had, up until the past few weeks, remained hidden and suppressed.

How her life had changed in just a few short weeks. She'd learned so much about what she was capable of that now even karaoke seemed easy. She'd killed a man and a woman, now she could kill a classic song. She thought it might be a way of attracting attention should a wealthy looking single guy walk into the bar. But somehow, she didn't think that was going to happen. All the guys were in twos or groups or with a partner. No-one stood out as in her catchment area when it came to refinement and potential wealth. But looks could indeed be deceiving. She would have to cast her net far and wide to attract the best catch.

The waiter who took her order spoke good English – it seemed everyone here did – but then again most of the holidaymakers were in fact English plus a few Irish. Maybe language wouldn't be such a barrier after all. Or maybe this style of bar was aimed at the British. It had certainly attracted her inside. Isn't it funny how, when you are at a bar on your own, you seem to siphon your drink in no time?

She was trying to catch the attention of the waiter to order another when in walked three girls. They looked confident and attractive, but not as attractive as she was in her unbiased opinion. They wore ripped jeans and tee shirts with band logos on. The waiter went straight to them and asked them what they wanted. Were she to get into a conversation, with them, or anyone, she didn't want to use her passport name of Steph. She wanted another layer of deception over the top. She needed a pseudonym or nick name. Unfortunately, she hadn't yet decided on her new, new name. As the waiter asked them for their order one of the girls said, "I think she was waiting to be served

John, keep up." He looked at her for a few seconds too long then turned to Steph. "Same again?" "Yes please." She had the money ready but the girl who had addressed the waiter said "put it back, this one's on us for barging in. I'm Mandy".

She was English with what seemed like a faint Northern accent. She was mousey blonde, tall and she had a nice figure. The girl next to her was older, a brunette, brown eyes and looked a little quieter. She wasn't fat but a little curvier and not necessarily in the right places. The third girl was ginger – it looked natural, but she wasn't quite sure. She was petite – around 5 feet tall so shorter than the other two, slim and quite muscly like she worked out. "These are my friends and esteemed colleagues Rach and Animal." Steph smiled and said, "Very pleased to meet you – I'm JC – and thank you for the drink." She had no idea where JC had come from but now it was out there. Mandy said "no worries – stick with us and you'll be fine. You on your own?" "Yes, just split with my boyfriend back in England and thought I'd get away from it all for a few days. How about you ladies?" They all laughed. "We ain't no ladies honey" said the brunette, Rach. We're sort of hanging around here for the season. JC thought about this for a moment then said, "You said you were colleagues?" "Yes – we're The Sisters Of No Mercy. We're a rock band." Mandy said – she seemed like the leader. "Well three quarters of one anyhow." JC, she must think of herself as JC from now on, smiled not quite knowing what to say. Then the penny dropped. You play here then? "Yes, not tonight as its karaoke night but every second Friday. We have a dozen or so places that we play regularly. We ain't rich but it pays for some spectacular nights out and we meet some real interesting people! The brunette, Rach, spoke with a Southern American drawl – like she was from Texas or somewhere. The ginger girl hadn't spoken yet. The ginger girl then spoke for the first time – I used to date the manager last year when I played with a different band. We stayed friends and we come in here quite a bit when we're not working. If you can call it working! We're so lucky. No nine to five, no boyfriends nagging us and spare time during the day to do what we want." "It sounds great." Said JC. And it did, to an extent.

They chatted for a few more minutes and Mandy ordered another round of drinks – JC offered to pay but Rach said it was her shout. "Better go do a song" said Mandy. "They like us to get things going in return for a couple of drinks." she said and winked. Mandy got up and had a go at The Boys Are Back In Town by Thin Lizzy. She didn't have a great voice, but she was confident and sexy and grabbed the attention of all the guys in there. A few came in from outside to take a look. A couple of guys got up and did a turn and the bar was filling up nicely within half an hour. Then Rach got up and grabbed one of the guys and they did I Got You Babe. Again, Rach could carry a melody but was by no means pitch perfect. Animal said she didn't sing – she played the drums. She asked JC if she played any instruments. "No, not really, but I like to sing when I'm in the shower." she replied. "Just what we're after – a singer and frontman. Get up there and strut your stuff! Think of it as an audition." Rach said. "But I'm only here for a few days." CJ replied. "Nothing is certain in this life. You never know this could be the making of you girl!" Rach said, very casually.

Having had four or five drinks now, she was more confident and less on her guard than usual. When they cheered her on to do a song, she actually went and got the song menu, picked one, and put her name on the list. I Love Rock and Roll by Joan Jett. She was familiar with it from the radio. It seemed simple enough! Next thing she was being passed the mic to screams and applause from her three new friends and the group of guys who seemed to like the look of her. She now felt overdressed a little but nevertheless she looked quite sexy and stylish. Not exactly Joan Jett, more like Cher or Celine Dion. Still, it didn't really matter.

She did look very good in her new dress – sexy but not slutty.

When the music started it suddenly became very real and sobering. She started to sweat a little. No words were on the monitor and she was beginning to panic when the first line of the song came up. Luckily, she came in both at the right time and in the right key near enough. She put plenty of attitude into her performance and before she knew it the crowd were cheering, and she was done. Her new friends were whooping and cheering and had already gotten her two more drinks in. She almost downed the first one in one go – were it not for the ice-cold temperature and bubbles she probably would have.

“You are full of surprises.” said Rach. “What a voice!” said Animal and Mandy just smiled. “I think we’ve found ourselves our new singer. You’re in!” JC just laughed and said “Yes!” – swept away in the moment – back to being a young girl again. She was having a really great time. After a few more compliments and listening to the lads do My Sharona, which was a lot harder that you’d think – they kept coming in at the wrong time, Mandy said they should meet up the following day and do a proper audition. They would run through the songs in their current set and load them onto JC’s phone so she could listen. JC said she had no stereo, just her phone. No worries they said – you’ll know most of the songs – they’re standard covers that we know go down well at the places we play. All you’ll need is a pair of headphones.

JC knew she’d need to buy a pair of headphones in the morning to take with her. She tried to slow down the pace of her drinking, but the girls were animals and she daren’t keep up in case she said something she’d regret or forget or both. At around one am she said she was tired after flying in and was calling it a night. Despite protests from the Sisters Of No Mercy, she finished her beer, said her goodbyes, and headed back to the Hotel California. She was both knackered and exhilarated. Singing with a band – could she really pull it off? What had she done! That was an occupation that certainly wasn’t on her list.

Back at the hotel her head was spinning. She'd need to find out if the band was serious, how much money she'd make – was it enough to sustain her there if she decided to stay with them? If not, she'd just say she was going home and move on to a different town. She'd made friends already; not just in the band but many of the people in the bar – they'd recognise her now. Still maybe the band was the perfect vehicle for meeting the right guy. An excuse to pile on the makeup and be a different persona – JC. She decided it was Jacey – spelled J A C E Y as opposed to the two letters JC – like Jesus Christ. That wouldn't do at all.

CHAPTER 13

Annie, or Steph, or Jacey even, woke up with a headache. It had been a most unexpectedly good evening and she had enjoyed the company and the freedom. Had she really gotten up and sung in front of a bar full of people? And had they really cheered? And had she really agreed to audition for that girl band Sisters of No Jersey or something like that? God. And that was just the first night! She now understood how single people can go on holiday on their own and actually have a good time. She got up, showered, got dressed and headed out to find a shop selling headphones. After about half an hour of wandering around she found a shop in a back alley that sold headphones. She bought a pair of over ear ones – Bluetooth – plus a pair of normal wired in ear ones for portability.

She'd arranged for the girls from the band to meet her at the hotel reception at 11 where they'd walk her to where they rehearsed. She still had time to rethink this whole thing and pull out, but what the hell. She had nothing better to do and she might enjoy it. She grabbed a sandwich from one of the shops and ate it on the hoof. She returned to her room, unwrapped the headphones and put the big ones on charge. Luckily the man in the shop had asked her if she had a charger. She took a few selfies in town, so her phone looked like it belonged to a tourist. Her new phone and headphones had European plugs – she had nothing with a British plug on. She put a selfie of her by the shops on the background of her phone and lock screen and installed some apps – Candy Crush Saga and a few other girly games she'd come across. She already had Samsung Music which seemed fine for playing music. She had a connecting cable and it had 64Gb of space - plenty of room for music. She hooked it up to the Wi-Fi in the hotel and put it on charge also. It was already two thirds charged and she still had over half an hour to charge before heading down to meet the girls. She would need to set up a brand-new Facebook account if the girls wanted her to use it. She'd say that she'd closed her old account so her ex couldn't find her.

She was wearing the nearest thing she had to rock chick – jeans and a tee shirt. Not ripped or anything but she thought she looked cool enough. Whilst being a little annoyed for making a spectacle of herself the previous evening and having drunk too much, she was also happy to have some friendly faces around her. She still didn't trust the girls yet, but she was fairly sure they were straight up. She put her passport and the small case of cash into her hotel safe and took only her purse with headphones and enough money in it. She didn't take cards as they wouldn't tally with her new name. Hopefully this wouldn't cause her too much of a problem. It would take time to make the connections to get a new passport or cards in her newly acquired name at some point and she had no experience of doing this anywhere let alone in a foreign country, wherever it may turn out to be. Still there would possibly be an acquaintance of the band that could help at some point. Bands knew all the right dodgy people it seemed.

By five to eleven she had freshened up, got dressed and collected her new phone and headphones plus the charger data cable and was heading down the stairs to reception.
As she arrived at reception, she spotted Mandy outside smoking a cigarette. She went out and said "Hi." "The others will be here shortly – they just stopped off for supplies - they'll be here in a minute." Sure enough, they soon appeared with a carrier bag containing bottles of beer and cigarettes.

"Where are we going?" asked Jacey. Animal answered this one – "we have the use of a villa that belongs to my father, well his company. It has a large basement that we use as a rehearsal studio. We keep our gear there and rehearse there too." "And that's not all" said Rach. "It has four bedrooms, and we all crash there. We have a room each. Beck, our old singer stayed with us too, but she moved out last week so there's a room free. If you make the grade and make the right choice to join us, and want the room, it's yours. Without it we wouldn't be able to do what we do, live life and pay rent from the meagre earnings we make. And it makes rehearsals easier, because they too are free. If we like you and you want to do this thing then it really should only take a couple of weeks of hard work to get the songs gig ready. You'll have a lot of words to learn and we might need to tweak a few keys to suit your voice – if so, we'll have work to do too." "I won't." piped up Animal. Then she added "There's no pressure. If you don't like it, or we don't like you, then no harm done. It won't be difficult to find another singer – they're ten-a-penny." Rach and Mandy looked a little uneasy at Animal's comment and Jacey knew herself that finding a frontman for a band that suited the band and who was good was more difficult than finding, for example, a rock drummer.

Things were indeed moving faster than she had anticipated. Still, she was under no obligation. She could walk at any point – she was still in control. Rach listed off some of their songs – I Love Rock And Roll, naturally, Sweet Child O' Mine, Hanging On The Telephone, Bad Case Of Loving You, Hot Legs, She's Got Legs, Sex Bomb, Nutbush, Simply The Best, and a couple of AC/DC numbers. All needing raunchy vocals. Jacey didn't know all the songs, but the titles were familiar – she'd have heard them at some point.

It was about a twenty-minute walk to their place – up a lot of steps and heading up the hill away from the town. They chatted all the way, mainly about music, influences, bands they liked, other songs they'd like to do if Jacey was up for them and able to sing them and so on. The three of them chatted away, although Animal seemed to talk the least. Jacey wasn't sure if it was because she was more thoughtful or simply because she couldn't get a word in edgeways. Or even that she didn't like Jacey. Maybe she sensed something wasn't right about her? If so, then the feeling was mutual.

When they arrived, the house was quite new and modern, much nicer than Jacey had expected. It was quite high up and overlooked a bay with shops and restaurants. It must have cost a fortune. And the girls stayed here for free? It seemed too good to be true. Seemed like Animal's father was nothing like her own – or was he? This was the first time she'd thought about her father in a couple of days, what with all that had happened. Her feelings towards him were still cold, no sense of missing him, no sense of guilt. That said she'd never really liked him much from being little. She'd also lost track of the latest news back in the UK.

She thought about her mother, she wasn't missing her either. Her mother was weak and she blamed her partly for the way her life had taken shape under her father's control. He tried to control her mother also and the only way she avoided this was by distancing herself from him, literally.

Animal unlocked the front door and they went inside. It was very modern and sparsely decorated. A three-piece suite in the lounge area with a large TV and big speakers. The kitchen had an island in the middle with four stools and a large American fridge. All the appliances looked state of the art and unused. "Do you guys cook much?" she asked. The girls laughed. "Maybe if we could work the cooker – it took us a week to master the microwave!" Rach said. They all laughed. Off the kitchen was a large door, wider than a normal door. It led to some steps which appeared to go down into the basement.

Mandy saw Jacey looking at the doorway to the basement and

said, "Shall we give you the tour?" Jacey smiled. The basement was amazing. One large area with some pillars for support. There was musical paraphernalia everywhere – a drum kit, guitars, amps, speakers, mics and stands, a mixer desk, books and an Apple Mac computer with a big screen. And lots of wires – everywhere. Why did bands need so many wires? she wondered.

The band gear seemed set up and ready to go. "And this is where it all happens" Mandy said. She added "The gear stacked up by the wall there is our gigging gear – most of the venues have drums there and a PA system so we just need backline and guitars and stuff. The gear set up mostly stays here for rehearsals. It makes things so much easier for us. We can fall out of bed, work for a couple of hours then do what we want. The great thing about a band is that, once you've nailed the songs, the only hard work is picking and learning new songs and you only need to do one a week, if that, to freshen up the set so you're not playing the same songs twice in a row at a venue and you've cracked it."

Mandy could tell from Jacey's expression that she still wasn't sold on the idea of living here and assuming this new profession. But Mandy had high hopes for Jacey. She was just what they were looking for. Pretty, intelligent, young looking, outgoing and she could even sing a bit. Her singing would improve with practise. Mandy knew they would be really lucky to find someone as fitting as Jacey in time for the next batch of gigs they had in the pipeline. Time wasn't really on their side.

They all took their positions. Animal sat behind the drums and picked up her sticks, spinning them around in her fingers like a marching girl with attitude. Mandy switched on the mixer desk and a few static lights which Jacey hadn't yet spotted. She then switched on her guitar amp and after a second or so a humming noise appeared from the amp. Rach switched on her bass amp and picked up her bass – it too made a little noise. Mandy and Rach tuned up silently using tuners sat loosely on their amps then when they were ready to go Mandy said "How about we start with I Love Rock And Roll." Jacey, over in the corner is a folder – go grab it – it has the lyrics to all the songs in there – just in case you need them. Jacey's face must have lit up with relief. She grabbed the folder and quickly read through I Love Rock And Roll. She stood in front of the drums between Rach and Mandy who were either side facing inwards, so they could all see each other. All eyes would be on Jacey. She put the words onto the music stand by the mic stand, smiled, and said one two into the mic. Nothing happened. "Sorry it's on mute" said Mandy and pressed a button on the desk and a light seemed to go off. The familiar hum then came from the speakers indicating all three mics were probably switched on now. Each had a mic except for Animal. She had a mic cable coming from inside her bass drum but that was it. "Let's do a level check" said Mandy and the three girls played what Jacey could only describe as a big chord... almost like the end of a song. She was able to hear everything OK. The three of them did one twos and yeahs and all three mics seemed OK to her. Hers sounded a little louder than theirs but she didn't say anything.

They did another big end with a bush then Animal went 1 2 3 4 whilst clicking the sticks together and they went into the start of the song. Luckily Jacey now knew where to come in from the previous night. She went up to the mic, lips touching it, and started to sing. It was strange to hear her own voice so loud from the speakers. She fluffed the timing in a few places but was able to read the words and even remembered some from the previous evening. They did the song three times and by the third time she was a lot more comfortable with the lyrics and the timing and thought it actually sounded quite good.

"Right time for a beer" said Mandy. She and Rach put their guitars back onto their stands, pressed what Jacey assumed to be a mute button as the humming went away, and Animal placed her sticks on the snare drum and stood up. They all went back up to the kitchen where Rach took four bottles of Super Bock from the fridge. "Lunch" said Mandy and they all laughed.

"So which ones do you fancy having a go at next?" asked Mandy. Jacey had brought the folder with her, so she thumbed through the song list picking ones she knew. Simply The Best by Tina, Rock and Roll by Led Zeppelin, Sweet Child O' Mine, Addicted To Love, Legs and Sex Bomb were the ones she knew from the titles and she had a rough idea how they went. She read these aloud and Mandy said "Sure thing – we won't get to nail all of them today, but as this is, strictly speaking, an audition, we'll have a run through of some of them just to check that you can sing them in the key we play them in – which is the original key detuned a semi-tone. That'll give us an idea of how able you will be to pick up the set. We don't want to be in a position of having to drop half the numbers or change all the keys just because the singer can't sing them or reach the high notes. Somehow I don't think that's gonna be an issue though." Jacey didn't really understand about keys and detuning, but she was caught up in the whole thing of making music and being at the front of a band. She knew that it could only ever be low key – she couldn't afford to become famous in case she was recognised.

Typical, her first band, she hadn't even done a decent gig with them, and she was already thinking about becoming famous. Shit. Still, she could change her appearance, give herself a new image, as part of being in the band which was good. If it got hot, she could simply up sticks and move on. This career had potential.

They took four more beers with them, one each, and went back down to the basement and worked through the first five songs on Jacey's list. Again, she was a little shaky to start with, but by the third or fourth run through she was sounding good. None of them were out of her range although Guns 'n' Roses was a strain. Mandy said that, with practise, her voice would get better and stronger as with any other muscles. This seemed logical. She seemed happy that the song would be do-able.

Between songs one of the girls went up for another four beers. By five pm they were finished – they'd done enough for one day. "That was pretty good for a first timer." Rach said and bumped shoulders with Jacey – she assumed this was an affectionate rock chick thing. By now Jacey was desperate for the loo – Animal directed her to the bathroom and off she went.

When she returned, the three of them were stood side by side, each with a bottle and a newly opened one for Jacey. After a few seconds of silent smiling Mandy said "We've had a quick chat whilst you were away for a piss and we all agree that, with some hard work, you could pull this off. We like what we've heard so far, and we think you'd be a great addition to the band. There's work to be done on you though, over and above the singing. You'll need an image if you're gonna be our front man.... woman. "We'll need to think about that" added Rach. Again, Animal was silent. She seemed in agreement though. Jacey couldn't imagine Animal getting too excited about anything.

"So how do you want me to look?" she asked Mandy. "Like a rock chick naturally!" Mandy replied and smiled. Jacey didn't know how to respond to this. Animal added "There's a tattooist we know – great guy, fantastically talented – I'd suggest you start off there – if you are brave enough. Jacey thought that she was somehow being tested. But a tattoo was a great way of effecting a change in appearance, but also a way of identifying her. But not the old her. Again, they could be removed – she had the money. "OK I'm up for that!" she said. Another whoop of approval. "That plus the new wardrobe!" added Mandy. Animal chipped in at this point "We can give you an advance – a couple of hundred Euros if you need it." Jacey was taken aback by this offer. "Thank you, that's really kind, but I've got a little money that my father left me. Not much really, but enough to get me started off. He always wanted me to choose a career, but I never could." They all laughed.

CHAPTER 14

After more chatting they finished their beers and decided they'd done enough for one day and it was time to go to town for a couple more drinks to celebrate the new addition to the Sisters Of No Mercy. Mandy led them to Vertigo Live Music Bar which just so happened to also be the place of their first gig with Jacey. There was no band on tonight though, sadly.

"So, you really have no ties back home and, if you really wanted to, could just stay here?" Animal asked. When Animal asked you a direct question it was never banter, there was always something behind it. "I guess so." Jacey replied. There was a pause, so she continued. "My mother died when I was young, my father brought me up but he also passed away a few months back. All I have is a rented house, a little money, not much, some clothes and stuff, and a few mates. No current boyfriend. So yeah, I guess I could just stay here. I'd have to go back to sort my stuff – or maybe Stacey would go get all my gear and stash it at her place. She could come visit and bring some of it over – that would be great." The rest of the band nodded agreement to each other. Clearly, they were concerned that she would want to return to England and leave them in the lurch. "You can always go back and see your friends when the season ends." Mandy said reassuringly. "I guess so." Jacey replied. "But for now I'm happy here." She added.

They stayed and chatted until around 10pm and by then they were all a little tired after their days rehearsing and drinking. They were also all a bit drunk by this point. Mandy said she'd pick Jacey up at her hotel the following morning at 11 or so.

From there they would go clothes shopping. This was an early start for Mandy. In the afternoon she could choose a tattoo. Then the day after they would start intense rehearsals to get Jacey up to speed with the set and to practise her frontman moves and banter. If they could do four or five songs a day, then they'd have plenty songs for the first gig.

Each day they spent a minimum of four hours rehearsing, sometimes as many as six. By the end of the week Jacey's voice was becoming a little hoarse. They'd been working on Sweet Child O' Mine and it had taken its toll. Animal suggested taking the following day off and spending that evening drinking to lubricate their throats. They all agreed. By now Jacey had been in many of the bars in the old town and traversed the escalators to the new town where the parties continued until sunrise. She was getting to know the place fairly well. She hadn't thought any more about her future career in criminality or how to make it big, she was totally focussed on being a rock chick and just enjoying herself. And why not? She had money and no responsibilities for the first time in her life. So far, she'd avoided the advances of all the guys they'd chatted to.

They had now got twenty songs sorted. Jacey still needed to go over the lyrics when she was alone, but she was confident she wouldn't need a music stand for the gig. For the odd song that she kept messing up she made a two-inch-wide, A4 strip and noted the first word of each verse in writing large enough to read in low light. This was enough to trigger her memory. Jacey now had a playlist of all the songs in their repertoire on her phone and this was all she played – over and over again in order to consolidate the songs, the lyrics and the phrasing in her head. She knew her performance would suffer if she wasn't one hundred percent happy with the song lyrics and format.

She had pretended to have organised the collection of her stuff from her flat and terminated the lease, wired the remaining payment and opened a bank account here and transferred two thousand pounds – that was all the money she said she had. It seemed enough to impress the girls. Although they were, in fact, all older than her by at least five years, they got on really well. She liked them all, but still hadn't got the measure of Animal. She always thought something was going on in the background with her. Maybe Animal felt the same way about Jacey. They hadn't really bonded and didn't really trust each other.

In the interim she'd followed the BBC news relating to her kidnapping, her father's murder, the terrorist attacks and nothing she heard gave her any concern. The British press still seemed bent on it being a terrorist attack. They were still digging into certain people's past but not apparently into her father's. He had some important friends with whom, no doubt, he shared secrets. The kidnapping seemed to have been buried by the terrorist attacks just as Dom had said it would. Poor Dom. But she didn't need a Dom anymore. Her apprenticeship had been short and quick, as had his end.
She still had the keys to his place in Horwich. You never know, they may come in useful if she found herself in the UK and on the run. He paid his bills well in advance so he could disappear for weeks or months and not have to worry about keeping his place back in Horwich. He was a good planner, but too trusting – well he was in her case.

By the end of the second week, she was now fully committed and a part of the band. After staying at the hotel for a week, as she had said she would, she had taken the step and taken up residence in the fourth bedroom at Animal's father's house. She'd had to buy more clothes, so she appeared to have had everything a woman needed for a two-week holiday, just to keep up appearances. She now had a reasonable rock chick wardrobe, affording her three or four outfit changes so she wasn't constantly needing to wash stuff.

Mandy had changed the band posters. They'd taken some pictures of Jacey in the rehearsal room and then, using her iPhone, superimposed Jacey's picture onto live pics of the band replacing the old singer with Jacey.... they looked quite good. They were only temporary as soon they'd have some new shots taken at one of the forthcoming gigs. By now Jacey's appearance was transformed. She had a tattoo on each arm and one on her shoulder and one on the small of her back. She had chosen colours that looked aged. Luckily, she had no infection and they were healed fully in time for the gig. She really looked the part. But equally they could be hidden if wearing something more elegant.

She had new jeans, new denim shorts, and a black leather skirt so she could mix it up a bit. She also had some new underwear as her bra was to be visible as part of her new image. Her long blonde hair was a thing of the past. She'd died her hair silver and cut it into a bob a little like Debbie Harry used to wear hers and it really suited her – and it served to make her look that bit older. She'd even put on a little weight, what with all the drinking and snacking, giving her a more curvy look, which her new wardrobe served to accentuate. Mandy had taken a few shots of the band in their gigging gear in the basement, using a camera fixed on a tripod using a timer. Jacey was amazed at how different she had looked. Even her own father wouldn't have recognised her or given her a second look.

She'd even picked up a little Portuguese. She could order beer and food and say thanks and please and where are the toilets etc. The fact that they were English girls, well with one American, was part of the bands image though, so they always spoke English at gigs apparently. It was part of their act and their British charm. Local people often thought they were either all British or all American. It must be difficulty to pick out an accent in a foreign language. Jacey struggled to tell Spanish from Portuguese never mind an accent.

They'd done a few karaoke sessions too in the evenings and Jacey had gotten up every time to do different songs from their set. Her moves were coming on nicely and she no longer relied on the crutch that was the TV screen bearing the lyrics. She had even added her own take to some of the phrasing which worked really well. She was now no longer worried about performing in public – she loved it. All the band's venues seemed to pay cash. The bigger ones, or those booked through an agent, paid by bank transfer and Mandy received all the payments to her bank and then paid the rest of them in cash. It seemed Jacey could get away without needing a credit card or bank account for a while until she got it sorted. She would need to open a bank account at some point but was worried about using Steph's ID. She still ideally needed a new passport and identity. At this time, she hadn't got the first clue about how to look at getting this done. Maybe by mixing with some of the seedier looking guys at the gigs she might strike up a connection. She daren't ask the girls in the band or they'd immediately know something was wrong – particularly Animal. She could spin them a story about someone looking for her but the stories she'd told so far left her an orphan, no boyfriend and few friends so who would come looking for her?

CHAPTER 15

Vincenzo was laid awake next to the beautiful blond girl he had spent the evening with. She was now flat out and snoring in a most unladylike manner. But there was nothing ladylike to her apart from appearances. What if the kidnapper took the money and the daughter and fled. He could have the letter. But if he had the letter, he'd have acted on it by now; either by reporting it to the police or in some kind of trade. Criminals usually wanted something in return. This letter was dynamite. Given the number of weeks that had passed, was it safe to assume the letter no longer existed? But for now, he had other, more pressing things on his mind.

He thought back to his meeting with Digby. Digby had described how he killed Devizes by drowning him. He knew that the scene was wiped clean before Digby got there and there was no sign of the girl. The receptionist had said that Devizes was with a girl when he checked into the hotel, but her description was vague. Young and attractive and speaking English. Could the girl be Montgomery's daughter? Was she in league with Devizes? But how so? They hadn't had time to meet and form a relationship. She was assumed dead, but no body found. Maybe Devizes was holding her against her will?

The receptionist hadn't said anything to corroborate this theory, but Devizes could have threatened the girl to make her cooperate with him and pose as his girlfriend. Another loose end. He remembered that Devizes was last spotted in an Audi TT. That TT had disappeared without trace. Digby said there was no trace of the girl when he got there to kill Devices. But her leav-

ing like that, leaving no trace of her having been there, no finger-prints etc. anywhere in that room was just too much, too tidy. If she had left beforehand in that fashion, she couldn't have done it without Devizes' support, but he was in the bath. Vincenzo couldn't see Devices helping her in any way. It was likely that she was the same girl that he had been seen with on the cruise and they were posing as newlyweds.
Could he really force her into pretending to be his girlfriend for all that time without arousing any suspicion? Surely not. If she was being held against her will then they couldn't have pulled that off for so long. One or both of them must have thought they were in a relationship.

His head was about to explode. He had a habit of overthinking things. So, Devizes checked in with a woman who then left leaving no trace whatsoever – probably the same woman he was seen on the cruise with – but not definitely. This was no ordinary woman. A random girl he just picked up would leave traces. There were none – absolutely nothing. To him it stunk of a cleaned-up crime scene. But the only crime committed in that room that he knew of was the murder of Devizes and that was by the hand of Digby. It didn't make sense. He ran though other possible scenarios in his mind. Only one made any sense at all. Could the girl have killed him, cleaned up and disappeared taking the Audi? That was a possibility, but it left a big question. Digby.

Digby was sent there to kill Devizes. He had told Vincenzo that he had done so. The only way to confirm this theory was to speak to Digby, look him directly in the eye and ask him did he kill Devizes or was he already dead. If he made it appear to Digby that it was no big deal then Digby might come clean. He picked up the phone and made a call. He told his contact to arrange a meeting with Digby the following day in a neutral place, a bar in the West End. It was a catch up over a few beers and a nice lunch. Soften him up a bit, tell him there was an upcoming project for him or something. Get him off his guard.

CHAPTER 16

It was Friday night – gig night. The girls had gotten a taxi and loaded their amps and guitars into it, squeezed in, arrived at the venue, and were now unloading their gear into the side door of Vertigo Bar. Jacey was chatting to the two guys on the door. They were both taken with her. She wondered what connections they might have. She assumed she wasn't needed to set up the gear, as she knew nothing about amps or wires. The venue had the drums and PA and desk already there.

Whilst the other three continued to set up their gear, Jacey went to the disabled toilet to apply her gig makeup. She really looked the part in her ripped tee shirt, showing her bra along with her short denim shorts and high heels. Nevertheless, she was a little nervous. The time had gone so quickly. It seemed like no time at all since she was stood on the stage at her first karaoke feeling nervous and embarrassed. But all that had changed. She had become the rock chick that had been hidden inside her, it had broken free and was about to take on a new life of its own. A reincarnation.

Their first set was to begin at 9pm sharp. It would last for forty-five minutes, though they usually played for fifty. Then they took a thirty-minute drink, fag and toilet break then retuned for the second set – another forty-five minutes plus encores, usually at least one encore if not two. Tonight, they actually played three. Having opened the set with I Love Rock n Roll they repeated it again for the final encore. The first set had had a few little moments where she forgot the lyrics and just made something up – which was better than freezing or saying nothing at all, as people usually tended to notice this. At the end of the first set they'd gone around the back of the place for a fag and she'd downed two beers in twenty minutes, which was a mistake, as she had wind during the second set and was a also teeny weeny bit tipsy, causing her to slip up a couple of times. Still, no one appeared to notice. She had changed into the mini skirt for the second set. It was even more sexy than the short shorts and the guys loved it. Rachel commented that she had observed more guys coming into the bar and staying on to the end of their set than usual. This was a really good sign as, more often than not, they would come in for a couple them move on. Live music was popular – so many different bands to incorporate into a pub crawl. It seemed Jacey was the thing that kept them in there. She flirted a little during the second set, appearing to sing parts of songs to certain individuals who caught her eye. Once she had established a rapport, they stayed until the end, maybe harbouring aspirations of their own.

When they finally finished their third encore, they took a bow and disappeared around the back again. "Don't mix with the punters at the end of a show." Rachel had said. "Leave them wanting more. We can go back in there in a bit. If they have stuck around, we can then have a chat, let them buy us a beer. It keeps the bar turning over – the more they take in a night the better chance we have of getting more gigs. It's all about what they take at the bar." Rachel added. "Then we load up and get the hell out and back to the house with the gear. We can't afford any of the gear to get nicked either." Mandy added.

They were breaking her in gently and had no further gigs until the next Friday. That was good as Jacey was already a little hoarse – no doubt tomorrow she'd struggle to do a repeat performance if they had one booked. She would need to practise on her vocal technique to reduce the fatigue on her vocal cords. She'd spotted a few things on YouTube about this. Only now did she understand the importance. She wished she'd listened more to her singing tutor back home. Animal said that she'd done well, that her voice had actually lasted right to the end of her first gig.

CHAPTER 17

Vincenzo walked from the tube station to the location of the restaurant and went and sat in the café opposite. This was the reason he used that particular restaurant. He had a vantage point to eyeball his quarry. Digby arrived ten minutes early and took a seat in reception. Vincenzo watched him from his vantage point. Digby looked a little nervous. But that was by no means out of the ordinary for anyone meeting Vincenzo. He remained in his vantage spot watching Digby until ten past and then strolled over to meet with him.

Digby stood up upon seeing Vincenzo making his entrance. They shook hands and the waiter immediately took them over to a table in the corner. This was Vincenzo's usual table for doing business. He tipped the staff here generously, so he always got what he wanted.

Small talk to start things off and put his quarry off guard. He asked Digby what he had been up to the past few weeks and Digby said that he'd taken a holiday and done some decorating at home. His wife had left him some months back and he was now in the process of making the place his own again. After the chit chat Vincenzo said he had some business to discuss. Business that was potentially very lucrative for Digby. The business in question required his peculiar skills. Digby seemed relieved to hear this. Whether it was because he needed the work, or was expecting something else altogether, he didn't know, as yet. But he soon would.

"Before we talk about this new project, I have a question for you. Don't worry it makes no odds in the long run, but I need to know. How did you kill Devizes – exactly, step by step." Digby immediately started to sweat. He hesitated with his response. Vincenzo had played this routine many times before. He let him stew for a few moments and then put him out of his misery. "It's OK, I know." He said. "I know and it doesn't matter. I'm disappointed you lied to me though. Why did you lie?" Digby continued to sweat. He removed his jacket whilst he gathered his thoughts. "Look, when I arrived the place was clean. I thought there was no one in the room. Until I went into the bathroom that was. Devizes was in the bath, dead. The water was still but was warm – you could even see a little steam rising, not much just a bit. I didn't know if he'd drowned accidentally or what. There was no splashing on the bathroom floor. I didn't go in there, I just looked in from the bedroom. I waited long enough to know he wasn't pretending. It was possible he'd had a heart attack or stroke of some other thing – I didn't fucking know!! I just knew he was dead. Stone dead and not long dead. I thought maybe I'd been set up – erm.... no disrespect intended of course."

At this he started to sweat even more. "I understand, carry on." Vincenzo said. "So I just wiped anything I'd touched and left pronto. That's it really. When you called me I hadn't got my head together. I should have told you, but I didn't. Fuck knows why I didn't... I just didn't. Maybe I thought you wouldn't pay me for the job. For that I'm sorry, truly sorry" He looked at Vincenzo to see if he could learn how he felt about this. He obviously knew this already somehow or suspected enough to prompt this questioning. Either way he knew now. Vincenzo just stared into his eyes until Digby looked away. "Let's order food." Vincenzo said and summoned the waiter. Vincenzo had made up his mind. Digby was no longer to be trusted. This was to be his last supper. The food arrived quickly – both men ordered pasta. A fitting last meal for Digby thought Vincenzo.

Washed down with three or four Peroni's, Vincenzo asked Digby to meet one of his men at the tube station in fifteen minutes where he would be given details of his new assignment. "You'll enjoy it." Vincenzo had said, smiling.

Digby's mood had lightened now, and he seemed more like his usual self. After saying goodbye, Digby left for his appointment and Vincenzo paid the bill. At the meeting point Digby was met by two guys. They just nodded, no words were exchanged and the three of them set off down the steps to the underground station saying not a word. At the bottom of the stairwell was a door marked 'Staff Only'. One of the men opened the door and stood back whilst the second man went through. Digby cautiously followed. The second man, who looked Spanish and had big hair, closed the door behind them. By then Digby was falling to the ground with a bullet in his forehead. It was just above his left eye and very neat causing minimal splatter. "I'll give you four out of ten for that one, Campo." He said to the one with the big hair. "You always were a better shot than me." replied Nolan.

CHAPTER 18

After the first three gigs the word had gotten out that the band had a new, hot member and Mandy had even got two new venues offering a gig every quarter. Their band diary was quite full for the rest of the season. They made between 250 and 500 Euros a gig depending on the venue and size. It was enough to live on given they had no rent to pay and even allowed them to go out most nights. If they stayed in, they rarely cooked and usually got a takeaway of some sort. Occasionally they ate out in one of the bars they played in as they either got a discount, free drinks or even free food occasionally. Rach knew all the ways to get a free drink or free meal.

Jacey had been worried that living with them would mean she was asked too many questions, but although they were quite close knit, they didn't live in each other's pockets, occasionally spending the evening in their own rooms or out with their own friends. But most nights the four of them went out for at least a couple of drinks.

Animal had continued to be the one that Jacey trusted the least having failed to bond with her. Whilst Animal was the quietest and most reserved member of the band, she seemed much closer to the other two than to Jacey. This was understandable. Maybe she still harboured concerns that Jacey would up and walk leaving them back to square one. Whatever was the case, she remained a little cooler with Jacey. Often Jacey would catch Animal looking at her as though she were a tiger studying its prey – maybe a kind of role reversal.

Jacey was enjoying her new role and intended to keep this part for quite a while longer. She was spending a lot less than she would have been without the band, so her Euro cash would last her a quite a long time. Nevertheless, she was still nervous about having so much other cash stashed in her little bag in her room. The house seemed quite secure, but she needed to be able to set up a bank account and deposit some of the cash for safety's sake. For this she badly needed a new identity. The only alternative was to use Steph's identity. If anyone was looking for Steph, then the setting up of a new debit card and bank account may trigger an alarm that would lead them to her address with the band as she'd have to use that as her address.

She had searched the internet for stories of a missing girl with the same name but had found nothing. Maybe Stephanie's father hadn't even reported her missing. Still, were he to do so at some point in the future, they may still track down a new account in that name and that would be bad. However, there must be several people sharing the same name. She could always say she found the girl's passport. She didn't think she'd face jail for that. No-one would be able to prove anything. Even if they suspected Steph was a stiff, they had no body, no evidence, nothing. What should she do?

At one particular venue in the new town, they were asked to play much later, starting at eleven pm and not finishing until 2am. Jacey had chatted to the two bouncers whilst the rest of the band were setting up. These two particular characters were much shadier than your usual bouncer, if that is indeed possible. They seemed to have quiet conversations with the odd supposedly innocent passer-by, as though they were ordering something or organising something. Drugs? The big guy was called Juan and the bigger guy was called Antonio – Toni.

When they finished their set and the others were packing up, Jacey said she needed the loo but went out front and found

Toni alone. Juan must have gone for a drink or to visit the loo. She approached him. "You were great tonight – you're a great band – everyone say so." Said Toni in a thick Portuguese accent. "Thanks Toni." She replied. And then she went for it. "Say Toni, don't take this the wrong way, but I had some trouble back home, it's my sister. She's a year younger than me, twenty-three, she married a year ago, but her husband is abusive, a real jerk. The police have done nothing, and that's because he is a cop himself. She's run away tonight; she's taken the bus to Liverpool where she has a friend. Trouble is, as her husband's a cop, he has access to trace her movements, credit cards and stuff so it's only a matter of time until he finds her. Next time he finds her he just might kill her." She tried to look sad and worried. "I think that, if she had a new identity, she could escape him for good, go somewhere else, like I did, and get away from him forever. Maybe join me over here. Do you know where I could get a passport made up? UK would be perfect but anything really, just to get her out of this hole. I just don't know what else to do." Tears were now welling up in her eyes. Toni looked at her. She was becoming a fine actress and playing the scared little girl was one of her best parts. "I'm sorry to hear that." Said Toni. He seemed to think about her question for a few moments then said "I know a few people, I'll ask around. I think I know who can help you, but it'll cost you." She looked up into his eyes. "I have some money, hopefully I can afford it." She said still with tears in her eyes. Toni smiled at her. "You're back here in two weeks. I'll see what I can do." She smiled at him and said "Thanks, you're a life saver. Literally. But if your friend can't help, don't worry, we'll think of something." She smiled, turned around and returned to the girls, they had finished packing their instruments and were chatting to a group of lads.

As she walked back into the venue, Animal was watching her, studying her. She went over to Rach and said, "Who are your friends?". Mandy introduced James who said he was an agent and he'd very much liked what he'd seen and would report back to his team to see if they had any work for the girls. They chatted about band stuff for a while then James and his friends left as the place was almost ready to close up.

Most people had already left or moved on to somewhere else but there still remained a few people who were nearly done. As they chatted, Animal still watched her. She caught fleeting glimpses of her looking at her, studying her. Did she suspect something, or was she just jealous of the attention Jacey was now getting when she had only just come into the picture? Animal rarely got male attention unless she was with the others. But they were all staying at her place, she had the power to take away their homes and rehearsal space. She was the undisclosed leader of the band.

Still, that shouldn't affect Jacey too badly – she could just move on, find a new hotel and continue being Steph for a little longer – back to plan A. Nevertheless, she needed to understand what it was with Animal. Maybe she should try and spend more time with her, become closer. She'd have to work on that. It wasn't something she looked forward to.

CHAPTER 19

Their next couple of gigs were even better, they made fewer mistakes and Jacey's confidence grew, which meant her performances were better too. Now she knew the lyrics and formats to all the songs in the set, her mind was free to focus on performing to the crowd. Each gig drew more people than the last. They already had a following but they were typically venue or locality based. People never used to travel to see the band but now it seemed some were. Jacey studied each guy that came to multiple gigs, to check them out, to ensure they were just guys looking for a good band. Or trying it on with one of the girls. So far none had stood out as being something else. Maybe she was being overly careful. But she knew there was no such thing. She was still on the run.

The following week they were playing a little further afield, in a bar in Carvoiero, called 'The Jailhouse'. It was a funny venue, accessed via a narrow side street and a little off the main road into the town. It was a really popular live music venue and had been for many years. The previous owner had played for a couple of British bands and he and his partner had moved to Carvoiero and bought The Jailhouse. She had run the place and he had organised the music and played himself most nights. Usually him, or him and another guitarist, they played to backing tracks and they were really great by all accounts. Apparently, they'd sold up and the new owners were now trying local bands.

Space was very limited. Animal was grumpy because she had to squeeze into a tiny corner and Rach and Mandy were at the extreme edges of the little stage. This meant Jacey was out front on her own – no room for her on the stage as well. The owner had given her a radio mic so she was free to roam the venue and even the first floor, where there was another bar and a pool table. Guitars adorned the walls – they looked old, dusty and some lacked a few strings.

As the girls set up their gear, Jacey chatted to some of the people in there who were sat close to the band by the small bar. She also chatted to the new owner. He told her that The Jailhouse was very popular with English tourists who loved live music. They'd had many British celebrities in, including a few names from Coronation Street that she didn't recognise. Apparently one of their posters had even been in an episode, pinned to a board in the background of a scene in someone's kitchen. Marvellous. But she kept smiling and appeared impressed. She then went upstairs. There were a few lads playing pool and a few older couples sat where they had a gallery view down onto the band. She thought this would be a good place to take some pictures of the band. When she went back down, she asked the owner if he could take a few pictures of them when they started playing. He said he would – he'd done it before for other acts that he'd had play.

Apparently, they were the first, full, four-piece band he had booked that featured a real drummer – hence the narrow space. He said that if it worked out, he'd get a larger stage area installed, he knew someone who did this, so it was no problem, just costly. He had borrowed a drum kit from someone for the night as he didn't yet have a house kit. Animal hadn't been impressed with it. It needed tuning and the lugs wouldn't tighten properly, and the cymbals were cheap ones. Still, it was better than lugging one to gigs. Jacey could tell by the body language behind her that there would be little appetite to return here again any time soon. Even Doctor Who with his Tardis would struggle to make space for a band. They needed space to perform, to move around, and to strut their stuff. Even so much as a two-step would mean bashing your knee into the drums or brushing your elbow into a cymbal. It was far from ideal.

When they finished setting up, they did a brief soundcheck. It sounded surprisingly good, but they were loud for a relatively small venue. The owner came over and asked Jacey if they could maybe turn it down a bit as it was louder than he expected, and people couldn't chat when they were playing. They shouldn't be chatting whilst we're playing thought Jacey, but she smiled and said they'd do what they could. Rach heard the conversation and went to the desk and lowered one of the sliders on an unused channel of the mixer. This seemed to appease the owner who thanked them and returned to the bar. Rach smiled at Jacey and they both giggled.

Next, whilst waiting to start, they all went upstairs where they found the pool table was free. They had a game of doubles – Jacey offered to play alongside Animal. Rach and Mandy were both quite good. Animal gave Jacey a few tips on which shots to play but nevertheless they lost both games. The girls kept glancing over the balcony to check on their gear between shots. You could never be too careful. As they finished their second game, Rach came back from checking on the gear and said, "I think that's James, the promoter down there, I wonder if he's here to see us or the owner?". "One way to find out." said Mandy and they replaced their cues and went back downstairs, all smiles.

James said "Hi'" to them but made no effort to engage in further conversation. They didn't press him and went over to tune their instruments before they started their first set. They assumed he was there to speak with the new owner. As they went through the first set, somewhat more staid than usual due to the lack of space, Jacey tried to make up for it by moving over to the punters and singing parts of songs directly to them or sitting on a guys' knees and singing to them. She even went behind the bar and poured a pint, very badly, whilst singing Born To Be Wild. The owner laughed. All attention was on Jacey. She made up for the limitations of the stage in performance.

No-one seemed to be looking at the band, just the singer. When they finished the first set, the bar was full and everyone applauded. “I need a fag.” Said Rach. “I need a drink.” Said Mandy. Animal didn’t say anything, so they took their drinks outside. “I’ll get a round in.” Jacey offered and went over to the bar. James was at the bar. He waited until the owner had gone upstairs then said to Jacey “That was some performance. But I’m surprised to see an act as good as you playing in this tiny place.” Jacey smiled, ordered her drinks then turned to him and replied “We just love playing. We’re the first four-piece he’s had. I guess this place isn’t really suitable for any more than a duo.” James smiled. “Have you ever considered going it alone? You could get backing tapes made up and then you could go solo. You’d make more money that way, than a quarter of your band fee.” Jacey said she had never considered this. She didn’t know if it was just banter or if it was leading somewhere. “Come to think of it, you could front any band you wanted. You have a great voice and you could pull off mainstream pop just a well as rock.” He obviously had no idea how new she was to the whole band thing. “I love playing in a band with great musicians. I’m just the icing on the cake.” She said and even sounded like she really meant it. “These girls are good, don’t get me wrong, but they aren’t in your league. Some might say they are holding you back.” Jacey looked at him now, not really knowing what to say to this. Should she be offended by proxy? The silence said enough to James to know that he may be on to something. “Look, give me your number and we can chat about this tomorrow, more privately. “

She thought for a moment and James passed her his pen and his business card. She wrote her number on the back of it and handed it back to him. “I’ll call you at eleven, we can go for a spot of lunch somewhere nice.” he said. Jacey smiled, and said “that would be lovely.” She then took two of the drinks saying, “Keep your eye on these, I’ll be back in a moment.” And headed outside with Rach and Animal's drinks. She returned for Mandy's and hers, smiled at James, and then re-joined the girls. They were all chatting about how cramped the space was, and how none of them fancied going all the way over here to play in such a small place ever again. Mandy said that there was a reason that they'd taken this gig. Apparently in Summer they had gigs on the beach, on an elevated stage, but when she had made enquiries they had asked if they played anywhere local. Mandy had organised for someone called Juan from the organisers to come and see them. She hadn't seen him yet, so they needed to ensure the second set was a good one, that way they may get the bigger gig. This seemed to change their mood a little. "Then why didn't you tell us this sooner?" asked Animal. "It was a last-minute thing and I forgot – sorry!" said Mandy. When they went back in and headed back to the stage area to start the second set, a Portuguese guy in jeans and a light-coloured jacket went over to the stage area and approached Mandy and shouted "Mandy?". "That's me, you must be Juan." Mandy replied. "Yes, I come to see you play. We can chat after you finish. I live up the hill so I will enjoy a drink or two. Me no drive today." With that he waved at them and went over to the corner where he sat with a couple of other guys that looked like locals.

The second set went well, better than the first one in fact. Jacey played up to some of the guys in the room but stayed away from going behind the bar this time, as she couldn't get to the bar for the people ordering drinks – there was a queue, three deep at all times. The staff were run off their feet and empty glasses were piling up. Juan and his friends watched the band, occasionally chatting, or shouting at each other, and more than a couple of drinks were consumed. One of them seemed to be queuing at the bar all the time. James had stuck around for the first couple of songs but as the place got really busy, he had left. He didn't wave or anything just left out of the front door.

When they got to the last song the crowd were shouting for

more. They went into their chosen encore track, Rock 'n' Roll by Led Zeppelin, and the owner came over to Jacey and signalled to her that this was to be their last song. He was sweating profusely; they had obviously been run off their feet. They finished it with the classic John Bonham drum roll and big end. Jacey then said "Thank you everyone and goodnight." She waved then returned the mic and nodded to the girls to say game over. They understood and replaced their guitars onto the stands and all four moved towards the front door to go outside for some air. A few people shook their hands on their way out, one patted Jacey on the shoulder. She was glad she wasn't living in the seventies where she'd have gone home with a bruised bum from all the pats. Or was that just on TV?

When they got outside Mandy said "That wasn't so bad. They loved us." "I'm sure they'll want us back." Replied Rach. "Do we? or don't we? I say no, there's no fucking room back there, it's a sweatshop and we have a taxi ride both ways. It's hardly worth the effort." Was Animal's contribution to the debate. No-one could argue with the taxi costs and it did reduce their income. The pub wasn't paying top whack either as it was only a small venue. "What happened to Juan?" asked Jacey. "No fucking idea." replied Mandy. "He wasn't there when we finished" "His friends were still there" said Animal. "Maybe he was in the toilet?" "I'll go check on him in a couple of minutes" replied Rach as she finished her cigarette and dragged the last of her beer.

Before they had a chance to go back inside, Juan came out to meet them. He went to Rach and said "That was some performance girls, you're good!! A little rockier than we usually have on the beach, but I think it could work! We're planning a series of beach party gigs and I'll like to put you forward to the committee as part of a rock weekend. It's advertised all over the Algarve and we usually get a lot of people. Rach gave Juan a band business card, she'd had them made up for the band for exactly this purpose. Juan said he'd get back to them the following week after his meeting. The girls nodded their approval. "I say we go for five hundred for this gig." Animal said. "I'll suss them out and get the best we can, don't worry about that." Rach replied, once again acting as the band manager.

With that they went back inside. There were a few less people in there now. They could hear the clicking of pool balls upstairs. When they walked past the bar, the owner called over to them "On the house!" He had lined up four halves of lager on the bar. "Thanks." replied Mandy and they took their drinks, downed them in one, replaced the glasses on the bar and went to pack their stuff. One of the guys sat with Juan whistled his approval. Very rock chick. Jacey stayed behind to collect their fee whilst the others packed.

They were just finishing up when they heard the toot of a horn outside. Mandy looked outside and saw their taxi driver waiting for them. He was blocking the narrow street outside, so they gathered their instruments and stuff, bid their goodbyes to the owner, and went outside to the taxi. By now a couple of cars were queuing behind the taxi. They put their amps in the boot and guitars into the back and got in. Jacey split the money four ways on the journey back. The taxi dropped them off at the house where they stowed the gear and sat in the lounge for one more drink before going to bed. It was late, too late to venture out and they were all tired.

The following morning Jacey went out at around 10.30am. She said she was going for a stroll in town and to do some shopping. Only Animal was up, Rach and Mandy were still in bed. Jacey wondered if Animal had only got up to check on her. She wondered if she would follow her. She decided she was being silly. She got her purse and phone walked into town. She arrived at Buddies Bar and ordered a Sprite. At eleven her phone rang. It was James. "I have taken the liberty of making a lunch reservation." he said. "I have a table booked at A Ruina on the front – you know it? It serves the finest fish." He added. Jacey said she knew where it was and agreed to meet him there at noon. She had forgotten about reserving a table there herself when she arrived, but with the band and all, she'd failed to show and completely forgotten about it up until now. It would be nice to check the place out.

She finished her drink and then had a stroll through the craft shops that were open and arrived at A Ruina at five to twelve. James was stood by the steps leading to the entrance. He looked very smart in a light suit and open neck shirt. He shook her hand and followed her into the restaurant. They went up the narrow stairs to the top where he had a table reserved with the best view, looking over the ocean and over the beach and restaurants below. She could see the escalators going to the new town and the large ships out to sea. There were people parascending and small planes flying, dragging advertising banners behind them for night clubs and who know what. This felt like both a first date and being on holiday. She was wearing the nice dress she had purchased when she first arrived, along with the belt and some light shoes she'd also bought later. Elegant but not too hot.

They ordered their drinks, and the drinks arrived very quickly along with menus. "Let's eat and then talk business over a cognac." James said. Jacey agreed. He was very charming. He told her a little about Albufeira, about Salazar and the war and about some of the places he liked to visit and some nice, private beaches only accessible from the sea. It all sounded idyllic. James recommended lobster, so they shared a lobster. It was delicious. By the time they finished, neither had room for a desert. James ordered two Remi Martin's and when they arrived, he savoured his first mouthful, then replaced the glass and said "Now let's talk business."

CHAPTER 20

Rach and Mandy had just surfaced and were in the kitchen having their first coffee. It was after one pm already. "Jacey gone out?" Rach asked. Animal replied "Out before ten, she's a strange one that one. She's hiding something and I'm going to find out, one way or another." Mandy looked at her for a long time, considering what she'd said. Both Mandy and Rach had come to really like Jacey. But they both knew what Animal could be like. They knew she'd had a tough upbringing, and something had gone on with her father that culminated in her stopping seeing him and this house being bought and effectively handed over to her. All the bills were paid, she paid nothing bar food and drink. It was very strange, but you never looked a gift horse in the mouth. She replied to Animal with a shrug and went back to her coffee. "Relax, she's fine." She's only just got here, she's enjoying herself, she might have met a guy, who knows." Rach said. Animal just nodded; she wasn't convinced. "Don't piss her off, things are just getting good again for us." Rach admonished. Animal replied with shrug. "What you need is a good shag." Mandy said to Animal. This made her smile. "You offering?" she said with a slight smile. "Fuck no. Go find your own bitch." Mandy replied and they all laughed.

No-one spoke for a couple of minutes whilst they all finished their coffees. "You heard back from that Juan man yet?" Mandy asked Rach. "Nothing; don't suppose you have either?". "He won't contact me will he?" Mandy replied. Rach nodded; Animal just watched. Then she chirped in with "So we gonna ask for five hundred Euros if he does get back to us?" "I reckon so." Said Rach.

Then she added "But fuck The Jailhouse. It was like being in jail playing in that tiny area. They should stick to duos." They all murmured their agreement. "Right, I'm off outside for a fag then I'll take a shower and go work on some songs." Rach said. "Yeah, I'll follow you down there later." Mandy replied. Animal just watched them.

CHAPTER 21

"What I'm offering applies to you and you only. Whilst your band is good, this particular client is looking for a glamorous, good looking rock chick lead singer to front their house band. The band are brilliant musicians, all guys by the way, been playing together for six years. They get on really well. They do exactly what their manager says. Consummate professionals. And I'd like you to become their seventh member; add some much-needed glamour to their line-up. Did I say they have two girl backing singers also? They play every day except change-over day, sometimes twice a day. Two forty-five-minute sets typically. You'll need to learn a lot of songs though. They have some seven hours of material, so they play mostly different songs each night, so the people on the cruise that choose to see the show every night get treated to a different set every night they are on the ship. On the one hand she was loving her new career as a singer. But part of that was the camaraderie of being in an all-girl band, playing bars and clubs and having a great time. But working with a professional band on a big cruise liner that was all blokes was something different altogether. It was more like a real job.

"Have you ever been on a cruise before Jacey?" James asked. She thought about this and then replied "No, never." "Well, you'll love it. The boat is absolutely massive. It's the fifth or sixth largest one in the world and it's the only one that is powered by liquified natural gas, I think that's it. It has more than two and a half thousand cabins and is over three-hundred metres long. It's unimaginably huge. You can get lost on there and not be seen for days." Jacey smiled. This was indeed unimaginably huge. She would need to think over the pros and cons of this. She'd need good ID to pull this one off – she could continue using Steph's passport, but she'd need a bank account to be paid into. She asked him how long she had to consider his fine offer. "Well the ship sails in four weeks. They want everything tied up as soon as possible. I have three other girls that are desperate to win this position, but you are top of my list. I can't give you more than 48 hours. Today is Saturday. Let's meet here again on Monday at noon. I'll treat you to another lunch to celebrate you joining my team." Jacey smiled. "OK that sounds fair enough. I need to speak to the girls and square things with them. Am I likely to be seasick?" she asked in a girlish way. "These ships are so large that you wouldn't even know you were on a ship. You feel virtually no movement at all. You wouldn't know if you were docked in port or full speed ahead out at sea, they are that smooth." She knew from her own experience that she would have no problems, but she was keeping up appearances. "If I agree, how long will I have until I need to board the ship?" "You'll need a week of rehearsals with the band to get up to speed with enough songs to get by. You'll continue to learn new songs every day so by the end of your first working month we'd expect you to be familiar with the complete set list. Are you OK with that?" "I think so. I learned our set in two weeks from scratch and we were hardly professional when it came to putting the hours in." Jacey replied. "I can assure you this won't be an easy job, at least not at first. In addition to playing you will have other duties. The captain likes to entertain some evenings you may be expected to join specially selected guests for dinner, or the occasional lunch. You might even get to meet some famous celebrities and even musicians – they just love these big ships." he said. "And how do I get paid?" she asked. "Monthly in arrears directly into your bank account. All your expenses whilst on board, except your drinks and lunches, will be paid for so you'll have relatively little expenditure. You will get a meal when you are working in the evening. You can bank it all. I have people who've worked these liners for fifteen years and retired at forty. That could be you." She smiled. "It's a great opportunity, I can see that. But it's a big step and it would mean being away from everyone and everything I know, so I need time to make the right decision." "That's OK, I understand. Until Monday then?" Jacey nodded. He said he had a tab there so there was no need to ask for the bill. They got up and left. He nodded at the waiter who nodded back politely. James was obviously a VIP to them. Jacey nodded too; the waiters eyes lingered on her a little longer than necessary. They shook hands and James headed off by the beach past the other restaurants and Jacey headed back towards the square. She stopped off at the Piccadilly Cocktail Bar and ordered a diet sprite. She needed time to think away from everyone else.

If she worked on the ship, she would have the opportunity to meet rich people, maybe extort or steal from them. But she would be a well-known face to everyone on board, a near celebrity. This was something that could work for her but equally well against her. If anyone was looking for her, they wouldn't think to look for her there. And they'd never look towards a singer as she had no experience whatsoever as Annie. It was a perfect hiding place. But did she still need to hide? It was a large ship. Maybe you could hide on one of those things, it was so big. All that said, she'd be getting a great salary with virtually no outgoings. She didn't need to resort to crime. But she needed it, she wanted to, it was something inside her that needed to get out. She needed the thrill and now that she'd tasted it she wanted more. She even enjoyed killing. She often thought back to how she had snuffed the life out of Stephanie. It even felt so good to think about it and replay it over and over in her mind. Killing Dom was more of a watery blur. She knew that she would have to curb these desires, so they didn't take her over. Maybe if she found a nice boyfriend on board it would take the place of her dark side. On the other hand, she was loving playing with the girls in the band. It was a relatively easy life, the only thing that nagged at her was Animal. She had no sound ground to feel the way she did about her, but her instincts had never let her down so far. Everything revolved around Animal – she had all the power. This wasn't good.

After she finished her Sprite she went back to the house. The following night they had a gig at the place Toni worked at. He had said he'd let her know about the passport. If Toni could get one made up soon, she'd have time to open a bank account before going onboard ship. If he didn't then she'd either have to use Steph's or turn the job down. She didn't want to mention the job to the band until she'd made her mind up. She considered her options as she walked back to the house.

CHAPTER 22

She arrived at the house and went straight to the kitchen to make a coffee. Animal was sat at the worktop with an empty mug. "Want one?" Jacey said. "Sure." replied Animal. "Good lunch date?" How did she know? She couldn't possibly know with whom she'd dined. Jacey smiled like a child caught stealing sweets. "How did you guess?" Jacey replied. Animal smiled, obviously pleased with herself. "One of the guys who has come watching us I assume. It's only a matter of time!" Jacey refused to be drawn in, she just smiled. She poured the two coffees and smiled again. Guitar sounds were issuing from downstairs. "Rach and Mandy hard at it?" Jacey asked. "No, they're playing their guitars." Animal replied with a grin. "I'd better check up on them." said Jacey and with that, got up and went down into the basement. As she was going through the door Animal shouted, "Call me if you need rhythm." Jacey waved her empty hand whilst holding the door with her foot and continued downstairs.

Whilst she held the pretence of being excited to hear the new song the girls were working on, she was fighting back the urge to go back upstairs and hit Animal over the head with the coffee pot. She knew that if she stuck around here then sooner or later, she would come to blows with Animal and probably kill her. This both excited her and appalled her, as spontaneity usually meant a lack of planning. She was far too clever to get caught. Good, reliable drummers were so hard to find. If they knew any, she could make waves, but they all lived in Animal's house. She was going nowhere. She was the band bedrock. Literally. She hoped Toni would have something for her later that evening.

The guitarists had been working on an old classic, Wishing Well by Free. It had some great guitar and would need some great vocals to finish it off. Jacey logged on the iMac they used for recording and production and found the lyrics and printed them out. "We'll need another hour or so until we're ready to try it out." Mandy said. Jacey said, "That's fine, I'll go up to my room and listen to the song to get the format and phrasing." And that's what she did. She went back upstairs and to her room. Animal was nowhere to be seen. Jacey changed into her jeans and tee shirt and then found the song on YouTube and played it over and over through her headphones. It wasn't too bad, she had heard it on the radio. Within the hour she was sure she had the format and all the changes. She was part way there with the lyrics too. Just then there was a knock on her door. It was Animal. "They're ready for us." she said, like a hospital nurse or a dental assistant. "Coming now." Jacey replied. She left her headphones on the bed, put the phone in her jeans pocket and went down to the basement.

That evening Jacey decided to check on the money. It was there in the safe exactly as she had left it. One thing she had never done was to count how much money she actually had. One problem was that most of it was in sterling. At some point she'd have to get some converted to Euros. She decided to count how much she had then split it into wads of five-hundred pounds ready to take to several banks and exchanges. She locked her bedroom door and went into the bathroom. She placed the piles of money into the bath. She counted the first – wad and it came to £5,000. There were over 40 of these wads – mostly the same but the values of notes changed so, without counting each note, she knew she had over two-hundred grand. It seemed a lot, but she knew it wouldn't last forever. None of the money spent had been tracked back to her and there was no more news on the internet, so she assumed she was safe to start to spend the money. But exchanging too much in one place may alert the authorities. She counted two thousand, placed it in an envelope and placed it into her bag. Tomorrow she would get it exchanged for Euros.

As she was putting the remaining wads back into the bag, she spotted something strange – a loose piece of paper, folded to a similar size to a note, mixed in with the wads. She hadn't spotted this before. She fished it out and looked at it. It was a letter, handwritten. It was signed by a Marco Ricci and disclosed details of three murders committed by someone called Vincenzo. This must have been in her father's possession and somehow ended up with the money. Maybe it was in the bag containing the money? Had he left it there deliberately so the kidnapper would find it? Or was the bag the place he kept his secrets and this one he had neglected to remove? Either way she had it now. She read it again. It contained details of three murders that Vincenzo had apparently committed himself and it also stated the names of the three victims. She went to google and searched for these three names. Sure enough there were news press articles, about all three, but nothing about anyone being suspected or convicted. It looked like the cases had gone cold.
Next, she searched for Vincenzo – nothing.

Lastly, she searched for Marco Ricci. Here she found newspaper articles about a Marco Ricci being killed. It was bizarre. A couple out walking their dog in the country had found his body up a tree of all places. Apparently, he'd climbed up there and committed suicide by blowing his brains out. But why go up a tree? She knew suicides often didn't make logical sense but going up a tree? She tried to put herself in that position. Maybe he was hiding up there. Hiding from something so dreadful that he would rather kill himself than face it, or him, or them. Or maybe it was a murder made to look like a suicide. Maybe this Vincenzo character was onto him and Marco wrote this letter to incriminate him in the event of his death? But how had her father gotten hold of it? Was it part of his job to handle stuff like this? Unlikely. She knew he was dodgy, maybe he was in with this Vincenzo guy? Maybe he was due to drop the letter off somewhere after the money drop off? That would explain him having the letter on him at the time. Maybe her father wanted to drop Vincenzo in it by leaving the letter with the money? so the criminal who was blackmailing him would find it. Knowing the criminal would find the letter too irresistible not to use as leverage. That would surely either get him killed by Vincenzo or caught by the authorities. All supposition. Without more facts she wouldn't know any more. She would of course keep the letter as it could come in useful at some point. Then a thought hit her. Maybe Vincenzo had killed Marco to get hold of this letter? If so, this Vincenzo guy might still be looking for it. That meant he may have looked into her father and seen he was blown up thus destroying the letter, if indeed he did have it and had it on him at the time. Whatever happened, this letter had value. She found an envelope and placed the letter inside and secured it with the cash in the safe.

CHAPTER 23

She didn't sleep well. She was thinking of the pros and cons of working on a cruise ship. Could she even pull it off? Playing pubs in a band was one thing but taking the step up to professional was something else. James had thought she could do it, so it was certainly a possibility. She needed to make her decision the following day. After trying to sleep she decided to read. Finally, at seven-thirty, she got up to make a coffee.

She went down to the kitchen and found Rach nursing a cold coffee sat by the counter. She looked up at Jacey with the appearance of someone with the weight of the world on her shoulders and who'd had even less sleep than herself. "What's up?" Jacey said. Rach then burst into tears. Jacey went to her and held her for a moment. She'd never seen any of the girls in this state before and expected Rach to be the last one to break down like this. "I'm glad you came down. I have something to say." Jacey looked into her eyes trying to read her intentions. She looked sad not confrontational. "I love it here, but I miss home. In a couple of weeks, when the season is done, I've decided to go back home. But I know it'll kill you guys after all the work and effort we've put into the band. But it's something I just have to do." "It's OK, they'll understand." Jacey replied. "You think so?" "I do. It'll be tough but they'll understand. We'll just have to find another you whilst we have no gigs. It'll work out." Rach looked relieved. "It's just something I've got to do." she said again. "You don't have to explain to me." Jacey said and poured them both a fresh coffee. "The longer you leave it the worse it'll be – you've got to tell them this morning." Jacey said. Rach nodded, welling up again. "It'll be better after you get some breakfast inside you." Jacey said, heading for the fridge. "Not for me – I couldn't eat a thing. My stomach is in knots." Rach said. Jacey got out the bacon and an egg and proceeded to make herself a cooked breakfast. This had made her own decision much easier.

They chatted whilst Jacey ate her breakfast and by nine o'clock Mandy surfaced. "Go get Animal, I've got something to say to you guys." Rach said welling up once more. Mandy looked at Jacey whose expression gave nothing away. "I'll go call her." Jacey said and headed upstairs towards Animal's room. Rach and Mandy looked at each other, Rach started to cry again. They could hear Jacey knocking on Animal's door and asking her to get up as they needed to talk. Rach got up and poured Mandy a coffee and then, almost as an afterthought, got out another mug and poured one for Animal. A strong one.

"What's going on, where's the fucking fire?" Animal said as she came into the kitchen, hair mussed up and dressing gown open at the front revealing her panties and bare chest. "Rach has something to say to us." Jacey said as Rach tried to get hold of herself. She took a deep breath. "I've decided to leave the band. It's not that I don't love you guys and what we do and everything, I do, I really do. But I've gotta go back home. I've been away a long time and I've got bridges to build." Mandy went over and hugged her. Jacey stayed put as did Animal. Animal wasn't looking at Rach but at Jacey as if she'd put her up to it. "The gear stays here." Animal said in an unfriendly manner. Rach just nodded. Mandy gave Animal the daggers.

"Actually, I'm leaving the band as well." Jacey said. As if Rach's bombshell wasn't enough. And this sideswiped all three of them. They just looked at her. "That fucking James has made you an offer, hasn't he?" Animal said. Jacey just nodded. Animal stood up and thundered back upstairs like the spoiled teenager that she was. "Fuck, that's the band gone in the blink of an eye." Mandy said sadly. "You'll find new members." Jacey said.

"What's the gig with James then?" Rach said, happy that the attention had been diverted away from herself. "He's offered me a job singing with a band on a cruise ship. Great money, all-inclusive and I get to see the world. It's just too good to refuse, a once-in-a-lifetime opportunity." she said like a teenager. "If I see any opportunity for any of you guys, I'll be straight in touch" she said. Mandy smiled. "I guess it's back to square one for Animal and I."

By now it was nine-thirty and Jacey, Rach and Mandy had finished eating and returned to their rooms to get dressed. The letter was on Jacey's mind. Somewhere she had an alarm bell ringing. Did Dom know about this letter? Was he planning on using it to his advantage? If he found it, she had no doubt that he wouldn't have just sat on it and done nothing – it was potentially dynamite. It was entirely possible that he had missed the letter too and knew nothing about it. All that mattered was that she didn't leave a trail behind her. She'd been very careful with her identity switching. She didn't think it was possible to track her all the way here from London. She was worrying unnecessarily.

She decided to do some research on people called Vincenzo in London. Although the name was probably Italian, everything led back to London so that must be where he was or even is, based. Naturally she found lots of articles on Vincenzo's in London. She needed to narrow it down a bit. This guy was bad, a murderer. But she found nothing directly related to murder. She did find a reference to some company building a big new office block in London and the company owners reserving the top two floors as their own pads. One was called Harry Rimmer – he must have been the top guy as he had the top floor, the other was called Vincenzo Dente. A little more digging into these two names gave her what she wanted. Both had been suspected of major crime and had connections to organised crime. Neither had been convicted of anything. They were squeaky clean.

Could this be the Vincenzo mentioned in the letter? She tried searching for combinations of Vincenzo and the victims' names – nothing. She then tried searching for combinations of her father's name and both Vincenzo and Rimmer. Bingo. A photo of her father and Rimmer at some big bash celebrating Rimmer's company receiving an award – Vincenzo Dente got a mention but wasn't in the picture. If the Vincenzo in the letter was indeed Vincenzo Dente, then now she had something to go on, a trail to follow.

CHAPTER 24

Once showered and dressed she went back downstairs to the kitchen. Rach and Mandy were there with another coffee. Rach automatically poured another one into a cup that was waiting and passed it to Jacey. "Thanks." she said and smiled. "So, it'll be our last gig tonight then Sisters. Better make it a good one!" Jacey and Rach both looked at each other. Mandy said "Don't worry, I understand and wish you both well. Animal will come around too. By tonight she'll be her normal self." Then all three of them managed a smile.

The band had been great whilst it lasted. But all good things come to an end. They laughed about some of the gigs they'd played and the people they'd met. After chatting for a while Jacey said she was going out to look around the shops and off she went. She had a wad of sterling in her purse that she planned on exchanging it for Euros. This went very smoothly indeed. No awkward questions. She then went around the boutiques and found a couple of nice, dressy outfits that she thought would work well on a cruise ship. They would also help to make her look that bit older. She knew Toni started work long before the band rocked up to the venue, so she thought she'd go there now and see if he was there thus avoiding any of the band seeing her later that evening. Toni was stood outside as always. There were a few people inside, but it was quieter compared to what it would be like in three or four hours' time.

He saw her approach and smiled. She walked up to him and he hugged her like an old friend. She knew this was for the benefit of anyone watching. "It's all good. I'll have it tonight." Jacey hadn't expected this – she hadn't given him anything yet - it meant the passport was already made up using a name – but in who's name? She smiled and asked, "What name will it be in?" "I don't know." Toni answered "The pick pocketers steal passports and then they sell them on. Very simple and clean." "But it'll be reported missing and then the passport will be useless – the authorities at an airport would know it was a stolen passport." Jacey said trying to not sound emotional. "I need a passport my sister can use safely for a period of time."

"Is she going anywhere nice?" Toni replied a little sarcastically. "Not without a passport." Jacey replied. She knew she could continue to use Steph's passport, but she preferred to not use that moving forward thus stopping dead any trail relating to Steph the stiff. "So, you don't want one then?" Toni said. "I need one she can use for a while, Toni. I thought you had passports made up from scratch. I have a photo ready and everything." Toni paused for a few moments. "Well, it can be done, but these passports don't stand up to close scrutiny." he said.

She knew her best bet now was to keep using Steph's passport. Whilst she had been very careful and she didn't believe Steph's father or family would look for her, someone, at some point in the future, may. It might be next year or in ten years. Still, she needed it for the cruise gig and that was it. She wasn't planning on working the ships as a career, just long enough to.... Well, to what? Land a rich guy? Steal more money? Work out her next step? Whatever it was, it would be sooner rather than years later. Steph's ID would have to suffice for now.

She thanked Toni and said that she really needed a new identity and a new life to escape her old life, so unless he could get her the real deal then she would look elsewhere. Toni said he'd make some calls and speak to her later. She wondered if this was Toni's sales pitch – offer something he knew wouldn't hit the mark, then come back later with the real deal but a whole lot more expensive. She'd find out later that evening. She had the cash; she would be out of Dodge soon with or without Toni's help. It was no biggie.

CHAPTER 25

There was an atmosphere between the girls at the gig. Animal was still the sulky teenager. Once she'd had a couple of drinks, she loosened up a bit. Jacey suspected that, by the end of the night, having had a few more drinks, she may have more to say. The gig went well. They decided not to announce any band breakup to allow Animal and Mandy to regroup ready for the start of the next season.

During the interval Jacey had gone outside and spoken to Toni once again. "I can get you one made up. It'll take a couple of days and I'll need a photo and the details of name, place of birth, birthday etc. If you can get me these tonight, then you'll have your passport within three days. "How much?" asked Jacey – the ten-million-dollar question. "Ten thousand Euros." Toni said whilst maintaining a straight face. Jacey looked at him. "And just where do you expect me to get that kind of money in a couple of days? I've pulled together a little over five thousand Euros. The most I can afford is five thousand. Take it or leave it." Toni looked at her and smiled. Five thousand must have been higher than his expected bid. He paused for some twenty seconds. Neither spoke. Then he said "Give me the picture and details then. I'll see what I can do." Jacey produced an envelope from her pocket. She told him it contained two pictures and all the required information. He took the envelope. Everyone was happy. On the third day she collected the new passport.

Amanda Macey was now alive and well. Aged twenty-four at her recent birthday. Born in London. Next of kin was her Mother, Jane. James knew Jacey was only her nickname – as was Animal's. She now had the document she required. When they got back to the house, they'd had a few drinks. Animal had gotten to the point whereby she looked like she might kick off, but she decided better of it and said she was knackered and retired first. Mandy went next leaving Rach and Jacey, the deserters, traitors. They finished one more beer chatting about their future plans and then they too retired. That was the last time the four of them socialised.

PART 3

CHAPTER 26

James was looking at Amanda's passport and noting down the details. That should be fine. He said. Two Mandy's in the same band – fancy that. "I never liked the name to be honest. No-one calls me Amanda anymore." "Well the ships like to use your full name so I'm afraid you'll be Amanda Macey whilst you're at sea. "That's cool I suppose." She replied. "So, Amanda, you asked me what you would need in terms of outfits for your performances. I've spoken to the relevant people and they say you need to look classy and a bit sexy but not too sexy. Bear in mind many of the clientele are quite old – we don't want them keeling over with heart attacks at the evening show now do we?" She laughed. She was wearing a summery dress. It met with James' approval. "Here are some pictures of the band. They aren't that recent but it'll be mainly the same people so you can see the type of image and outfits they use. Get yourself three or four outfits that you think will work. Remember you can buy just about anything onboard one of these babies, so don't worry about being able to get hold of more outfits whilst on board. They like consistency too. I'm sure you'll find something absolutely perfect." Amanda smiled. So tomorrow we'll meet here for lunch then the taxi will pick us up at three sharps where we will head to Faro for our flight to Barcelona. There we will head over to the ship. She's called 'Bellisima Barcelona'. Or 'BB' to those that know her well.

In the past few days she'd been listening to the songs from the new set list to familiarise herself with them. She'd walked on the beach, away from people, to practise singing along to the songs. She felt she knew them pretty well now. Apparently, the new band weren't into rehearsals onboard ship as they were professionals. Everyone was expected to perform note for note perfectly at every gig. They only rehearsed to bed in new songs or new band members. Nevertheless, they'd pencilled in two full rehearsals prior to their first gig. James was the perfect host. He kept hold of Amanda's travel documents and presented them when required throughout their journey. They looked, to all intents and purposes, like a couple going on their holidays. Her new passport was accepted without issue or delay. James had several engagements on the cruise lasting the whole week. He would then disembark with the rest of the holidaymakers and go back to work leaving Amanda with her new friends and colleagues. Being under his wing somewhat helped her to remain calm whilst travelling. She hoped it would also mean she would be quickly accepted by her new colleagues and the crew.

The band was an eight piece – James on lead guitar, Ben on acoustic guitar, Ian on drums, Howard on Bass, Nick played piano and percussion instruments and then there was Gill and Gemma on backing vocals. The girls danced during most of the numbers. All the guys, except Ian and Nick sang too. Their voices together were amazing. She wondered how she could make this truly great band sound even better. Her self-confidence pulled her through the first rehearsal and by the end she knew she'd be fine. Her preparatory work had paid off. They'd nailed ninety minutes of material in the first practise – the objective for both practises. This meant she could focus on other songs for the second practise. Any songs she hadn't nailed would then be added to the set one at a time using the soundcheck as a one or two song rehearsal.

At the rehearsals the band had worn their gig gear. Amanda had chosen to wear a dress – the kind of dress you'd wear to a posh restaurant. It was bright red and shiny. It hugged her figure, but it had a high neck, not exposing too much skin. She wore heels, made by Castaner, that she'd picked up at the airport. They too were red, but elegant. She decided to make Red her colour – her trademark. It suited her well. She'd also coloured her hair silvery blonde. It really suited her and worked well with the red dress and made her look more mature.

Onboard the ship she'd purchased three more elegant red evening dresses. She'd also found a couple more pairs of red shoes. She was now ready to make her debut in the 'Theatrium' as it was called. There were two similar large event rooms the other being named simply 'The Club'. The band performed in 'The Club' for afternoon performances and then in 'Theatrium' each evening. Apparently, they were also to perform at the odd gig up on deck. These were to celebrate special events like someone's ruby wedding, or a birthday party. The guests could book this as an extremely expensive, optional extra. Often, they took their family and friends with them on the cruise and it was like having your very own party on the deck of the ship. They weren't exclusive – anyone could join in. The band received a bonus for these additional gigs, and they had to be fitted around other engagements which often meant a long day. She was looking forward to this next stage of her career.

CHAPTER 27

Over the past couple of weeks Amanda had been creating her past and going over it in her mind to consolidate the story of her youth and life so far. Some of it was true – the part about singing in Albufeira. She also made up UK bands she'd sang with after leaving school and before moving to Portugal to fill in the missing years. She didn't intend on getting close to any of her colleagues. The salary was good. As the singer she had the least work to do – no songs to learn, no hours and hours of practising scales or vocal harmony parts. She just rocked up and put on a show. But the putting on of a show was more physically demanding given the dancing and moving around the stage and the engaging with the audience and creating banter. And it required a lot of concentration. James had told her that, after a performance, all the guys in the crowd should want her and all the girls should want to be her. A strange thought given most of the crowd were over sixty.

With two rehearsals under her belt, she was to watch the band at each and every appearance this week for their short, seven-day trip to Italy and France returning back to Barcelona. Other places included Gran Canaria, Tenerife and Madeira. Most cruises were seven days. The current singer, Alexandra, was to leave at the end of this cruise and Amanda would take over from her. Alexandra, was that even her real name? Was quite tall and leggy. More legs than figure, lacking the vital upper assets somewhat. She had a good voice. She seemed to be more of a crooner singing rock songs than a rock chick. She thought that, once settled in, she herself would be a better front person for this very talented band. Ben and James were quite animated during the songs, with classic guitar poses during their epic solos. They seemed to be extremely tight, giving the impression they'd played as a band all their lives. They probably had. Gill and Gemma didn't set the world on fire, but both were pleasing on the eye. Gill had jet black hair and Gemma, who looked Afro-Caribbean, had brown dreadlocked hair. Something for everyone. Ian the drummer had very dark skin – she wasn't sure from where he originated. He was energetic and kept a tight groove, rhythmic but not too much going on. Howard was short and wore a trilby. Each of the guitarists had two instruments. She thought this was both for show and as a backup in case of a fault or something. She wasn't great at being able to tell the difference between the sounds of each pair of instruments. To her they sounded the same. She wondered if the audience would be able to tell.

Alexandra was quite good with the crowd. Before each gig the band was briefed on any birthdays or anniversaries or newlyweds known to be in the audience and Alexandra would dedicate a song to them, or the band would pipe up happy birthday to two or three people. Altogether it was an enjoyable set. They played for around an hour and fifteen minutes. Then returned for an encore featuring a further two songs. An hour and a half's work on stage all in. After that the resident DJ played some tunes to keep the dancers on their feet. Many people disappeared to the bar. Others preferred to stay at their table and wait for table service.

She could see the attraction of cruises, but she also likened the guests to caged animals. All inclusive. Not much need for cash except for the drinks, presents and tips. The band didn't really get tips, except for an outside private party. But the salary was enough for most – not massive but, given the living costs minimal, most of it went into the bank – the rest back to the cruise line via the bar. She'd been told that many of the bar staff would give the band free drinks if you were nice to them. Alexandra had mentioned one or two of the staff during her little chats between songs. She always had a couple of drinks lined up after a performance. After the gig the band went backstage, changed or showered and changed and then some came out to the bar and mingled with the guests, sometimes signing autographs. They had signed band pictures for sale also. Amanda was due to have a photo shoot the following day so that new posters could be made up to sell featuring her. The band signed them during the day then the cruise line sold them with none of the proceeds going to the band. Still, it was easy work. It didn't take long to sign forty or fifty posters. They were even given markers to use. The gulf between a pub singer and a celebrity was so wide with so many stops in between. She'd managed to miss a few stops by landing this gig. Alexandra seemed closer to celebrity than pub singer. She was older, maybe thirty or so, very graceful and well-rehearsed. After seeing her a few times Amanda became a little bored of the same moves, the same chit chat and the same performances. She had no spontaneity. It was all very repetitive. Probably exactly what was wanted. But she would make things more interesting, more alive. She was not a robot.

Maybe she would find a wealthy but unhealthy widower who could fall for her. A quick marriage then early departure leaving his fortune to her. But who to pick? She knew that Americans were keen on pre-nuptial agreements and this was becoming more popular outside the US – all to discourage gold diggers. She'd need to be careful in choosing someone for this line of work. She wouldn't want to throw away her career as budding starlet singer. She giggled to herself.

A smart dressed man in his early fifties came over to her. "You must be Amanda. I'm Lawrence Brown – chief purser." "Very pleased to meet you." she replied. One of his roles was to distribute tips to designated staff members. Apparently, this often happened. Alexandra, as the singer, received more than the band generally but had agreed to split any tips relating to the band evenly. She agreed to do likewise. That should help her make her first impressions with the other band members. They chit chatted for a while. He advised her of some of the procedures on board. She knew from research that you had to be twenty-one years of age to work aboard this ship and with no criminal record. Luckily, they hadn't followed up on this. With her false passport there would be no such record, but any search could potentially highlight the fact it was a false passport, a missing history. Still, they had no reason to suspect her being bad. She was young and pretty, but not bad!!

James had brought her onboard personally. She didn't receive holidays whilst on board but apparently, once you'd been working on the ship a while, you could take pre-planned and agreed holidays, but they'd need to organise cover. She told him she had no family to go and visit, worth mentioning anyway. So, no holidays or anything else to worry about. She was happy to work for the next six months or maybe more. Maybe by then she'd need a bit of time off. This seemed agreeable to him. He had arranged the necessary training for her, and he explained what it comprised and when and where it was to take place. That was it. She was free to enjoy the ship and its facilities before starting her stint on Saturday night. She was both excited and a little nervous. No-one knew how little experience she really had. James had swayed everything her way. Tonight, she was to have dinner with him, and he was to introduce her to more of the ship's crew. She was quite looking forward to it.

CHAPTER 28

Vincenzo Dente had had two things bothering him recently. The mysterious girl assassin, capable of murdering a hard man in cold blood, cleaning the scene and leaving one of his own so confused he claimed he'd done it himself and because of this ended up dead – a man down. The second was the missing Weasel. He knew from his myriad of contacts in the police that the Weasel had gone to them to say his daughter had been kidnapped and he wasn't for parting with any of his cash for her return – safe or otherwise. But apparently, he'd then gone AWOL and very shortly afterwards ended up in bits. There was still no trace of his daughter. Maybe she too was a weasel – Little Weasel. Had she inherited some of her father's greed and guile? Could she somehow have been in on the kidnapping? Or even faked the whole thing herself to get daddy's cash. If that were the case, then she could have disappeared with the cash and the letter Montgomery had. If she had the letter would she understand the contents? If so, then she'd have acted on it by now surely? Or would she be too young to appreciate the implications. Maybe she had found it and decided it was too hot to handle and got rid of it. Or just thrown it away, unaware of its importance and value. The letter was the biggest loose end of all as it could, in the wrong hands, leave Vincenzo in deep shit. Shit so deep even his big wig copper friends couldn't dig him out of. One letter and two mysterious young women.

He tried to put himself into Little Weasel's shoes. He'd only met her once that he remembered. She was pretty and her father used her to soften up negotiations at his place. She'd eat with them then leave early, prior to their discussions. Vincenzo made a point of meeting his high-profile contacts in person as infrequently as possible, and only with an above-board, fully legitimate explanation. One sighting could start a chain of events that could run out of control. He preferred to remain elusive. And he hated photographs.

If Little Weasel had taken Devizes out, what would she do next? Where would she go? And how the fuck could a sixteen-year-old girl, slight of stature, take out a fit, healthy, big, muscly villain so professionally? It was just too much to take seriously. His imagination was running away with him. But there was no one else in the picture. That meant it must have been a hit man, a silent assassin, who entered the room, killed Devizes, cleaned up and left. The Little Weasel must have come back into the room and found Devizes dead and fled. But why would she be out of the room on her own in the first place? None of this added up at all. And in the end, he still didn't know if Devizes girlfriend was indeed Little Weasel in the first place. This was a mess. The country was still at a partial standstill due to the terrorist bombs going off all over the place. She can't have bargained for that. And then it hit him.
This was too much of a coincidence. Weasel under a bridge, possibly with wads of cash and the letter, and then BANG he's gone. So is his cash and the letter. Little Weasel wasn't dead, so she had gotten away. She must have been in on it somehow. But what about the other bombs? She couldn't have planned all that. Was she in league with a terrorist cell? Maybe she was shagging a terrorist? Or brainwashed by them.

He knew that, if the attacks were planned and orchestrated so well by a terrorist cell, that they would have claimed responsibility. His contacts had also told him that no viable claim had come in. Just lots of bogus ones. If he were planning on killing Montgomery, he wouldn't have considered a bomb. And multiple bombs? Maybe they were intended to kill other targets in one fell swoop? And make it look like terrorists. Clever. But likely too clever. It didn't make sense. Why all the bombs? To distract from the one that killed Montgomery? It was true that all the police manpower would be put into finding terrorists not one missing daughter and would-be kidnapper. Or even a dead diplomat. The world needed more dead diplomats he thought to himself. Was Little Weasel working with someone else? Someone clever enough to plan a series of bombs, make or acquire the bombs, distribute them and set them off in such a fashion as to appear like a terrorist attack? Someone who had about as much compassion in his soul as he himself did, not caring about how many innocent people died in the process? Who did he know that fit the bill? And was Devizes in on it too? Again, nothing added up. He should stick to the facts.

CHAPTER 29

The restaurant required formal evening wear. Amanda wore a blue dress and blue shoes purchased on the ship the day before. She had decided to wear red in the band and anything but red outside of the band. She didn't want to draw attention to herself when she wasn't working. James wore a lounge suit with black tie. He looked very dapper. He ordered a bottle of red wine and the waiter brought it over and poured their glasses. They left it to breathe a while. He asked her how she was settling in, how was she getting on with the band and how ready was she for Saturday's performance - the usual stuff. She could tell he liked her. If he made a pass at her would she oblige or play hard to get? He was on here for this week, she didn't know how often he visited the ship. She asked him a few questions and learned that he was single, never married and came on the ship about once a quarter. He also visited a couple of the other ships in the line. Half his time was spent at sea, the rest on land hiring staff and negotiating contracts. She could tell he was a man of means. She didn't think he had sufficient means to tempt her away from this gig so soon. She would be fishing for bigger, richer fish. Most likely older and iller too!! She needed a much lower life expectancy.

It was a set menu, with something for everyone, including vegans and vegetarians. She wasn't really fussy. Everything she saw looked of the highest quality. The lamb she chose was tender and not overcooked. She finished with a crème brûlée - light and sweet, like her. If she continued to eat like this, she wouldn't be light for very much longer she feared. After the meal she had a large Baileys with ice and he a Remy. She wondered if he would ask her to his cabin for a night cap and if he did what would her response be? After finishing their drinks, he suggested they went to the bar for a last drink. He had another brandy and she a half of lager. Rock chick naturally. By now she'd had half a bottle of fine wine and a Baileys. She was by no means drunk, but she was relaxed and ready to enjoy herself. She asked where the best place would be to go and maybe do some dancing. He said they had a club where the young ones frequented but said that he had never been there. She took this to mean he wasn't interested in joining her. So, after their nightcap, he bade her farewell and she ordered another half of lager as he returned to his cabin. She mulled over the evening to see what she had learned from this nice dinner. The ship catered for the old, the young and all things in between but the bulk of the punters were on the old side. She liked this.

The only problem with her plan of finding an older, ailing rich guy was that she was so young it would inevitably be shunned upon by one and all. She'd be seen as a gold digger – which of course she would be. Maybe she needed something that was less in the public eye involving only the victim and herself. Maybe she could chat up an older guy on board then video them together and use the video somehow – maybe to threaten to expose their affair to his family or wife back home. She'd need to work on this a bit. But it all seemed too personal. She needed one big hit then get the hell out, with another new identity and on to the next challenge. She still had stiff Steph up her sleeve. For now, she had this gig, it paid well, provided accommodation, food and everything else she'd normally pay for. She could enjoy herself, earn a few quid legitimately, build up a legitimate image and plan her next move. There was no rush. Being a singer would potentially open up a lot of doors for her. Life was good.

CHAPTER 30

It was three am... on the dot. Vincenzo sat up in bed and looked at the clock. Suddenly it made sense. This was no easy jigsaw, but he now had a theory. And the worst thing about this theory was that the importance of the letter would have been understood immediately. And now he knew the reason why it hadn't been acted on. Little Weasel had killed Devizes before he had chance to do anything with it. He was now sure that she had dispatched Devizes. She was the woman he checked in with and she had disappeared in the TT before dopey Digby had tracked them down. No-one else was in the frame for this role. It had to be her. How she had met Devizes he may never know. Maybe she started as a hostage, then gained his trust, manipulated him to dispose of her father, get the cash, then dispatched him also. And was there an explosives expert, or radical in on the plan as well?

So now he had to work out where she was and how to get to her. At the point where Devizes was dispatched, they were heading South through Europe. Did they have a destination in mind? The TT was never found. She could have driven it anywhere and dumped it. It was now far too late to try and find CCTV footage of the car. If she was capable of tricking Devizes into transforming her from hostage to lover, then she had indeed inherited some of her father's cunning and callousness. What she had done made her somewhat of a sociopath and a serial killer. Some woman. He was growing to like her.
Either she had his letter, or it had been lost or destroyed at some point prior to Devizes demise. She seemed too clever to destroy

anything of potential value. He felt sure she would still have the letter but maybe hadn't decided what to do with it. She may be totally unaware of its relevance. He had two options – try and find her or wait until the letter surfaced with some sort of demand probably for money. If she was going to use it as such then he would have the march on her as she would assume that he had no idea who she was. But he wasn't one to sit and wait. He'd adopt both strategies. Get some men out there looking for her, with the help of the police, and he'd remain vigilant in the event that she came to him. If she did, she would sure regret it. But now he had some idea of what she was capable of.

CHAPTER 31

The following day, Amanda woke with a headache. She shouldn't really have headed down to the club last night. She'd had enough to drink before she made the decision to go check it out. She didn't go to pull or to dance but to see the lay of the land, who visited this place, was it crew or customer, was it expensive and what opportunities could arise from a place like this. The music was loud, and you had to shout into someone's ear to be heard. She had ordered a pint of lager and sat on a table close to the dance floor. Her nice dress was a little dressier than most of the people in there, but she didn't attract any undue attention. She didn't look like she was dressed to pull, but then again why else would a young, single girl go in a place like this alone?

It wasn't long before a young guy, probably twenty-five, sat beside her. He seemed worse for wear. His pulling lines were terrible. She dismissed him and off he went. But within five minutes another man came to her. He didn't try shouting to be heard he used his hand to point at the seat beside her and smiled. His meaning was clear – can I sit with you? She smiled back and nodded. He sat beside her. He looked around thirty, well dressed, in nice jeans and a short sleeved pink shirt. He offered her his hand;"I'm Dean – Deano to my friends." "I'm Amanda." she replied. Luckily, the song being played had a long passage that featured a more melodic, less loud section which allowed them to talk without too much shouting. "I work here, how about you?" Deano said. "Me too, I just started this week." Amanda replied. "That's good, so we may see a little more of each other over the coming days then." he replied. "I'm the head of entertainment here onboard." "Then we shall be seeing more of each other." Amanda replied. "I'm the new singer for the showband." "I know." Dean replied. He had obviously known who she was as soon as he had seen her. She didn't like this, she felt like she had been hunted. Only she was the huntress. Deano offered her a drink but she politely refused saying it was time she retired for the evening - she'd only come into see what the place was like - research. They said their goodnights and she left. She'd have to keep an eye out for Deano.

She slept well and when she awoke it was light. A couple of paracetamols would help see her through the morning. They had a final rehearsal scheduled, to cover off a few additional songs for the repertoire. They'd have an additional half a dozen songs over and above what she had been asked to deliver. She was looking forward to her first show tomorrow night. Today she might look for another outfit. She decided to change outfits in the middle of the show – from dressy to more sexy. One of the songs had a long guitar solo, where she could go backstage to the dressing room and change. She'd start off with the red dress then move to a red minidress with a lower cut top. Not too low, glamourous with a hint of sexy. A big hint. She needed a pair of higher heels for the miniskirt.

By now she'd found all the clothes shops on the ship and knew the best one for her tastes. She intended to make friends with Janet, the lady who managed it. Much of the merchandise on board had the ships name on it. She'd ordered the red miniskirt with the addition of the ship's logo on the back. The guy had said he had the necessary equipment on board, but it would take a day or two. This afternoon she'd collect it and buy a pair of shoes to go with it.

Today was changeover day. They docked at around 4pm and the passengers disembarked. A few would stay on for another week. Some couples stayed for six weeks! She thought it would get a bit boring after two weeks but each to their own. Alexandra would be gone. Amanda's day had dawned.

She had a light lunch on deck then headed down to the shopping parade. Janet had made a fantastic job of her dress. The logo was stitched into the back in coloured sequins. She'd also stitched a few sequins onto the front in matching colours. The dress was still red, but it had a shimmering, glitter effect across the front and the logo on the back. "It's absolutely brilliant, Janet. How much do I owe you?" Janet said she too was really pleased with the outcome and that she didn't often get a chance to be creative. She only charged the normal price for the dress. Amanda tipped her twenty-five Euros to show her appreciation and said she'd buy her a drink this evening if she was up for it. Janet said that she was. She looked about forty, attractive with a penchant for anything bright or glittery.
They agreed to meet in the bar on deck, for dinner and a few drinks. They knew it would be quiet as the passengers would still be embarking. Amanda thanked her once again and left her for the time being. She mooched around some of the other shops but didn't buy anything. She then went back to her cabin to go over the lyrics of the new songs again just to make sure she didn't get brain freeze.

She remembered her first gig back in Albufeira with the girls. She'd done alright. That was a much bigger step than this would be. She'd been on stage, albeit never done anything like this one! Later this afternoon, whilst the exchange of passengers was going on, they were having a dress rehearsal and playing tomorrow night's set. They'd have a go at the new ones too if they had time. She changed into her first outfit, packed her second outfit into a bag which held the shoes as well, took her lyrics and headed down to the Theatrium.

When she got there the rest of the band were on stage tuning up, setting up and generally making that horrible noise whereby they were all playing something different at the same time.

It reminded her of jazz. James and Ben waved at her. Howard shouted, 'Break a leg". Not a very comforting thought being up on a stage in high heels. She placed her lyrics on the floor at the front of the stage and adjusted her microphone stand. Whoever set it up for her it was always, always too high - even with these heels! The PA wasn't on yet. She could see the sound and lighting engineer at the back of the room by the desk obscured in semi-darkness. His name was Jonny Fontaine. Jonny Fontaine? Was that even his real name? He was a throwback to the 60's. He looked about fifty, well dressed and fancied himself rotten. He claimed to be able to play the drums too, but no one could vouch for this. He looked over at Amanda and waved and she gave him a thumbs up. He used his desk mic to announce that he was turning up the vocal mics.

The musicians seemed to fizzle out like a pub band who hadn't rehearsed the ending well enough. She did the proverbial one-two down the mic. She had a radio mic in a vertical stand. For some songs she released the mic and walked about. Other songs she used the stand, so her arms were free to wave around to the melody. Everything she did just came naturally. She didn't plan things but when something worked, she kept it. She knew that by the end of her first week she'd have her own personal show mapped out in her subconscious head.

The first two numbers, which ran into each other, went without a hitch. Her voice was clear and bright and even dancing to an empty room felt good. The third song wasn't so good Something went wrong in the transition from the first verse to the chorus. She couldn't pinpoint which element of the music had gone wrong, but something definitely, wasn't right. Still, she resisted the urge to turn around and glare at the guitarists. Jonny didn't look up from his desk, so he hadn't noticed – drummers never do. It appeared like they'd gotten away with it. When they finished the song, James and Ben berated Howard for playing a bum note on the bass. It was funny how you often didn't notice the

bass when it was played well but one wrong note stood out like a sore thumb! Still the remainder of the first half of the set went smoothly. They had decided to change things a little and have a short break making the show two sets instead of one long set. It afforded a toilet break, drink refill and a chance for Amanda to change outfits.
So now they stopped for a break and Amanda went backstage and changed into her second set outfit. No-one had seen this as she'd only just collected it. When she emerged from stage right the guys in the band all whistled at her! She'd been told by James 'not too sexy' – had she overstepped the mark? As she passed the girls, she said "Too much"? "Hell no!" was Gill's response! "Makes a fine change!" said Gemma.

Ben's bottom jaw nearly hit the stage. "Put your eyes back in." Amanda said, in a friendly but flattered way. He just smiled and returned to tuning his guitar. The second set started with a bang – I Love Rock And Roll. They'd tweaked the set list a little that week. This was a great opening song but deemed a little too rocky for the first set. The second set was indeed rockier and her outfit matched this. Having two sets afforded them the chance to mix it up a bit. The guitarists enjoyed the second set more as they now had a little more freedom to shine. During the guitar solos she danced on the stage. She could feel the guy's eyes burning into her rear as she moved - she liked the feeling. But she didn't like Jonny letching at her from the other side of the desk. Even in the gloom she could see him, he was probably drooling. At the end they agreed to run through the six new songs. Surprisingly these went smoothly too, but they had to stop straight after so the room could be set out for dinner for the new arrival's first night. It was after six pm, so time was tight. They all agreed the rehearsal had gone really well and that they were all set for the next chapter of the band's history. By changing to two sets, and introducing the new songs, it seemed that the band had gained more personality and spontaneity in the music. Everyone was upbeat.

They went back to the changing rooms. Amanda had neglected to bring civvies as she'd come on down in her first set dress. Only now did she realise her mistake. "I forgot to bring anything casual." she said to James. James said "That's OK. Keep a low profile on your way back to your cabin and you can change there. We're meeting in the bar shortly for pre-match drinks." "Thanks, I'll be there. "Amanda replied. "If you're worried you might be attacked on your way back to your cabin, I'd be happy to escort you." Ben said with a wry smile. "You wouldn't know what to do with me!" she replied with a wink and then collected her things and headed back to her cabin alone.

She quickly showered and changed into jeans and a shirt and headed up to the bar. In the thirty minutes she'd taken, it seemed the guys had drunk three beers already. The empties were still on the table. "I got you a beer." Ben said and pushed a pint glass of lager in her direction. "Cheers!" she replied and proceeded to down half the pint in one go. Ben's eyes nearly popped out. "Bottles are for girls." She said to Ian and James who were drinking bottled lager. They both smiled not knowing what to say. It seemed Ben had taken a shine to her.

They'd already ordered food – a selection of finger food. By now she was hungry, so she filled her plate with chicken, nachos and some chilli. Gill and Gemma were sat together huffing and puffing that the chilli was too hot. Amanda was already on a second helping with no side effects whatsoever. She couldn't decide whether getting too close to the band members was a good thing or a bad thing. Maybe it was something she just couldn't really avoid.
During their conversations, Alexandra's name had popped up a few times. Never anything bad but never anything you could call fond either. She was now long gone in their minds, but it didn't appear that she'd be missed.

Jonny Fontaine had joined them too. It transpired he too had returned to his cabin and showered and changed. His arrival was proceeded by the thick smell of cheap aftershave. He'd piled it on like plaster. Who was he trying to impress? He'd looked over at Amanda when he arrived, but she was sat between Ben and Howard and there was no room close by. So he'd sat at the other side with Gemma and Gill. They didn't look too enamoured with his arrival. Three or four drinks later she decided it was her round. By now she'd memorised everyone's drinks. It wasn't difficult. Draft lager, bottled lager or a spritzer. "My shout." She said as she stood up and went over to the bar.

Whilst she was waiting to be served, Gill came up behind her. "Slimeball has the hots for you, baby." Amanda turned around. Gill was smiling in a sort of 'you'll find out' way. "I think I can handle him." she said and smiled. "Is that really his name?" she added. "We don't know but Gemma and I reckon he's called Shirley Shufflebottom from Blackburn." They both laughed. Gill helped her carry the drinks over to their table. It was the norm that everyone got a round each, then they retired to their respective cabins, all a little worse for wear. That was quite a lot of booze. Now she knew why some of them drank bottled lager. She'd moved to halves after the first pint. Good job too. She was now very much looking forward to tomorrows performance and the start of the next chapter of her short life.

CHAPTER 32

Vincenzo had dispatched two of his best men on the trail of Little Weasel – Davo and JJ. They'd gotten hold of photographs of her and DNA from her belongings left behind at her home. How helpful the police could be when they wanted to be. One of his best assets over the years, Bernard Traynor, was retiring at the end of this month. As a final thank you, and to secure his loyalty, Vincenzo had agreed to pay for a cruise for Traynor and his wife to celebrate his retirement. She had always wanted to go on a cruise but Traynor's work schedule had never permitted it. But he wouldn't be fully retired. He was still an asset to Vincenzo. But the incoming wasn't. This was indeed a big blow. But his tendrils still ran deep into the foundations of many police forces and agencies across the globe. He had enlisted the support of key individuals to assist Davo and JJ in their hunt for his prey. Already they had determined that there was nothing in the system for the missing TT. Not surprising as in that it had never been reported missing and likely had false plates. They found a report of a burned-out TT a couple of days after Devizes demise. It could be the same vehicle; it might not be – they were a popular car even in France. He was sure that Little Weasel would have been long gone by now – but was she even able to drive? They would have likely switched plates on the TT before heading through France. She could have just left the car, with the keys in, in some dodgy neighbourhood. It would be gone in no time - free disposal. You couldn't do this with a hot vehicle but a disposable one like this was fine. But you'd need an alternative method of transport after dumping the car. Either another car, train or plane. Air travel was inherently riskier given the additional security checks – especially in the midst of an apparent terrorist attack on British soil. Everywhere had a heightened security level. Europe would be on high alert seeking fleeing bombers. If he were in her shoes, he'd have taken a train, paid cash naturally, after all she had plenty, then disappeared far away from the UK. He assumed that the ransom cash would be in Sterling, so she'd have needed to either get some of her own Euros or exchange some of the ransom money. Vincenzo had a habit of noting the serial numbers of any cash, usually fifty-pound notes, given to his associates. That way he could stand a small chance of tracing their spend with the assistance of the police that is. One of his operatives had collated a list of the notes that Montgomery had been paid over the previous months. It was a long shot, but maybe one or more of these would surface and form a trail to lead him to her. If he had enough long shots, then the chances of one coming in were multiplied. This was how he worked. Lots of fishing lines in the river meant you would likely catch something, even if you had no idea where the fish were. Davo and JJ were armed with this info. They were to start at the hotel, interview the receptionist and staff, then meet with the local head of the police task force that had worked the murder. Vincenzo needed information to help him understand if it was indeed her and to where she was heading.

CHAPTER 33

She awoke a little later than usual, again with a thick head. More paracetamol was required. She put the TV on. They had hundreds of channels in every language you could think of. She went for the BBC World Service. The bombings were now very much old news, but still featured in the broadcasts. No organisation had been named and blamed. The clean-up operations were underway. But that didn't interest her. So long as there was no mention of a Montgomery, she was OK. This new phase of life had begun. How lucky was she? Free board and lodgings, money to spare and that's without touching her nest egg. She was safe in her floating home. The work schedule was quite punishing, but it wasn't real work, it was doing something she enjoyed. Strutting her stuff, singing songs she loved. How her life had changed in a few short weeks. Her education had begun the minute she stopped going to school.

CHAPTER 34

Vincenzo was having a good day. He was sitting up in bed, his partner from last night having just left. He was checking his Inbox. Bingo. One of Montgomery's fifty-pound notes had been flagged up. In Portugal of all places. Still, this made sense to Vincenzo. Full of tourists and lots of British tourists. She'd blend right in. Apparently, it was part of a large amount of sterling that was exchanged for Euros recently. They knew the date and time of the transaction but nothing on the ID. He knew that banks required proof of ID when exchanging money. The name of the person would be in their system. Whilst Davo and JJ hadn't come up with anything of real value, this would speed them along. The bank was in Carvoeiro on the Algarve and it was here that his two operatives were heading. They'd be there tomorrow and, with a little persuasion, be able to obtain the name and any document numbers of the person who exchanged the cash. He knew this could lead him to her. She was a clever Little Weasel, but she would have left more breadcrumbs like this and these would inevitably lead him to her. He might even be able to recover some of the ransom money as well to boot - bonus. Still, in monetary terms, that was chicken feed to Vincenzo, but nevertheless part of a trail that he would need to wipe clean. The game was afoot.

CHAPTER 35

The lights were off, the crowd were seated and quiet in anticipation of the performance that was about to begin. The intro music had started, and the band members left her alone backstage as they headed out to the crowd. A lively crowd, for this was, for most of them, their first night of a holiday of a lifetime. The intro music built up and she could hear the tell-tale clicks of guitars being picked up and made ready to play. As the intro music finished, she heard the one, two, three, four clicks on the sticks and the show began! Another ten seconds and she'd herself would be appearing stage left in her beautiful red dress making her debut. She took a swig of water from her bottle and headed out. The room was full – she couldn't see an empty seat anywhere. When the crowd saw her a huge roar erupted. She felt like she'd hit the big time. The crowd gave her energy, and her performance was so much more than during rehearsals or with the old band. This was something else. She had a big stage and room to move. She could visit the guitarists at each side of the stage and flirt with them. The first song was over in what seemed like no time at all. "Thank you and welcome aboard our beautiful ship. We'll be here to entertain you each evening with our rock themed show. I'm Amanda and this is Born To Be Wild." Another cheer as James' guitar brought the song in. She skipped over to James who was playing the intro and played air guitar with him cheek to cheek. She could see him blushing. Ben on the other side looked over and laughed. Her motor was certainly running. It looked like Ben's was too.

And so, the first set went really smoothly. No slip ups, no massive lyrical blunders and all the transitions went as they had rehearsed them. They finished the set with Hotel California, James excelling with the solo and Ben doing his bit as well. The dual solo at the end had the crowd standing. Amanda left the stage waving to the crowd just before the end and the number finished with a dead stop – der der der der! The lights went down and Ben shouted, "Thank you – see you again in a few minutes."

Backstage they were bouncing. All the band congratulated Amanda on her performance. "Mega!!!! well buzzin'" said Ben. "Well played." said Gill. They had a crate of beers and everyone took one and chatted about the set. Several conversations were going on at once. "She's a way better showman than Alexandra ever was." she could hear Gill saying. "She's hot." Ian said. Ben came over and sat next to her and offered her a second beer. "Better not." She said. "Rules and all." "Fuck the rules." Ben said opening his second beer. James looked over with a hint of admonishment. But then even he smiled and opened his second beer. All was good. Before they had time to finish the second one it was time to go back. Amanda had changed into her sexy outfit and for the second set she went on stage first, alone.

The crowd went quiet as their chattering subsided. "How ya all doing?" she said in a mixture of British and American. She had no idea where the accent had come from, maybe she had subconsciously noticed it with other bands? The crowd responded with a roar. "I might be wrong but I'm guessing you all love Rock 'n' Roll?" With this the band emerged and with a four click they launched into I Love Rock 'n' Roll. Then on through the second set. All was going great. She'd finally found something she was good at that was above board and legal. What a turn up.

CHAPTER 36

Back in the dressing room the band were still buzzing. "That was the most enjoyable gig we've done for ages." James said. It seemed that Amanda was a great match for the band. After downing a couple more beers, the band members were both more accepting of Amanda and more open to sharing their views about Alexandra. "It was always about her" "She used us......" and so on. One thing she'd learned in the past few weeks was that musicians could be a funny bunch. Still, she was beginning to like this funny bunch.

She changed back into her jeans, which she had remembered to bring, and hung her outfits up in her dressing room. Well it wasn't hers, the three girls shared it. She would leave her costumes there for the next performance. She suddenly thought about washing her outfits. Shit, it hadn't crossed her mind. She'd need another couple of outfits too. James was right when he had said she'd need three or four outfits. And this was doubled now with her change at halftime. Still, that would wait until tomorrow. She felt sure that her choice of sexy outfit for the second set was just sexy enough, but not too sexy, as James had warned her about. No-one had complained that was apparent.

The guitarists were picking the bones out of the mistakes they'd made, of places where they felt they could improve things by changing an accent here or a note there. Everyone seemed excited with this new lineup. She wondered how long it would last before they tired of her like they tired of Alexandra. She imagined it could be difficult being in the shadow of the front person. The front person who did the least work but got all the credit. Still it worked for her! The band then went into the bar to mingle with the guests. They found that if they mingled a little, they got more repeat business, people came back for more. They only stuck around for half an hour or so, to avoid getting too sozzled. They went downstairs to the club for that part. When they arrived, there was a row of bottles on the bar waiting for them. At this time, it was mainly staff in there – the band arrived, to a round of applause and whoops from the people waiting for them. "Great show guys." "Fantastic job!" "Way to go!" "Amanda you really nailed it!" were just some of the remarks she picked out from the cacophony of voices at the bar.

The first beer didn't last long! Amanda got the next round. As she was paying, she noticed James coming down the steps and heading in her direction. He was due to leave the ship shortly, so she guessed he was saying his goodbyes. He walked over to her. "What can I get you?" she asked him. "One of those would be fine, thank you." He replied pointing at the array of bottles of lager on the bar waiting to be taken back to their table. She ordered one more, paid for them, and then they took the bottles over to the table together. James sat beside her. The rest of the band nodded or said "Hi" to him. "That was some show you guys put on back there." He said addressing the whole band, but they knew he was really referring to Amanda. "You did well this time Jimbo, you did really well!!" Ben said and the rest of the band laughed. James was visibly irked by being referred to as Jimbo, but he didn't say anything. He drank his beer, wished the band farewell, wished Amanda luck and they walked out together. "You did great today. I'm really pleased you chose to work with us." "So am I. So am I." she replied. He then kissed her on the cheek, bade farewell and he disappeared, ever the gentleman. He wasn't sure when he'd be back – he had a busy schedule over the next few days and weeks. But she had the feeling that she would indeed see him sooner rather than later. And she was looking forward to it.

CHAPTER 37

Davo could be very persuasive. He was originally from Barbados but having been brought up in London his plummy British accent defied his appearance. JJ, on the other hand, was born in Milan and grew up in London. His accent was East End. Chalk and cheese. Davo had shown his warrant card and the girl was looking through the bank records relating to the transaction. "Here it is. The lady in question was Stephanie Garcia." They would be able to find out who she was, where she was living and close in on their quarry. They thanked the bank staff for their cooperation and asked them not to mention this to anyone as it was an ongoing enquiry. They didn't want to cause any trouble for the bank given the nature of the transaction. Despite the fact that the bank couldn't have known anything about the supposed money laundering, it could have a negative effect on the bank's image and reputation if word got out, and no one wanted that. Either Stephanie had gotten hold of the cash downstream of it being used by their quarry, or their quarry was now using this identity.

Davo and JJ left and reported back to Vincenzo. He then assigned one of his police associates in Spain to look into Garcia. Was she working with Little Weasel or was this a fake identity? Either way it was a lead. When Vincenzo heard back from his operative, only thirty minutes later, what he had to say came as a surprise. Stephanie Garcia was a real person, of similar age and physical description to Little Weasel. But she hadn't been seen for a number of weeks. Her father had said she'd run away from home. He hadn't reported her as missing, as he was confident that she'd left of her own accord. She wasn't happy at home and was old enough to make her own decisions. So, either she had gotten some of the money and exchanged it or Little Weasel had taken her identity. Interesting.

Vincenzo then leaned on his friends in the police in Portugal to find out any other transactions that had been made using this identity. It was possible that this girl was innocent and had merely been in receipt of one of the notes after it had changed hands several times. But this didn't ring true – it was sterling, and this was Portugal. Logic dictated that the original owner, likely British, would have exchanged it and that was seeming to be Little Weasel. But how had she come to be passing herself of as Stephanie Garcia?

Vincenzo now knew that his quarry was indeed more formidable than even he had considered. This Stephanie Garcia looked like Little Weasel. She must have met up with this runaway and targeted her because she was a similar age and appearance to herself. Logically she would have stolen her ID. Equally likely she could have killed her and assumed her identity. That must have been her plan all along. Find a donor and do away with her and assume her identity. Clever. But, also very stupid. He now knew the identity she was using and could track her down far more easily. He just hoped that she hadn't disposed of this identity and assumed a new one.

CHAPTER 38

It was midnight and most of the band had gone to bed. James, Ben and Gill remained, and Amanda said she'd get the next and final round before hitting the sack. Ben offered to help her bring the drinks over. As they stood at the bar Ben put his arm around her. "You really did well tonight, we're all still buzzin'." She wasn't sure where he was from, but she thought she detected a slight northern English accent. She knew James was also from up North as well. Ian the drummer was from Lapland, Nick was from Yorkshire and Howard the bass player was from Bolton. She'd heard them talking about football earlier and she remembered he supported the Trotters whoever they were. She had no interest in football or any other sport really.

Ben and James were chatting about the old guys that came to watch the band and how they letched at the girls. James said that it wasn't unusual for there to be the odd passenger who drops dead on a cruise. She wondered what the best way was for her to benefit from an additional person dropping dead on each cruise. She could rob them but that would only work for a single person who didn't have a partner to report missing items. A single middle-aged bloke would be a good target. Hook him, reel him in, fleece him and give him a fatal heart attack. One per cruise tops. Maybe she'd have been better off on a Saga cruise! She knew there were poisons that could induce a fatal heart attack and be almost undetectable. She wished she'd paid more attention in chemistry.

After they bade their farewells Amanda was still on a high, so she went upon deck for a stroll. It wasn't warm, but it wasn't really cold either, so she was OK with no coat. The bar was still open, so she decided to have one last drink on her own. She ordered a bottle of lager and stood at the bar reflecting on the evening's events. It was getting late and there were only a handful of people left in the bar. At one side were a young couple who looked deeply in love. They were sat side by side and holding hands. Their conversation was quiet and punctuated with soft giggles and coos. She wondered if that is how she and Dom had appeared to other passengers on their last cruise. The remainder of the people were also couples, but the majority were older. There were two couples sharing a table for four in the middle of the bar. They were quite loud - it was apparent they'd all had a few to drink. Apparently, they were celebrating one of their party's retirement. She had no idea which one. The blokes had glasses of whisky and the ladies each a glass of champagne. She wondered if that had been their tipple of choice all evening. From the sound of them it may have been. But for her it was now bedtime. It had been a memorable day.

CHAPTER 39

She awoke at 9am with no headache. Maybe the adrenaline had consumed the alcohol? She did have a drink of water before going to bed and that probably helped. She got up, showered, dressed and went up on deck to grab a breakfast. She fancied a full English; she had a mega craving for a fried egg. She returned to the bar on deck where she had ended the previous evening. In contrast, this morning it was busy, she got the last remaining table – a table for two. Whilst she waited to order she looked around at the clientele. Again, mostly couples, middle aged or quite old, all chattering incessantly. Two tables along she noticed the same four people that had been celebrating in the bar the previous evening. They all looked surprisingly well. They must have eaten early as their plates were empty and awaiting collection by the staff. Their tipple of choice was now coffee. That was definitely what she needed first off.

“Hey, Amanda.” She looked up to see Gill walking towards her. “Mind if I join you?”. “Be my guest.” she replied and pulled out the chair for Gill. She sat down. “Some night last night – you did really well.” “Thanks – I really enjoyed it.” Amanda replied. Just then the waiter came over. “What are you ladies having then?” he said. “Full English and a large pot of black coffee for me please.” Amanda said. “Same here please but can I have some milk too?” Gill said. The waiter nodded, wrote it onto his pad in what looked like a cross between shorthand and scribble and left.

“How long have you been doing this cruise thing then?” Amanda asked Gill. “About two years now. I enjoy it. It’s hassle free, better than singing in pubs and paying for a bed sit in London." "I know what you mean." Amanda replied and went on to say how she'd been working in pubs and bars. As always, she tried not to open up any more personal conversation about her past – the less she said the less likely she was to trip herself up at some point. Remain a bit elusive and mysterious, it was a girl's prerogative, she thought. The coffees arrived first, then, only some five minutes later, the breakfasts arrived. They both asked for red sauce. Amanda also wanted brown to go on the sausage. "Red and brown?" Gill asked in amazement. "That's the only way." Amanda said and laughed. As they ate their breakfasts, they continued to chit chat about the ship, the typical punters, what usually happened, the private parties the band had played in the past and which of the crew were fit and which were to be avoided. It was all useful information for Amanda. Gill warned Amanda to watch Ben as he was the band Casanova. Amanda said she'd already ascertained as much. She said she preferred Ian as he was tall and more reserved. Amanda told Gill that she thought she needed another outfit or two to allow for laundry turnaround. Gill said that the band had asked for the laundry to be collected from backstage and returned there between gigs. Amanda agreed this would be much easier for them. Gill then said that, if it was OK, she'd tag along to help her pick something. They split the bill then they headed off for the shops.

CHAPTER 40

Vincenzo put the phone down after speaking to his police colleague in Spain. The guy, who was a senior police figure, had dispatched a uniform to go visit Garcia's address to speak with her father and family in order to ascertain her whereabouts and contact details. According to the uniform she had left home a few weeks ago, just packed a bag and left. No arguments, no plans, she just wanted out. Apparently, she'd been saving all her money, never went out, no boyfriends or anything. A complete mystery. She hadn't been reported missing as she was old enough to look after herself. The uniform said that her father, whom he had been speaking to, didn't seem unduly worried about this daughter. Her father explained that her mother had died some time ago, and he had remarried and now had twins. His daughter resented his new family and couldn't wait to get out of Dodge. So that was that. Not missing, just looking for a new life.

Vincenzo now strongly suspected that this Garcia girl was most likely dead, with Little Weasel using her ID. Great, this was a big step forward. Now all he had to do, was find her. He got back onto Davo and JJ. They hadn't come up with anything over and above the ID. He sent them back to the bank to ask the person who had handled the transaction if they remembered anything at all about this person. Anything at all that could give him a clue to understand if it was Garcia or Little Weasel that had changed the money. He sent them pictures of both girls.

An hour later the phone rang – it was Davo. I've got something for you. "The woman that dealt with her had met her before, in a pub". "Nothing unusual there." Vincenzo said with a tone of admonishment in his voice. "Yes, but the girl in question was playing in a band. And she had an English accent. Apparently, she'd spent a lot of time in England." Vincenzo knew this wasn't the case for the real Garcia girl. It had to be the Little Weasel. He told Davo to track down this woman via the band or venues. There can't have been many bands working in that area. Speak to the organisers, managers, venue owners and track down the band and the person in question. He wanted an update that evening. The net was closing. When they found her, Vincenzo himself would come over in person to question her.

Vincenzo took a swig from his whisky glass. He decided to take a nap and then grab a bite to eat. Hopefully in that time Davo and JJ would have found out a bit more. As soon as he had enough, he would organise a helicopter to get him down there. He needed to speak to her face to face to find out what she knew about the letter, retrieve it, and retrieve whatever cash or assets she had, before sending her back to her father.
You learned more from people's eyes than words alone. That was why he needed to do this himself.

At 8pm UK time he called Davo again. "What have you got." "Well, she was singing for a band called 'Sisters of No Mercy', or something like that. I spoke to the venue owner; he gave me contact details for the band. I spoke to a girl called Animal who lived in Albufeira. She said the band had broken up and she wasn't interested. She put the phone down. I called back a couple of times, but the bitch didn't answer. So, we found her address and paid her a visit. She had a nice, big pad at Albufeira. When we arrived JJ rang the bell, but no one answered. I went around the back and gained access through the rear doors. We found this Animal woman upstairs asleep. We knew it was her from the description the landlord had given us, grumpy cow she was. So, we made her talk and had some fun in the process. Turns out the girl we're looking for turned up out of the blue, supposedly on holiday. They met at a karaoke bar, they asked her to join the band and she did. Trouble is, the band split up recently, and...." At his point Vincenzo interjected and said.... "So, where the fuck is she? That's what your paid to find out." "She's gotten a job singing on a cruise liner somewhere. She didn't know the name of the boat, believe me. By the time we'd finished with her she'd have told us anything. We know the agent that offered her the job, so he is our next port of call. We need to research him, get his contact details and then use him to find out where the bitch is. If she's on a cruise boat, she's a captive audience. We can take a cruise on her ship and sort her out." "No." Vincenzo said. "Find out the name of the ship, where it is and let me know. I'll be going there myself, alone. That, my friend, is a job for me, not you. Get me the details and call me back – any time day or night." "OK we're on it. Shouldn't take long." said Davo and hung up.

Vincenzo didn't ask what had happened to this girl Animal as he knew they would have done what they were trained to do in this situation. Silence her and leave no clues. By now the fire engines would be there and they'd be scraping her remains up from the debris. Mystery gas explosion or something similar.

CHAPTER 41

The next gig was even better than the first one. Any nerves that Amanda felt, or indeed the rest of the band had felt, were gone. They blasted through the sets and did an encore. They recognised many faces from the previous night. It was another sell-out with hardly any empty seats. After the gig and formalities were complete, the band went down to the bar for a few drinks as was their habit. They discussed other possible songs that they wanted to play. They felt that Amanda's vocal style gave them more flexibility and opened doors to different material. Alexandra had been very unreceptive to new material, apparently because she wasn't that keen on rock music at all. They discussed artists like Billy Idol, Led Zeppelin and even early Heart stuff – Barracuda was pencilled in for a rehearsal as was Boys Of Summer by Don Henley. They could drop a Blondie track, or one of the other middle of the road set fillers they were used to playing. If anyone requested them, say at a private event, then they were simple enough to play again.

Speaking of private events, they'd been asked to play a gig up on deck in the afternoon later in the week as part of some guy's retirement celebrations. His wife and friends were organising it as a surprise for him. Strange as it's usually birthdays or anniversaries James had commented. The woman's name, who was organising it, was Susan Traynor. They were only aboard for a week, so it had to be this week. Her husband's retirement obviously didn't stretch to several weeks, just the one. Still, not bad. Amanda wondered what she would do for her retirement. She intended to retire early, very early, and live a life of luxury. She just hadn't figured out the intervening years part yet.

They stayed in the bar until well after midnight and then left together to return to their cabins ready for the following day and evening performances. Their booze expenditure was a lot more than Amanda had envisaged. Keep this up and she'd be working for drinks and not much more.

CHAPTER 42

Vincenzo picked up the phone. It was 9.30am. "Found him boss, but he's left Portugal. Apparently, he went over to the ship. He's left now but we have the details and without having had to speak to him." Davo related the details of the ship and cruise line to Vincenzo. After putting down the phone he got up, dressed and then made a call to organise his transport to the ship where he would accept a VIP cabin. These things were always possible when you knew the right people. Maybe he'd stay on the ship after completing his work, treat it as a mini break. Then again, he may have more work to do.

CHAPTER 43

The following day's performances both went very well. By now there was a bit of a buzz going around the staff that worked in the areas where the band performed. It seemed that everyone was enjoying this new line up and the freshness it brought. They sound checked Boys Of Summer both in the afternoon and evening and it was sounding good. They were considering adding it to the set for the private party before slotting it into the set proper, which had to be note for note perfect with no slip ups. Once that was in the set the next one was to be Hot In the City by Billy Idol. They'd discussed White Wedding but decided it was a bit of a cliché. Amanda had wanted to do Rebel Yell, but she'd been overruled. She would continue to push this number as she loved it and sang it well. Maybe she'd have a word in the ear of the retirement guy's wife to get her to ask them to play it. Another cunning plan. Still she had no idea who the woman was so dismissed it. The retirement party was organised for the following day at 1pm. The party would have lunch then the band would play from 1.30pm through to 2.45pm. Then they could go and rest ready for their 4pm and 9pm gigs later that evening. It would be a long day. She hoped her vocal cords would go the distance.

She'd never played a private party before. Still, a smaller audience and a smaller stage area, and a shorter set, but apart from that the same. Given the advanced ages of the couple, him being retired and all, they picked the more 60's end of songs rather than the rockier ones but they included the two new ones but put them later in the set for when people had had a few drinks.

Part of her role at these private events was to introduce herself, as the band spokesperson, congratulate them on the retirement or anniversary etc., get them a bottle of champagne on the house and ask for anything they wanted her to say or announce during the set. Maybe even get someone up to say a word or two. As she couldn't switch outfits, she went with the first set outfit, less sexy, and headed up on deck around forty minutes before show time.

She could see a group of people milling around near their stage area. The back line and drums were already set up and ready to go. She casually walked over to the group that were standing talking. As she approached, they all turned to look at her and their conversation snuffed out. "Susan?" Amanda said. "Hi, that's me. You must be Amanda. We've heard a lot about you and the band." "Thank you, how has your day been so far?" "Great, it'll be so nice to have Bernard back at home again. He works, or worked, so hard. He was a chief of police you know." "That's amazing." replied Amanda. "Oh, speak of the devil, here he is now. Bernard, over here, it's Amanda from the band." Bernard smiled and came over to them.
It was then that Amanda realised that Susan and Bernard were one of the couples she'd previously seen at breakfast and in the bar. "You look amazing." Bernard said. He was looking at her closely, not looking her up and down like many guys, but he seemed to be looking at her facial features. Their eyes met and he extended his hand to shake hers. "So how long have you been a singer then? Bernard asked. "Oh a few years now. I was singing in a rock band on the Algarve before I joined the ship." "Ah that's nice. We love the Algarve." Bernard said. "Yes, we've been all over, we especially like Silves." Susan said. "So, you are British?" Bernard asked her. "I was brought up mainly in London." she replied. Bernard offered her a drink, she accepted, and he went away to collect a glass of bubbles for her. Whilst he was away Amanda asked Susan "Is there anything you want us to say or announce during the set?" Susan went into her handbag and pro-

duced an A5 piece of paper with large handwriting on it. "Just say this if you are able, dear." Amanda took the paper and read it. "No problem, no problem at all." Susan smiled and then they chit chatted a while until Bernard arrived with two glasses of bubbles, one for Amanda and one for Susan.
Again, Bernard seemed to be studying her. "Do you mind me asking your age? I know a gentleman shouldn't ask such a question." "That's fine, Bernard. I'm twenty-four." She replied. They continued to chat for a few more minutes, then one of the other guests approached Bernard and he disappeared with the guy who wanted to speak to him about something.

When she had finished her drink, she thanked Susan, wished them both well and went off to meet up with the band. They were due to start in ten minutes. There was a dressing room area behind the bar. The barman let her in, and she went over to the band. They were all chatting but quietly so as their noise didn't pollute the bar. "What're they like?" Ben asked Amanda. "Nice, I think. He's a retired policeman." Ben pulled a face. Gill's face went red. James didn't say anything. "Is everything ready guys? All tuned up?" Amanda asked. "All good." James said. Ben picked up his acoustic guitar and proceeded to plug it into his tuner. Had he forgotten to tune up? Probably.

Just then the barman bobbed his head in. "It's showtime." he said, winked at Amanda, then went back to the bar. As they left for the stage, they each collected a bottle of beer from the bar. The barman had them ready. He'd have another one around halfway through the set when he'd deliver them to the stage area for them. That was a nice touch. There's nothing worse than playing in a bar or pub for a set, then having to queue up for a beer, then no time to chat or pee but straight into the second set.

The guys plugged in their guitars. Ian sat at his kit and proceeded to adjust the seat height up a bit. He seemed to be getting taller with every gig. Amanda took her vocal mic from the stand and held it. The mixer man gave them the thumbs up to say the

PA was now unmuted and they were ready to go. One two three four and off they went.

The mixer desk was at the side of the bar, so Johnny Fontaine, the sound man, kept moving around to get a feel for the sound reaching the punters from different locations. After the second song Amanda said her little spiel, wishing Susan and Bernard a happy retirement, and did the shout outs for the people Susan had named on her paper – these were friends and family that had joined them on the cruise and kept quiet about this fantastic party! They then went into Jailbreak by Thin Lizzy. Appropriate they had thought – a little joke. By now many of the guests were up dancing. They may have been in their sixties, but they could still move! She kept glancing over at Susan and Bernard. They were dancing and chatting. She often found Bernard was looking at her, or in her direction. Still he wasn't the only man whose eyes were on her. But whilst the other guys were looking mostly at her body, Bernard always seemed to be studying her face, looking right into her, not in a sexual way but in a policeman way somehow. Mid way through the set the barman arrived with their drinks and placed them in front of each band member and two by Amanda. She took one and passed it to Ian between songs. The trouble with drinking beer from a bottle during a gig is that it never lasted more than two gulps between songs. Amanda was careful not to drink too much in one swig to prevent the bubbles affecting her voice.

Boys Of Summer and Hot In The City both went down well and had everyone dancing. They would be part of the new set moving forward. They finished the set with Purple Rain by Prince, a bit of a smoochie, and popular with all ages. The crowd shouted for more, so they finished with The Boys Are Back In Town, then thanked everyone and left them wanting more. They headed back to their dressing area behind the bar and found another round of beers back there waiting for them. They couldn't really get changed there in any privacy. The guys could change their shirts, but Amanda had to stay as she was. They drank their drinks and then the band all left. Amanda went back and found Susan. As soon as Susan saw her, she virtually ran over to her and gave her a big, daughterly hug. "That was brilliant. Absolutely brilliant. You guys are brilliant." It was obvious she'd had a few more to drink by now but she wasn't quite slurring her words yet... not quite.... well maybe just a bit. There was no sign of Bernard. Amanda said her goodbyes, explaining that they had two more shows that day. Susan said that they wouldn't be at the shows today, but she'd leave a round of drinks for the band behind the bar. Amanda thanked her and headed back to her cabin. She didn't have much time before their next set and she needed some rest.

CHAPTER 44

Vincenzo took his case and placed it on the bed in his VIP cabin. Apparently, he'd created quite a shit storm by pulling the necessary strings to secure a VIP cabin. Still, he didn't care. The helicopter had dropped him off a little after 8pm. Time to unpack, shower, get dressed and catch the band's gig and get his first glimpse of the Little Weasel herself in action.

He had brought one of his many, hand tailored suits. Some came from Italy, some from Saville Row. All were exquisite and oozed class. Naturally they all fit him perfectly. He couldn't afford to gain or lose more than two or three pounds. But no matter what he drank or ate, his weight remained exactly the same. Must be his metabolism. He didn't go out of his way to exercise either.

After liberally applying his favourite cologne he left his cabin and, following the directions he'd been supplied earlier, headed off to where the band would shortly be performing. Apparently, they did two shows on some days. Today was one of those days.

CHAPTER 45

The afternoon show had gone well with the inclusion of the two new songs. The room was almost full. By the end every one of the band was quite tired. Afterwards they went back to the dressing room for a beer, but they only had the one as it wouldn't be long until their third show. "It's a real killer, this three shows in a day malarkey." James had said to Ben who nodded. Ian was drenched in sweat but said nothing. Amanda knew she'd had to use her new outfit for the first set of the last show as she'd worn the usual one twice already today. If they had two days running where they had three shows she'd need yet another outfit! Still that was unlikely. But a girl can't have too many clothes.

After a twenty-minute power nap in her cabin, apparently that's what musicians do. She felt a little refreshed, but somewhat drained at the same time. She had donned her new first set outfit and looked at herself in the mirror. The outfit looked great, but she really was looking a little tired. She redid her makeup and off she went, taking with her the once worn second set outfit and her jeans and tee shirt for afterwards. Although she didn't think they'd be partying tonight.

The room was once again full. She couldn't see any empty seats at all. They had mixed the set up a bit, keeping the two new songs but bringing back all the songs they hadn't played in the previous set – this was for the benefit of anyone choosing to watch them twice or even three times.

Their set lists were pre-printed by James, he had a printer in his cabin apparently, and laid out in their respective positions on stage where each band member could see them, but the set lists weren't obvious to the audience. Tonight, they opened with The Boys Are Back In Town - a somewhat brave move. When they performed Amanda was in a world of her own. During the guitar solo sections, she sometimes swayed and observed the members of the audience watching the band or watching the lead guitar player in action. They always looked enthralled. She hated to see people playing on their phones whilst the band were playing. She understood that business people needed to check their messages and notifications frequently but it still irked her. Tonight, everyone seemed to be watching the band. It was difficult to see the back of the room and the bar area with the lighting. Sometimes, when the lights were bright, she caught a glimpse of the bar and the bar staff and people stood watching from the bar. Usually, the bar area was quiet but tonight there were a few people stood by the bar watching the band whilst waiting for a drink to be served. Maybe they couldn't get a seat. A full house was exactly what was required of them. They were doing well.

After the first set they went backstage and downed a bottle of beer. Amanda also had a bottle of water. She didn't want to be dehydrated from working and drinking on and off throughout the day. "Hey, I think this is for you." Ben said and passed her an envelope. Was it one of Ben's windups? She opened it up expecting it to have a spider in it or talcum powder or something. But it contained a letter, very brief and in exquisite handwriting. "Please meet me at the bar after the show. I'd very much like to meet you and buy you a drink." It was signed Vincenzo. An Italian, nice. This was the first time she'd received such an invitation. She read the letter aloud to the band. Ben whooped. She asked Gill "What should I do?" "You should go meet this guy. He's a paying punter. You can always down a drink then make your excuses – it's no big deal." "When was your last invitation from a punter, Gill?" Ben asked her tauntingly. "Fuck off arsehole." She replied and everyone laughed. Gill was a good-looking girl and she'd confided in Amanda over breakfast that Ben had asked her out, but she didn't like dating band members as, when things went wrong, it affected the dynamic of the band and her work. She'd done this once before and, as a backing singer, was more expendable than her then boyfriend and ended up having to leave the band. She didn't want to lose this gig, so she'd spurned his advances. Plus, she didn't fancy him. She'd tried to explain the situation to him, and whilst he had said he understood, he still occasionally had a pop at her, like just now. Guys didn't like being turned down and often had fragile egos. Amanda knew she couldn't turn down this Vincenzo guy. Something in the back of her mind was flashing red. Vincenzo, where had she heard that name before? It was Italian and unusual – except maybe in Italy. She'd never been to Italy though. Still, probably just some old rich guy who fancied her. She'd definitely meet him and, who knows, it might prove beneficial to her in the long run. Right now, good things were happening to her and everything was just seemingly falling into her lap.

She changed into her second set outfit – it was still a little damp from this afternoon. She hated that feeling. Still, needs must. She still looked great as she looked into the mirror, in the girl's dressing room. Gill and Gemma had also changed their outfits but to fresh ones she hadn't seen before. Gemma caught her looking at them. "Emergency dress number three." she said and smiled. "It's been a long day!" Gill said and sighed. "But the show must go on." Amanda said and they headed back to the guys for the second set, their fifth set of the day. Amanda had never worked so hard in her life! More than a full day's work! But strangely she had still enjoyed it.

The band went on stage first and started up with Proud Mary. They started slow, like Tina Turner had done. The intro was stretched out a bit then the lights went stage left and Amanda slinked onto the stage, walking slowly and sexily. When she arrived at the front of the stage, she casually picked up her mic and started the first line of the song. They did two verses slowly then 'bang' into the fast version.

At the end the crowd went wild. "Thank you." Amanda said and James went straight into Teenage Kicks – always a crowd pleaser regardless of the age of taste of the crowd. They finished the set with Comfortably Numb. Both guitarists also played keyboards, so they had one of those electronic keyboards stage left. It could sound like a piano or an organ or whatever, in addition to whatever Nick was playing. It had been programmed with the sounds for Comfortably Numb and a handful of other tracks that only needed one guitar but benefitted from additional keyboards. It sounded great and added a new dynamic to the band.

When the number had finished the crowd again showed their appreciation. For an encore they played Legs by ZZ Top and Amanda had all the moves. Still wanting more, they concluded with Rock 'n' Roll by Led Zeppelin. "Lonely, lonely, lonely..... time" followed by one of those big endings. After a round of thank you's they all stood in line, took a bow, then skipped off stage left waving as they went. This was a sort of fun thing they did for a laugh. When they got backstage, they all looked drained. They drank their bottle and as a group decided to call it a night. Then Amanda remembered she had to have one more drink with this Vincenzo guy. And that's when it hit her – where she'd seen the name before. It was on the letter; the letter she had found with the cash telling of murders committed by a Vincenzo. Could it be him? She was drained and tired, but now fully awake. It was probably just coincidence. Would she know a murderer just by looking? She doubted it. She was one, a serial killer in fact, and everyone else was clueless. If it was him then how the fuck had he tracked her here? It was impossible. She'd been careful to leave no traces anywhere. She'd used multiple names never using her own name at all. The last person to use her real name was Dom. It can't be him – she was letting her tiredness cloud her thinking. She said her goodbyes to the rest of the band and said she was going to get changed. Gill shouted over to her "I wouldn't bother getting changed, stay as you are, it's the singer in the band he wants to meet, not you, nothing personal." She looked at Gill and then grasped what she had meant. It was a rich guy's fantasy to meet the singer from the band. If she rocked up in jeans and tee shirt it might shatter his illusion. "Good thinking." She said and turned around and headed in the direction of the bar.

As she walked across the room there were still quite a few people in there. A couple of guys shook her hand and said how they had enjoyed the performance. A young woman accosted her telling her how great she was, and that she too had also sung with a band once, on holiday. Amanda was polite but told her she was late for an appointment. The woman wished her well and then Amanda headed towards the bar. The barman was watching her approaching. He nodded to the far side of the bar towards a guy dressed in a snappy suit. She understood this to mean that the suit was Vincenzo himself. As she walked along the bar to meet him the barman whispered "Arrived by helicopter today. Must be well rich!" and he smiled. She wondered what he thought of her – had he assumed that she would welcome the approaches of older, rich guys, and that she was nothing more than a slapper? Who wouldn't she thought to herself? Things like that don't happen when you work in a factory, a shop, or a bar.

As she approached Vincenzo, who was trying to appear like he hadn't been watching her approach all the way from the stage, he looked over and extended his hand for a handshake. He then pulled her towards him and kissed her on both cheeks, which took her by surprise. "Thank you for accepting my invitation to meet with me. I watched you last night and I knew that I just had to meet the beautiful lady who sings with the band." He was lying. She knew this immediately from the barman's comments

– he had only just arrived today by helicopter. Alarm bells were now ringing.

CHAPTER 46

"So, you saw me last night – did you enjoy the show?" She was testing him. He looked into her eyes, probing, whilst his face told a story of delight and joy, his eyes were black, but were they the eyes of a murderer? After a brief pause, he said, "actually I only arrived today. I didn't see you yesterday as I was at home in Italy. I have no idea why I said that. I just lose my marbles when I'm in the presence of a woman as beautiful as you are." Had he realised that she knew that he was lying or was it her who looked for these signs all the time. She knew she was beautiful, especially in her current outfit. "I was fortunate enough to secure a VIP suite." Now that sounded like an invitation. The alarm bells grew louder.

All the guys around were looking at her or glancing at her. She was something special and she knew it. It wasn't that surprising that some rich guy had seen something he wanted and made a bold move for it. That was probably how he had gotten rich in the first place. "Excuse me, I have something for you." He turned around and retrieved two large glasses of champagne. The remainder was still in the bottle on ice on the table. He was planning on more than one drink. "Why thank you" she said and took the glass. He clinked his glass to hers and said "Salut." "Cheers." was her reply.

They both took a drink of their champagne and he then took her glass off her and placed them both on the table. "I'm sorry, Vincenzo but I've had a long day; this is the third show we've done today actually – we've been working since noon. I'm absolutely shattered, and I can only stay for the one drink." "No problem, my dear, I expected as much. But please stay for a few more minutes whilst we finish our drinks.

Please tell me a little about yourself, you are so... enchanting. I've seen many bands and many singers, but you are... you are special." She smiled "Thank you. I've been singing for a few years now, initially in bars and I've only just started on the ship. It's a big change for me." He smiled at her but didn't say anything. She felt a little awkward, like she was being interrogated in some way. As she spoke his eyes, although almost totally black, seemed to be processing her every word, verifying if she was telling the truth or lying. It was like she was being assessed or something. "What do you do and what brings you to this cruise, especially when it is part way through?" she asked. Now she was the interrogator. "Ah, nothing more than a whim. I have just closed a nice little business deal and I wanted to celebrate. I have no wife, so I celebrate alone." he replied.

He turned around and retrieved their glasses. They both took a drink. She envisaged only one more such drink before the glass was drained and she could take her leave. "It's lovely champagne." she said, struggling to think of anything to say. She was trying to process all the thoughts going around in her head. Was this just some rich guy who fancied her, or was it THE Vincenzo, the murderer, the man her father had had dealings with. "So, you are from where?" he asked. "London originally but I've lived all over – the rock and roll lifestyle." And she giggled. Vincenzo didn't laugh. It was as though he hadn't heard her answer or wasn't interested in what she had to say. "I can see you are tired, my dear, I don't want to impose on you, would you mind if I were to come and see your show again before the cruise ends?" "Please do." She replied, hoping that she wouldn't see him again. He had confused her, and she felt vulnerable for the first time in what seemed a lifetime. "We've only got the one show tomorrow I'm pleased to say." "So, you can have a lie in tomorrow – that's nice." He didn't say that she looked knackered, but she could tell that's what he was thinking. He retrieved the drinks once again and they both emptied their glasses. "Your parents must be so proud." He said looking into her eyes. "They are, although it wasn't the career they envisaged for me, after paying for private schooling." she joked.

His piercing black eyes were drilling into her head. She knew she was a good liar, capable of fooling almost anyone. But this Vincenzo was cold, like a hungry wolf. "I am sure they most certainly are, my dear." he said, smiling in the way the Big Bad Wolf smiled at Grandma. By now her gut was telling her that it was indeed him, THE Vincenzo, the murderer. The fact that he was a murderer didn't scare her too much. She'd killed one murderer already. He was obviously rich from his clothes and watch. She thanked him for the drink, wished him well and left.

As she walked back past the bar the barman looked at her, his expression showing a little concern. She nodded at him and said "Goodnight." He nodded back and she headed for her cabin, all the time looking back to see if she was being followed. Tonight, she would be vulnerable, in Grandma's cabin in the woods.

CHAPTER 47

She didn't sleep well. In her dreams, she was running away from someone or something, legs like treacle, unable to gain any speed, sure that she was going to be caught and killed or eaten or something worse. She awoke with a start, sweaty and anxious. This had happened two or three times already tonight. It was now 4.15am and she needed to think. She put the light on and filled her glass with water. She then retrieved the letter and read it again. It seemed that Vincenzo was responsible for several murders but these three listed he had committed personally. How many had he presided over? And why did he do these three himself? Why were they killed in the first place? Were they a threat to him? Did he do it for fun?
She felt certain now that the Vincenzo here on the boat was the one in the letter, the murderer. Still, she'd vanquished murderers before. But this one would be different. She was the hunted, not the huntress. But she had the advantage that she knew who he was. He didn't know this and thought that she had no idea of who he was. But he was being cautious, nevertheless. He was a professional.

She went over in her mind how he could have traced her. Did he know about the girl she'd killed for her identity? Would he tell the authorities? Would he tell the British police that Annie Montgomery was alive and well and on a cruise ship? She thought not. But it seemed he was a formidable opponent. Whoever had written the letter had done so for insurance. What did she have for insurance? The very same letter. Whether he knew of the letter or not, it would serve her well as her insurance. She wondered if Vincenzo knew what was in the letter.

She decided to make a copy, in ink, by hand, that could be passed off as the original if it came to that. All she could find was branded paper. She searched through the side pockets of her bags and found a single A4 sheet folded into four. She unfolded it and used one of her own biros, in a different colour to the one provided by the line, that was sat on her desk untouched, and copied the letter, word for word, trying to make the handwriting look similar. She didn't make a conscious effort to reproduce every detail, she wrote it quickly, rushed, much as the original had been written. She popped it into a standard issue line envelope and wrote on the front – 'Gill – please can you keep hold of this for me – Amanda' and added a cross for a kiss. She then wrote 'In case anything happens to me, hand it to the captain immediately.' She followed it with a smiley face to detract from the serious implications of her message. She had licked and sealed the envelope. She then left her cabin momentarily and slid it under Gill's door – Gill's was the closest cabin to her own of all the band members.

Once this was done, she then went back to her own cabin and put the kettle on. She knew she wouldn't be able to get back to sleep again. She needed coffee and time to make a plan. She knew it was dog eat dog – one of them wouldn't live to see the end of this cruise. She felt that, currently, the odds were in her favour, as she knew who he was, and she felt sure that he thought that she had no inkling of who he was or why he was on board. He would be thinking that she would make easy prey.

She folded her duplicate letter and sealed it in an envelope, wrote Annie on the front and then placed it back into her bag. One option was to offer Vincenzo the letter, were he to visit her cabin, and say she hadn't opened it claiming ignorance. Say something like her father had given it to her to look after. But given Vincenzo had followed her here, he must have put the pieces together meaning he knew she was complicit in her father's murder and that she'd killed Dom. How else could he have put the pieces together and tracked her all the way here? She could maintain the pretence of not knowing who he was, that was her most powerful asset. He thought he'd been so clever, and he'd even used his own name; such was his level of confidence in her not having a clue as to who he was or why he was here. Sheer arrogance. But it wasn't her that was clueless. This was the one thing that could put Vincenzo down, arrogance, his Achilles heel.

So, what next? If Vincenzo knew where she was, then surely, he must have confided in someone else – this would be big news. Even if she saw him off, who else would be coming for her next? She knew that, much though she loved this new life on the ship, this was to be her last week. Two more days until the ship docked at Malta and it was there where she would need to alight and disappear – this time for good. But for him to get so far, he must have worked out the identity of the girl she killed. Had he? She still had her passport. She'd need a passport to get off Malta pronto. She couldn't hide on such a small island. Or could she? This was all so complex – so many things to think about and so many unknowns with so little time. One thing was for certain, she needed a weapon in case she ended up alone with Vincenzo. Later on she would pay a visit to the kitchen and acquire three or four knives of differing sizes. They had lots of knives; they wouldn't miss them. She could return them later. She would place one under the mattress, one in her clothes bag and a smaller one on her person somewhere maybe. Her show outfits left nowhere to conceal a smartie, let alone a weapon. But as long as she was in a public place, especially on a stage, she was safe.

It wasn't his style to shoot her down from his position at the back of the room, plus he'd have nowhere to hide on a ship. He would need a plan and he'd need to dispose of her body, if he didn't want her being correctly identified.

Was there a way she could finish him off whilst she was performing, offering her the perfect alibi? She wouldn't need an alibi. No-one would suspect her. Should Vincenzo go missing, she doubted anyone would report him missing, or even notice the fact. This was another thing on her side. If he was as dodgy as she thought then no one would involve the police, they would just either look for revenge or rub their hands together, glad that someone finally killed the bastard. But which? She had no allies here. She was on her own. But that's how she worked best. She had plans to make, contingencies to consider, weapons to acquire, frocks to buy and songs to sing. Such a complex life.

CHAPTER 48

"You're a bit quiet, Bernard. That makes a change!" Susan said as she made their morning coffee. "Ahh, I'm just knackered that's all. This retirement has hit me hard. I'm not used to having time on my hands. I can't stop thinking like a cop. You know something silly, when we were speaking to that girl from the band yesterday, Amanda, I couldn't help thinking that I knew her face from somewhere. And this morning it hit me. Impossibly, it was someone involved in a case my team were working on before I finished. And you'll never believe which one?" "Not those evil bombers?" she said. "No." he replied. "The other one, the kidnapping. She looks very similar to the daughter that was kidnapped and never heard of again, assumed dead. We never did get to the bottom of that case as the bombings took all the resources away." "Shame." Susan replied, not really bothered about either of his old cases. "You know you're no longer in the police. Everyone agreed, even your Doctor, that it was in your own best interests to take retirement. At your age, most men would jump at the chance. And you – you're still thinking like you're still working. Give it a rest. We're on our holidays." She was getting more than a little annoyed at him. Again. He smiled at her, kissed her on the cheek and said "You're right. I think I'll go grab some air, back soon." She acknowledged him and he left to go for a stroll on deck.

Bernard headed straight for the purser's desk. "Hi, my name is Traynor. You organised the band for me yesterday for my retirement party." "Yes, sir I did. I trust everything was satisfactory?" "Oh yes, the band were excellent – everything is excellent to be honest. I'd just like to have a chat with Amanda from the band. You see my wife has gone and bought her a big box of chocolates and some flowers and I'd like to deliver them to her room. "No problem sir, leave them here and I can get them delivered." "Thank you so much, but I rather wanted to deliver them myself and pass on a message from my wife." "I'm very sorry sir but, as you can understand, I am not permitted to give out staff member's personal details." "No, you are quite right, I understand, after all I do work for the police service." Bernard said. "How about you leave her a message and ask her to meet me in the bar on top at say noon. I can pass her the gifts there. If she chooses not to come then we'll understand." he said. "Well, it's a little unusual but, given the circumstances, I don't see a problem. What cabin are you in sir?" Traynor gave him their cabin number and the purser agreed to get a message to Amanda to meet at noon in the bar on top if she was available.

All Traynor had to do now was decide what to say to her, how to ascertain if she was indeed Annie Montgomery, and if so, what to do about the whole affair. He had so many questions, well the cop in him had, that is. He wasn't sure where his allegiances lay now he was retired. Whilst he was retired from the force, no one ever got to retire from his other role, not alive anyway. He went back to the cabin where Susan was still getting ready.

CHAPTER 49

The phone rang. Amanda picked it up. It was the purser telling her the couple they played for yesterday had a gift for her and would she like to meet them in the bar up top at noon. She agreed and put the phone down. How nice. It would give her a chance to sit in company and take in the people in a search for the elusive Vincenzo. As long as she was in company, she was safe. She was most vulnerable here alone in her cabin.

She left her room at 11.45 and went to the purser's desk. "No-one ever gives me chocolates." he said. "Chocolates?" she replied. "Shit, I wasn't meant to say anything. Don't say anything, just pretend it's a surprise. She took her chance. "OK, now you've put your foot in it big style. How about you tell me the cabin number of the big wig that arrived by helicopter yesterday and I won't say a thing to the Traynors. He thought about this knowing he wasn't supposed to give out cabin numbers. But she smiled at him and he could feel a blush coming on. God, he was forty-two and she was, what, twenty-five. Nevertheless, as a single man, he would have loved nothing more than to spend time with her and make her happy. All he could do to make her happy right now was give her this guy's cabin number. He looked on the system and said to her "Oh he must be really rich. He's in a VIP suite – number four." She smiled at him again causing him to blush even more. "And where might they be? she asked. "Easy – up top." was his reply. Great. She smiled again and headed for the restaurant. She knew there was a VIP restaurant up top as well, but she hadn't seen it. She guessed the rooms must be nearby.

She arrived in the bar at 11.58 but she didn't see Susan. She did see Bernard though and he was waiting for her. No chocolates though which was strange. "Hi Amanda." he said. "Susan would have been here but she's a little under the weather, you know, too much booze to be frank but I can't say that to her." "Oh that's a shame." Amanda replied. Bernard was studying her face once again. But why? Traynor seemed to read the question from her expression. "You remind me of the daughter of someone I knew in England, someone who is sadly now dead." Where was he going with this? "You see, my job before retirement was chief of police. It's related to one of the final cases my team worked on." "I see" she said, trying to look interested and not concerned. "You remind me of someone who disappeared, assumed dead. Sadly, those bombers took all the resources away and we never really got to do a full enquiry. By the time the dust settled it was too late." "Too late?" she asked." "Yes, the girl I am referring to was kidnapped." "Oh, I see." she said. Her head was spinning. Miles away from anywhere, on a cruise liner and now two people were after her. "So no-one knows what happened to the woman in question then?" she said. "No. Actually she was a girl, sixteen years of age. I can't say too much, but she was kidnapped, and her father came to me to get her back. But then he too disappeared only to turn up as a victim of one of the bombs. "That's just dreadful, how awful." she said. "To be only sixteen and left with no father." They sat in silence for a moment.

She was hoping that the clothes she'd chosen, jeans and a blue shirt, didn't either look like any of her old outfits. Which they most certainly didn't or made her look her true age. She had applied her usual makeup and she felt sure she would pass for twenty-five even under close scrutiny. "Would it help you if I went back to my cabin and showed you my passport?" she said innocently but testing him. "No that's fine. I'm sorry I troubled you, I really should have kept my big mouth shut. For God's sake don't tell Susan about any of this. She'd go absolutely crackers."

Amanda smiled at him. "Don't worry. So, if the girl was missing then will she be dead by now?" Bernard sat in silence for a whole thirty seconds. "I don't know." he said, again studying her. She thought her lines were convincing, but he still had the enquiring look in his eyes. But nothing like Vincenzo's eyes, these eyes were hardened but still with compassion. He was trying to look after a missing girl. Should she confide in him? Tell him about Vincenzo? If she did that, she'd be admitting to murder. She had to play the innocent. "Well please pass my fondest regards to Susan when she surfaces. I'll keep my eyes open for you over the next couple of days. Will you be coming to any more of our shows?" "Oh, I hadn't thought about it. I'll see what the boss says. We have plans for this evening, but tomorrow is our last, we might come to the evening show, I'll see what she thinks.". "That would be lovely. I'd better head off too, things to do." They said their goodbye's and she headed back to her cabin. The conversation had knocked her sideways and she had completely forgotten to undertake her surveillance. She went downstairs and arrived back at her cabin door. She hoped that Vincenzo hadn't been watching her. If he had, he may assume that she was talking to the ex-chief of police about him. Now she was assuming Vincenzo knew who Traynor was as well! God, in her overactive imagination Vincenzo knew everyone! But nevertheless, she had gone from feeing safe and sound to be being hunted. Both as a missing teenager and as a criminal.

CHAPTER 50

He watched her as she disappeared in the direction of her cabin. Why was she talking to him? Was he warning her? If he was, he'd find out and make him pay. Was it coincidence? Never. Traynor knew who she was. There was no kind of confrontation, so he hadn't told her he knew – maybe it was all innocent. Vincenzo felt sure that Traynor hadn't played his hand. Not yet at least. This complicated things immensely. Maybe he should have brought back-up like it had been suggested to him. It was too late now. Vincenzo was alone and had to tidy up this mess himself. He had to find out if Little Weasel had any knowledge of the letter. If so, he needed to find and then destroy the letter. Either way she would die. But not today. Sadly, with her unmissable job she'd be missed too quickly, within half a day. He would have to wait until after her last performance tomorrow night before offing her. She was only small and light, an easy package to bundle over the side. She might survive a little while, but not if he crushed her skull first. Or broke her neck – that was clean and quick and quiet. With his strong hands he could snuff out her tiny life in seconds. This was his plan. Get her alone, kill her, then send her over the side in the early hours before the ship docked.

CHAPTER 51

Bernard watched her as she walked back. She was a very beautiful young woman, nothing like Annie Montgomery, she was a tired, controlled teenager. But nevertheless, something in her facial features, her eyes, and her expressions when he laid his cards on the table, lead him to believe that she was indeed Montgomery's daughter. His gut still told him it was her. But how? How had she gone from kidnap victim, past her father's death by bomb, only to reappear, reinvented with a new career and new identity on a cruise ship? He didn't even know she could sing. And what about the kidnapper? What had become of him? Had he taken the money and just let her go? He knew from experience this just never happened. His brain said no but his gut disagreed. Just then Susan appeared. "You took your time." she admonished. "Sorry, I got chatting. Are they coming to meet us?" "Yes, they're on their way, let's get a drink and look at the menu." she said.

"I fancy salmon." said Susan. "What again?" Bernard replied. "You had that yesterday." "Yes, but it was divine." was her reply. As a cop, or ex-cop, Bernard had this annoying habit of always watching people, perp spotting, and never trusting anyone he met or didn't know well. He found himself looking around the deck at the other people. Mostly couples having fun, strolling hand in hand. A single man or woman stuck out like a sore thumb in this type of couples-oriented environment. The thumb he was looking at had a familiar fingerprint. One he thought he would never again have the displeasure of seeing or speaking to in what remained of his lifetime. He was looking at Vincenzo Dente. But the worst part was that he felt sure Dente was watching Amanda and had, therefore, spotted her talking to himself. Any doubt he had around Amanda's identify was quickly settled. His gut was right once again, his copper's instinct.

But now he had a problem, a big problem. What did Vincenzo Dente want with Annie Montgomery, or Amanda as she was calling herself now? What was the connection? Was she running away from him? But how? Or was she working for him in some capacity. Could he be forcing her, against her will? The last thing he knew she was a kidnap victim assumed dead. When he had alluded this to her, she had done an excellent job of reaffirming her new identify. Even at the sound of her father's death she hadn't flinched. That was strange for a young girl. He wouldn't have expected floods of tears, but he should have seen something. His coppers gut feel was kicking in again. She knew more about her father's death than anyone had thought. His head was spinning. What was he to do? Was he himself in danger? Was Susan in danger? Should he tell her? He would have to play it by ear.
Whatever was to transpire, it would happen over the course of the next two days. So much for a this being a holiday. So much for retirement. But now he had to decide where his allegiances lay.

CHAPTER 52

Amanda's head was spinning. Had the cop fallen for her lines? She thought so. Was it coincidence that he was on board? Could he, in fact, be after Vincenzo himself? Or was he in collusion with him? Should she have told the cop, ex-cop, of her real identity? This was a definite no as it would be admitting her part in crimes, she wanted no part of. She had to remain the innocent victim. If they proved that she was Annie, then she could say she escaped from Devizes and hid; then landed this dream job. Very unbelievable that one. But it was probably her best idea yet. Claim to be the victim.

She had two shows today then one tomorrow. If Vincenzo wanted to harm her, he would surely wait until after tomorrow's show so that her disappearance didn't arouse suspicion aboard ship. If she failed to show for a gig, then the heat would be on. She knew she had some time on her side. But she would need to be ready and at her best to survive in order to once again disappear and reinvent herself. A part of her was cursing the time and effort she'd put into becoming a great singer – all of that would be wasted and it was down to Vincenzo. Now, were she to strike first, bump him off and dispose of him, then the cop would be none the wiser. He'd assume he'd made a mistake and life could go on.
This seemed her best course of action. Unless the cop knew and had seen Vincenzo on board. Still, even if he had, he probably wouldn't say anything. Or would he? But how the fuck was she gonna overpower, kill and dispose of this formidable murderer. He was cold, callous, clever and an experienced killer. He would

assume that he was the hunter, Arrogance. But now he was the hunted.

CHAPTER 53

The kitchen would be really busy, all day, today. Her best shot would be after tonight's gig. She could have a drink with the band then head off to her cabin... via the kitchen. She'd have her bag with her in which to conceal her necessaries. After thinking this through, she felt a little safer knowing that it was unlikely that Vincenzo would try anything today or up until the end of tomorrow's performance. That would be around midnight. She'd have the company of the band. Maybe if she pulled a big strong guy and took him back to her cabin, he could help her deal with Vincenzo. Ben fit the bill perfectly. But no one would then simply help get rid of the body and keep it to themselves. Plus, they'd be a walking risk. She had to do this herself. Maybe she could arrange for Gill or Gemma to swap cabins, that way if Vincenzo did get in and kill her whilst she slept it wouldn't be her. She'd be dead, again, and able to leave and start another new life. It was worth thinking about. But someone would know. And there would be two girls missing then.

The cabins allotted to staff weren't particularly large. There was nowhere to hide bar the bathroom, which was the obvious place. Vincenzo, however, had a VIP suite. His room, or rooms, would afford lots of hiding places. She needed to know when he was out and about, so she could break into his cabin. But how could she kill him? He would have a sea view, a veranda or something like that. Surely it wouldn't be difficult to man handle a body from his apartment to the deck and overboard? She needed to see his apartment and make a plan. But there was no time now. She would have a little time between shows and she'd just have to do it then, in daylight. She had a feeling that she would see him again, either at this afternoon's show or this evening's show. The thing still on her side was the fact the Vincenzo thought that she was completely oblivious as to who he was, what he did and why he was here. She had to appear to be acting normally to ensure he continued to believe this, as it was her best defence. Keep him calm and not force him to do anything rash before tomorrow evening. She needed the time to get her shit together.

Damn, she hadn't washed yesterday's outfits. There wasn't time now to wash and dry them for this afternoon's show. Then there wasn't time between shows either. She'd have to either wear the dirty ones or wear something different. Fuck. She'd have to wear the same ones, no time for hopping. Extra deodorant and fragrance might hide the stale smell. She cursed herself for forgetting this, but she had a lot on her mind. She put on her worn, first set dress, packed her jeans and worn second set outfit and headed out to the Theatrium.

When she got there Gemma, James and Ben were there, but the others hadn't arrived yet. Gemma went over to Amanda and said, "Can I have a word with you?" "Sure." "Don't worry, it will only take a minute. I know you're new around here, but I know you've spent more time with Gill and me over the past week or so." Amanda looked at her, wondering where this was going. They both stopped walking and Gemma continued. "Has Gill said anything to you?" Amanda looked at her as though to say "And…" Gemma shuffled uncomfortably. "She's been a bit quiet the past couple of days. I think she's been seeing someone.". "So?" Amanda asked. "Well I don't know really. She's not mentioned it and we usually tell each other if we meet anyone on board, you know?" Amanda nodded. "I am just a bit worried it's a married man that's all.".

Amanda looked at her, it was obvious she was indeed worried about her friend. "So what, she's a big girl." Amanda said. She continued "I'm sure he wouldn't be the first guy have a fling with a pretty girl on a cruise.". Gemma smiled and said "I know, I know, but it just seems strange she hasn't mentioned anything. I'm a bit worried about her." "Well let's both keep an eye on her. If she invites me for breakfast or anything, I'll see what I can wheedle out of her shall I?" Gemma smiled, "Thanks, I feel a bit better now." Amanda finished their conversation with "I wouldn't worry, I'm sure she'll be fine." and with that Amanda left Gemma to ready herself for the gig. Gill and Ian had just arrived, only Nick was still to show up.

After the first set they went back to the dressing room. Amanda made her excuses to go to the loo. Instead she went to the back of the kitchen – the staff were over the other side talking. She could see an array of knives in the sink and on the worktops. For a moment they all turned to look the other way as someone had apparently shouted over to them. With that she sneaked in and went to the sink. She saw two identical knives around five or six inches long in the sink. She took both these knives, plus a smaller knife and some kitchen roll and quickly left. When she was out of sight, she wrapped the knives in the kitchen roll and placed them in her bag in the ladies dressing room with her clothes. She then changed into her second set outfit, which ponged a little, and went back to the rest of the band. The whole thing had taken less than five minutes. No-one had missed her. As she walked back Gemma looked up at her and smiled. Gill was talking to Ben.

She had decided she needed a sheath of some kind, in which to carry one of the knives, and avoid touching it to carry out the next part of her plan. It may not be needed but better safe than sorry. She had an umbrella in her cabin that came in a sort of case. It seemed around the right size for holding the knife. She could also use one of those clear, plastic bags required for cosmetics at airports. They were easy to get hold of. From now on she'd keep it in her bag just in case, disguised as an umbrella.

The second set went well but the band were visibly less animated than earlier in the day, tiredness creeping in. Nevertheless, the audience loved their music and two encores were required to finish the night off. They had decided to have one or two beers after the show, to wind down, but then have an early night. They got changed into their normal clothes and headed back to their cabins to drop off their clothes for laundering, then they were to meet in the bar. As Amanda entered her cabin, she saw a piece of paper that had been pushed under the door. She put her bag on the bed and picked up the paper. She opened the envelope. It contained a brief, hastily written message. "I need to speak to you urgently Annie, you are in danger. We'll be in the bar on deck till around 1am, please head up there and I'll make my excuses so we can talk. It was signed Bernard Traynor. She stared at the letter.

She was right, he had recognised her. Fucking cops. She didn't think he'd have shared this with his wife, and if he'd called the cops there would be no need to send her a letter. There was still time to fix this somehow. But why was Traynor saying that she was in danger? Vincenzo? Traynor must have seen Vincenzo and put two and two together. Maybe he knew of Vincenzo from his job.

So, she wasn't apparently half as good as she thought she was, at switching identities and hiding in plain sight. How could she get out of this one?

The only way she could see now was to get rid of both Traynor and Vincenzo. A top cop and a top bad guy. No easy task. She knew that if Vincenzo disappeared then no police would be involved. No doubt he had enough enemies that wanted him dead. No-one would suspect a small young woman to be capable of this. But how could she off him? More to the point how would she silence Traynor? She knew another sleepless night lay ahead of her. She had to make plans and act on them tomorrow. That's

if she survived the night that is.
Now she really needed a drink. She went back and met the band, but after two drinks they were all ready for off. They said their goodbyes and Amanda went up on deck to the bar where she saw Bernard sat on a table facing the entrance, opposite Susan, who wouldn't see her. She stood still.

Traynor spotted her almost immediately. He said something to Susan and then got up and walked in the direction of the toilets. Amanda followed him. Susan was still facing the other way so didn't spot her. The toilets were down some stairs. They met at the bottom. "No time to talk, but I know who you are and there is someone on the ship that I believe also knows who you are and, for whatever reason, is after you. He arrived by helicopter and as the cruise finishes tomorrow when we dock, if he is going to do something it is likely to be tonight or tomorrow morning." He looked into her eyes. "Given you recognise this guy, I am assuming he is wanted for something. Can't you just call the police to come and pick him up?" she asked innocently. "It's not that simple. He is above the law. He is a very senior guy in an organised crime outfit that owns half of London and half the police there. He is untouchable." At this she knew she had no option but to kill Vincenzo and soon. "Have you told anyone else?" she asked him. "I can't – it's complicated." he replied. "OK, I'll lie low – it's a big ship he'll never find me." "OK but don't go back to your cabin, stay the hell away. He'll know where you are, and he'll have been watching you. He'll know your movements, who you see. I think he saw us the other day in here" "Are you in danger too then?" she asked. "I can handle myself." he replied.

Her head was spinning. He was a retired cop that wouldn't call the cops. He must have been in Vincenzo's pocket at some time but thought he was free with retirement. He would probably like to see Vincenzo dead almost as much as she did. Could they team up together? Before she had decided what to say, Traynor said "Look, I need to go back. Susan doesn't know a thing. No-one does. You're on your own. I don't know why or how you pulled this identity switch off and to be honest I don't care. But after all the trouble you've gone to, you must have your reasons. I knew your father; he was a bastard. I'd hate for it to end with you as just another one of Vincenzo's victims."

She sensed there was still something good left inside Traynor. "What if I said I had something he wanted that incriminated him in murders, that could give your guys what they need to convict him." Traynor looked at her. "To be honest, he's so slippery I don't know if anything could stick to him. But if you have it, and he knows you have it, then you're in deep, deep trouble. Give it back to him and hide and never come back. He never forgets. A week, a month, a year. He'll be back. I know some of the crimes he's committed and they're brutal. But nowadays he has people he can call on. The fact that he's here in person is what really makes me worried. I've told you, hide and disappear. If you don't give him this letter, he'll hunt you for all your days. Leave it in your cabin for him to find but don't let him find you or you're as good as dead. Or worse.". He was about to leave.

She produced the knife from her bag. She was careful to hold it by the case and not to touch the knife which she'd wiped clean. She held it out to him, handle facing him. Instinctively he took the handle and removed the knife. He touched the steel blade and felt its sharpness. "This won't help you; you'll never get a chance to use it, he'll probably use it on you. He put it back into the sheath and passed it back to her. She put it back in her bag. "I've told you, give him the letter and hide." And with that they parted company.

He went up first, returning to his wife. She waited a few moments then followed whilst checking the coast was clear. She was heading back to her cabin, all the time looking for Vincenzo. Traynor had told her not to stay in her cabin. Was Vincenzo in there? As she arrived in her corridor, she saw Gill stood outside her room. It seemed like she'd been waiting for

Amanda. "I've been waiting for you; we need to talk. Where have you been" she asked. "Toilet. What's this about?" she said. Gill opened her door and they both went in. The letter she had posted under her door was on her bed, open. Gill had opened the letter. Her prints would be on it. "What the fuck?" she asked. "Just who are you?" "Look, it's nothing to do with me, it's something that just came into my possession and right now that murdering bastard is after me. He's on the ship right now and I don't have time to stand here chatting with you. Just give me the letter back and forget all about it. I'll leave and we won't mention it again – OK?" Gill just looked. "I can't just forget. You're mixed up in something bad. I had a funny feeling about you all along. You're too...perfect, little miss fucking Perfect. They should have given me your job, it's not fair. But they will when they find out whatever it is that you don't want anyone knowing."

Amanda saw red but her acting abilities came to the fore once more. She pretended to cry and said, "Can I use your bathroom?" Gill nodded. Amanda went in and retrieved the knife from the umbrella case. She got some wads of toilet roll. The knife was covered in Traynor's prints. She left her bag in the bathroom and gently opened the door. Gill was standing looking out of her window across the sea, obviously deep in thought. She held the knife, handle wrapped in toilet roll, and went up behind Gill. With her left hand she grabbed her hair and pulled her head back. Instinctively Gill's hands went to her head to her hair where Amanda was tugging. This left her throat exposed. With her right hand, Amanda used all her strength and sliced through her neck in one, clean stroke. She held on to her hair. By now her hands had moved to her throat and were interrupting the pulsing flow of red liquid that by now had splashed all over the windows and wall of her cabin and was dripping down onto the floor. Gill made gurgling sounds, but still faced the wall minimising the splatter that could have covered Amanda had she not been so careful. Gill fell to her knees and into the pool of her blood. Her head lolled forward and into the wall. When the spurting had stopped Amanda let go of her hair. She returned to the bathroom and wiped the blade of her knife with more toilet roll and placed the dirty paper into the toilet but didn't flush it. She left it there to be found. This knife had more deeds to do before the night was out. She placed it back into the sheath, being careful not to leave her prints on it.

Now she had something similar to do to Vincenzo. She suspected that he would pay her a visit later that night, when he expected her to be asleep. Her cabin was small and had nowhere to hide except the bathroom. She collected her things making sure she hadn't left anything and took the letter and envelope and placed it in the side compartment of her bag. She hoped Vincenzo wasn't waiting for her in her cabin. She had gambled on the fact that he would leave his visit until later.

She inserted her key and opened the door and switched on the light. Her room appeared just as she'd left it. She'd taken the precaution of leaving an empty lipstick box by the corner of the bathroom door. If it had been opened the box would have been disturbed. It wasn't possible to replace it from within the bathroom. A trick she'd used to see if her father had been inside her home. The box was in the same place. Nevertheless, she put her bag on the bed and retrieved the second knife. She held it by the handle and boldly kicked the bathroom door open. There was no one inside. She hoped the bang wouldn't arouse anyone's attention as it was late. If she got a knock, she'd pretend to be drunk and apologise. They'd forgive her. But no knock came.

But now she had to prepare for her visitor. She placed the dirty knife in its sheath and bag in the bathroom under the sink away from view where it wouldn't be disturbed. She took her casual clothes – jeans, tee shirts and shoes, and put them into her bed arranging them like she was asleep. She went into the bathroom and, using scissors, removed a long lock of her hair and then placed it on the pillow, arranging it to look like a large tuft protruding from beneath. Hopefully that would fool Vincenzo upon his arrival. She knew he would be very stealthy and arrogant. No kicking her bedroom door open. He would be quiet as a ghost cat.

She had purchased a Bluetooth speaker which connected to her phone and allowed her to play music in her cabin or wherever she was. It wasn't very large, but it was heavy. It had cost a couple of hundred quid, and whilst she'd bought it for the sound quality, it's size and weight made it a suitable weapon to stun someone, but not necessarily kill them. Her plan was simple. Wait in the bathroom in the dark with the door open. There was no way Vincenzo would put the light on. He would open the door and sneak in quietly, closing the door behind him. His eyes wouldn't have time to adjust to the darkness of her cabin. The blackout blind over the window was very effective indeed and it was closed. He would need to dispatch her quietly so she expected he would try and strangle her in her bed, or possibly stab her, but that may result in a scream.

CHAPTER 54

It was now 2.15am and Vincenzo was making his move. But he had already been busy this night. He had paid a visit to his old friends, the Traynors. The fact that Traynor had spoken to Annie meant that he knew too much. Vincenzo had come onto this ship for one reason – to kill. It was just the number of kills that had changed. Bernard had let him in – he couldn't really do anything else. Vincenzo had introduced himself to Susan as an old friend. She thought it funny that he was wearing gloves. As she went to shake his hand, he quickly grabbed her arm and spun her around so she was in front of him, facing Bernard and Vincenzo held his knife to her throat.

"Spill or I kill" he said. Traynor looked into Susan's terrified eyes, she was clueless. Whatever happened now his life was changed forever. "The Little Weasel, Annie, you spoke to her didn't you. I saw the two of you together. I've been watching you both." Traynor just looked at Susan, fear and tears in her eyes. Traynor was now in survival mode. "We can help you. She has a letter, we can help you get it back." This was all Vincenzo needed to know. He didn't need anyone's help to get the letter back. In a split-second Susan's expression had changed; her eyes had widened, and blood was spurting from a wide gash in her throat. With one swipe Vincenzo had almost decapitated her. He let go of her and she crumpled to the floor, twitching and gurgling.

It was over in a flash. Blood all over Traynor but very little on Vincenzo himself. Traynor hadn't moved, he'd just been an observer, a rabbit in the headlights that was about to be run down. Before he could say a word, Vincenzo threw the knife and it hit Bernard in the throat. With a flash of pain, he grabbed at the knife, but Vincenzo was upon him, pushing him to the floor and Vincenzo was wriggling the knife whilst Bernard's hand was still clutching at it. Bernard was now choking and beyond reprieve. So much for his happy retirement, it had lasted just a few short days. Vincenzo was looking him in the eye, watching the life ebb out of him. Traynor so wanted to say something to Vincenzo, but words failed him. The pain went away, and the lights faded down to black.

Phase one of his night's activities had gone well and to plan, easier than he had thought. This was by far the toughest part of his assignment, a double kill. He left the knife embedded in Traynor's throat for the authorities to find. But the next part would be easy. Little Weasel was next, and she suspected nothing. But she needed to tell him everything she knew, including the handing over the letter itself, before she found everlasting peace.

CHAPTER 55

Amanda had been stood at the back of the bathroom, in the dark, for over two hours. She was becoming very sleepy. Her adrenalin levels of earlier, having dispatched Gill, were waning. She hoped that no one would discover Gill until late tomorrow morning. If they did it would scupper her plans. As she stood in the darkness, she could make out the drone of the ship's engines. She'd never noticed this before. They sort of blended in and were filtered out somehow by your ears. Her eyes were accustomed to the dark like they had never been before. Any light now would effectively temporarily blind her, but she didn't expect to see light until she switched it on herself. As she waited, patiently, in silence, she could hear her own engine pumping blood around her veins. But for how much longer?

CHAPTER 56

He didn't encounter a single person on his way to her cabin. He was wearing jogger bottoms and a hoodie – both black. A man out for some exercise in the evening before going to bed, nothing unusual, indeed quite ordinary, it could have been anyone. He paused outside her door. He inserted his key card and the light went green. He slowly pushed the door open. He didn't want to open the door any more than necessary, as it let in the light from the corridor. It wasn't too bright, but the cabins had backout blinds and it appeared that hers was drawn. He slid in through the narrowest gap and quietly closed the door behind him. He stood in silence for a minute to allow his eyes to adjust. He couldn't hear her breathing, but he could see her shape under the quilt. He wondered if it was indeed her in bed, but, as his eyes adjusted to the near total darkness, he could see her hair protruding from the top of the quilt, and he knew it was her.

He waited another minute or so, drew his blade, and went quietly over towards the bed, knife in hand. His plan was to sit on her and in her confusion, place this blade to her neck and make her tell him everything she knew, what had happened to Montgomery, Devizes and the location letter, it mut be here in this room somewhere. As his eyes were adjusting, he looked around the room.

The bathroom door was open but pitch-black inside. He saw the outline of an envelope on her dressing table. Could this be it? He reached over and retrieved the envelope. He opened it and could see it was a handwritten letter but there was insufficient light to be able to read it. Still, when he had her in his control, she could turn on the light and they could read it together. He placed the letter in his hoodie pocket and removed the hood from his head. He then removed the hoodie and placed it on the floor behind the door. That way it wouldn't get covered in blood – he couldn't risk returning to his cabin covered in blood, even though there would be hardly anyone about. This was just too easy.

CHAPTER 57

She could see him in her room, her eyes like a stealthy cat, a big cat. He had looked at her bed and had spotted the copy letter she had left on the dresser. He had taken it and opened it. She didn't believe that he would have been able to read it in the near darkness, but it was now in his pocket. For some reason he'd removed his hoodie and placed it by the door. He must have been planning to make a mess, probably with a knife. But she too had a knife. Slowly she moved from the back of the bathroom to the doorway. He now had his back to her as he stealthily approached the bed. He took a knife from his back pocket and as he removed it, holding the handle, she lurched forward and hit him over the head, as hard as she could, using her nice Bluetooth speaker. She was surprised at the sound it made, a horrible sound, and the blood, more than she expected. He slumped onto the bed but still with his knife in his hand. He had tensed, the blade's position had moved, and it had cut through his fingers. Before he had time to turn around, she plunged her second knife into his back, hard and deep. She heard him gasp as he arched his back. As he collapsed forward, she lost hold of the handle. He went face down onto the bed. As she made a move for the knife, he started to twist around to face her. His injured hand was now holding the knife by the handle once again and he was intending to cut her. But he was wounded – mortally? She didn't know.

He lurched forward with the knife and she instinctively reached out. He missed her hand but cut her arm – it began to bleed quite badly. She was incensed – she hadn't planned on being cut. She grabbed his wrist, twisted his knife and jumped onto him, her knees smashing into his chest pushing him back onto her knife which must have embedded itself even deeper into his back. She took his knife from him and put out both his eyes. He tried to scream but he couldn't breathe properly, her knife must have punctured his lung. She then plunged her knife into his heart. A few seconds later he had stopped moving. She got up and turned on the light to survey the damage. Her bed was covered in blood, her own arm was quite bloody, she went into the bathroom and washed it. Luckily the cut wasn't too long or too deep, it wouldn't affect the next stage of her plans. Now she had to dispose of his body.

First, she searched his pockets. She found his room key card, VIP suite 4 she recalled. There were only a limited number of these so it shouldn't be too difficult to find, she pocketed his card. He had nothing else on him, no wallet or ID. She wondered how he had paid for his drinks.

It wouldn't be easy to get him up on deck and dump him over the side, especially doing this unnoticed. She thought about dragging him out of her room and down the corridor to Gill's room. If she left him there everyone would assume that he'd attacked Gill and she'd somehow managed to kill him in the ensuing fight. But Gill couldn't have inflicted those injuries on him simply in self-defence. And they'd probably identify him, and his people would know what happened. They'd know he came looking for her and then they'd come after her too. No matter how hard it was, and the risk, she had to dump him over the side.

CHAPTER 58

She was physically tired. A dead body always seems heavier than one that is still alive. She had worked her way to the VIP suites. There was an access door that blocks the great unwashed. She entered his cardkey and it opened. So, he did indeed have a VIP suite. They must have been large as the distance between the doors was four times that of her cabin area. She stood outside the first door – silence. It had a number one. She moved past the second and third then bingo. She entered the cardkey and got the green light. She hadn't heard any sound issuing from within, so she slowly pushed the door open in case there was indeed someone else in there. Maybe he'd gotten lucky? But he was too careful to allow anyone to remember him, so she felt confident the room would be empty.

She stood in silence. Nothing, no sounds of breathing. As her eyes once again adjusted to the darkness, she realised that he hadn't employed his blackout blind. Maybe he didn't like the darkness. She could see the outline of the freshly made bed – still pristine. She quietly went over to a doorway which led to a lounge area; it too was empty. Finally, she ventured towards the bathroom – the door was closed. She stood outside for a couple of minutes listening and then opened the door quickly and ducked to the side. Nothing. She turned on the bathroom light, again nothing, save a few meagre toiletries and some expensive cologne. Back in the bedroom there was a single suit hung in the wardrobe and one clean shirt. One pair of leather shoes stood beneath the suit. These looked like the ones he had worn when he had watched her band. She gathered up everything that was his and inserted everything back into his fine Italian travel bag. She liked this bag – maybe she'd keep it as a souvenir. She'd searched all the internal pockets and found nothing. No ID, no passport, no credit cards – absolutely nothing, he was living gratis. Maybe his company paid for everything directly. When she left his room, it looked like it was freshly turned around and waiting for its next guests to arrive. In fact, as though he had never been there in the first place.

As she returned to her room Amanda was physically exhausted and she still had to dispose of his body. By now the ship looked deserted, it would be safe, or as safe as ever, to do the deed. She put his hoodie back on, to cover the blood somewhat, and heaved him over her shoulder. He wasn't a large man luckily and she was strong for her size and pretty fit. She moved as quickly as she could, resisting stopping to rest. The final leg of getting him over the barrier at the side took all her strength. By now the body was getting cold to the touch. She expected a huge splash, but none came. It was as though the sea had been expecting him. She returned to her cabin once more. Next, she emptied his bag on her bed and sifted through his clothes, checking the pockets and lining for anything. She found nothing. She put all his clothes into a plastic bag, tied the top, and went back to the top and threw it overboard along with his phone that she had retrieved earlier. Every trace of him, save his fine bag, was now in the sea. This was her finest achievement yet. Assuming that she wasn't ultimately caught or killed that was. She once again returned to her room. The last outstanding item was Gill. She retrieved the well packed knife from her bathroom.

She went back to Gill's room. She took the knife out of its bag and sheath and, using a piece of toilet roll, sank it back into Gill's neck. She'd been careful not to leave any of her own prints as she knew Bernard's would still be on there. They'd be able to lift even partial prints if there was a bit of smudging. She then took Gill's hand and placed it on the knife as though she'd tried to remove it in her death throws. She loosened the knife but left it still partially in the wounds. She took the toilet paper with her and, after a final check, closed the room door, again being careful not to leave any prints, and returned to her room.

If she had left prints in Gill's cabin, she would admit that she had previously visited Gill in her cabin. She then retrieved the second knife and took it and the toilet paper up on deck and threw those overboard. Now all that was left was to tidy up her own room.

She took the bed sheets and bundled them up for the laundry. She then cleaned any blood splashes she could find on the wall or carpet as best she could and then replaced the sheets and duvet with clean ones. There would be no cause for anyone to check her room for blood etc. as none of this was anything to do with her. She was just a colleague of Gill's. She had no connection to her soon-to-be-identified murderer prior to him trying to chat her up after their private gig. He must have moved from her to Gill and poor Gill copped it.
It could have been her. She could feign tears. It could have been her! If the police entered her room, they would find nothing out of the ordinary. The wallpaper in the cabins was designed to allow the removal of dirt and spillages quickly and easily as was the carpet. It made her final job of the long evening that bit easier.

She was now exhausted, but there was still some adrenalin left to course through her veins. Her arms and back ached from her strenuous efforts earlier. She took a beer from the fridge and gulped it down. She took a second and then sat on her bed going over the night's events to make sure she hadn't missed anything. By now it was approaching 4am and she could do no more. She got into bed, turned off the light and slept like a baby.

CHAPTER 59

The following morning, she got up and went up for breakfast. She saw James and Ben sat together – it looked like they'd just arrived. "May I join you?" she asked. Ben's eyes lit up. "Sure, take a seat." James said. They waited for the waiter, or waitress, to come and take their orders.

When she eventually came, the waitress appeared a bit flustered. "Have you heard? There's been a murder." James looked at Ben and Ben looked at Amanda. "Two murders. The couple who you did the gig for, you know, he was recently retired. Well last night something happened and now they're both dead. The security police are looking into it – they don't know if anyone else is involved."

Now this really did get Amanda's attention. She was horrified. The person who she had framed for Gill's killing was now dead. Was he dead before he killed Gill? "What time did this happen?" Amanda asked, her concern now genuine. "No idea yet. Probably the early hours." Then it hit her. Vincenzo had killed Bernard and Susan before going to kill her. The timeline was probably intact. Bernard was now a double killer and he didn't even know it. Maybe it would be OK after all. "That's terrible. They were so nice." James said. Amanda just looked at the table, deep in thought.

They ordered three full English breakfasts, apparently it hadn't put any of them off their food, and the waitress went to the next table who had been waiting some time to place their order. She wasn't there for long, so obviously wasn't sharing this news with the passengers yet. "You think he killed her then himself?" Ben said. "Who knows" said James. "Who knows what goes on in other people's lives." James added. This had been one hell of a week. In her experience, cruises were anything but relaxing.

Their talk revolved around Susan and Bernard, what they were like, their friends and of course what had happened the previous night. Their suppositions ending with the idea that Bernard had killed his wife then killed himself, as opposed to her killing him then herself. The guys didn't suspect a third party. The food arrived and they began to eat. Her head was spinning. As she ate her food, she tried to work out the ramifications of finding three bodies. Vincenzo would have left no clues or weapon at the scene she felt sure of this. She had left the knife embedded in Gill. They'd find Gill later this morning. When they examined the knife, they'd find the prints.Three murders in one night – they'd naturally assume they were connected, which of course they were. It was too much of a coincidence for them not to be connected. But how could the knife be left in Gill? Bernard would have had to have killed Gill first, then gone back to his cabin, killed his wife and finally himself. But had the late Vincenzo left the scene to appear as a murder suicide? She hoped so. It seemed to make sense to her, a way of leaving no loose ends, something she had to improve in her own life.

She couldn't return to Gill's cabin now. She had to wait it out and see how the story panned out. "What will happen when the police arrive on board?" James had asked. He continued "Normally they'd secure the crime scene, keep all the witnesses together to question them. But there's fucking hundreds on here. They can't hold everyone. "They'll have everyone's names and details I suppose." Ben added. Not Vincenzo's Amanda thought to herself. Clever. Now she saw it. A murder suicide would be the easiest explanation and cause least fuss; and the cops would want it to be so. The cruise line would want it sorted as quickly as possible so as not to disrupt its schedules or passengers.

They'd want it hushed up as well if that were indeed possible.

But she'd unwittingly complicated matters by adding a third person. If they assumed Bernard had killed Gill, then Susan then himself it would still be pretty tidy, just not as tidy. She decided to set the scene. "That Bernard was a funny guy." She said. "I don't know, you are the one who spoke to them. What makes you say he was funny?" asked James. "Well the morning after their party, he contacted the purser who contacted me, to ask if I'd meet him and Susan in the bar up top at noon to thank me on behalf of the band for playing at their party. The purser said he had chocolates and flowers for me, that was the only reason I actually went." She looked down and tried to look embarrassed. "But when I arrived no flowers, no chocolates, no Susan just Bernard." She added that he had gotten a little too friendly for her liking, so she'd made her excuses, refused lunch and left.

Now it may appear that he had tried it on with his first choice, Amanda, then moved on to Gill. Under some pretence, possibly to again thank the band, he had visited her room and bosh. It was worth a go. Her alibi was the band. The thing playing on her mind right now was should she stay on board for another week or more, or should she get the hell out of Dodge when the ship docked?

CHAPTER 60

The head of security was speaking to the purser. He'd been asked to tell him everything he knew about the Traynors. He'd explained about their booking, arrival, retirement, requesting the band, asking for the singer's cabin number, passing the message to her, and generally seeing the couple around the ship. All this was duly noted. All the main staff who could have had dealings with the Traynors were interviewed. The band would also be interviewed. After lunch he'd track them down. He wanted to gather as much information as possible before the police came on board.

CHAPTER 61

Leaving now would look suspicious, she knew that. Why point the finger at herself needlessly? And they'd need to stick around for questioning. The band would be questioned as they had performed for the dead couple. Plus of course Gill was dead and soon to be discovered. If they didn't think Bernard had topped her himself, then the band would be their likely next port of call as they were closest to her. She had to stick around. But what were the ramifications of Vincenzo just disappearing. Had he told anyone why he was visiting the ship? Did his cohorts or underlings even know, and would they come looking for her? If he had told them he was after her then he would have told them about the letter. The letter didn't affect anyone except him, so no one would come looking for the letter. She suspected he would have kept the letter secret so far as he could. If his cohorts suspected that Vincenzo was now dead, then they would likely be shit scared of the person who had managed to overcome him. They'd think it was a hardened criminal like himself, one of his many enemies. Not a frail young singer, and a girl at that. No doubt there would be a power struggle in his wake, and they'd be vying for his spot and that would take all their time and attention. She wasn't too concerned about one of Vincenzo's guys coming looking for her. After thinking things through, she had little choice but let things run their course. Stay here, sing with the band and behave as normal. For now. It was her only option.

After breakfast they decided to sit by the pool and have a drink. Ben phoned the rest of the band to assemble and tell them the hot news. Gemma answered first. "Really? I'll get Gill and we'll be there shortly." He then called Ian who was still asleep, as was Nick. They both answered after several rings and, upon hearing the news, both said they'd shower and get there in half an hour. Howard had already arrived by this time and was eating a bacon sandwich covered in red sauce.

Ten minutes later Gemma arrived. "No Gill?" asked James. "Dunno where she is. I knocked on her door but no answer." "Maybe she's got a fella." Ben piped up and winked. They all smiled, Amanda too. They ordered a round of beers and sat discussing the news. Ian arrived in due course and was appraised on the situation. Nick arrived shortly after.
By now Gemma was getting a little worried about Gill. "Even if she picked up some bloke after last night's show, he'll be long gone and she should be packing" she said "We'll be there in half an hour." Howard said between mouthfuls of his second sandwich. "True." replied Ben. "Give her another few minutes then I'll go back and knock on her door again." said Gemma. "It's not like her to miss out on a changeover last beer day." and they all laughed. "So that's what happens on changeover." Amanda said gently changing the subject.

The chief of security walked over to them. "Hello you guys - you are the band I take it?" "Yes. Is it about the murders?" Ben asked. "News travels quickly on a boat like this." he added knowingly. "Sadly, it is. I need one of my team to speak with each of you. We need to know everything you saw or heard about the Traynors from their arrival up until last night. We need to know as much as possible before the police board when we dock. No doubt the British will send their own police over too at some point so I'm sorry, but you'll need to make yourselves available. It isn't good for business." The band agreed and said they would stay put and wait. Each of them was called one at a time to pre-prepared room where they each told everything they knew about the Traynors. Amanda knew the most. She told them of her encounter with him. They'd already spoken to the purser, so it all tallied. Just then there was a knock on the door. Another security person entered and beckoned towards the interviewer. He left the room momentarily. When he returned he looked a little flustered.

"Amanda, how well did you know Gill from the band?" "How well did I know her?" she said, noting the past tense. "Not well at all. I only started recently; this is my first proper week performing. I've known her just under two weeks. But she seems a nice person. She kept herself to herself. I wasn't aware of any boyfriends. She was tight with Gemma, the other backing singer." After a pause she added "You said Did - has something happened to her? She was supposed to join us this morning, but we couldn't rouse her." He looked at Amanda, wondering how much to say. "I'm afraid so'" and he paused again. "I'm sorry to tell you that she too is dead. Looks like we now have three bodies on our hands." Out came the tears. Amanda tried to hold it together, the security man comforted her. "Who will tell the rest of the band? Gemma will be devastated." she said. "Leave that to us. For now, please return to your cabin where we will know where to find you."

She returned directly to her cabin. About ten minutes later there was a knock on her door. When she opened it Gemma was there, crying. Amanda turned on the tears again and the two of them hugged in the doorway. "I told the security I'd be here with you. I couldn't face being alone in my cabin." "I'm so glad you came, it's just awful." Amanda said as they comforted each other.

CHAPTER 62

It was early afternoon. Gemma and Amanda had exchanged theories about what linked the three victims. They agreed it was too much of a coincidence not to be connected. Gemma had shared some stories about Gill and shared even more tears. It looked like Gemma was coming to terms with things now she'd had a chance to digest the facts and talk things through with Amanda. "Will they cancel next week's cruise? That would leave hundreds of unhappy people." Amanda said. "I don't think they could afford to do something like that. The police will have to work around the clock whilst the ship is docked. They could close off the cabins and leave them closed for further investigation. The line always keeps back a couple of cabins for contingency." Gemma said. Maybe that was how Vincenzo had gotten his cabin – but a VIP suite? Maybe they'd moved someone out and downgraded them to accommodate him? He had pulled some strings. Someone senior on board must have arranged this, but who? And how much did they know?

There was another knock on the door. Amanda went to answer. It was one of the ship's security team. "The Maltese police are here. Please could you come with me – they need to speak to everyone as soon as possible." Amanda agreed and the two girls followed him to a large room that had been assigned for the use of the police as an incident room. It transpired that they also had some vacant cabins to use as interview rooms. As they walked past the incident toom the door was open and they could see it was a hive of activity. Computers were being set up and boards with papers and photographs attached. They were led into a cabin. It was much nicer than both Amanda's and Gemma's. "Nice cabin." Amanda commented to Gemma as they went in. Gemma didn't respond. Waiting for them was a policeman. They assumed he was local to Malta where the ship currently stood. His English was excellent. They had decided to interview the girls together, which seemed a bit strange.

He asked them some background information about the band, their performances, everything they could recall about playing for the Traynors and everything they could add about Gill, her movements and mood over the past few days. Did she seem worried? Did she seem scared? Did she act differently? Was she seeing anyone? They both answered "No" to all these questions. Amanda then shared her lunchtime meeting with Bernard and said she'd felt uncomfortable in his company, especially as he hadn't brought Susan along. She said she was concerned at the time, but only now did she believe that maybe Bernard was trying to get more than friendly with her. This was all new to her and she was still learning the routine. Had he tried the same with Gill? The policeman was very interested in this aspect and proceeded to ask Amanda questions on the subject. Gemma didn't add much, apart from saying that Gill was a nice girl, she wouldn't entertain the advances of a passenger, let alone a married one who was forty years older than her. It wasn't her style and could affect her career. What if Gill had spurned his advances and she hadn't been quite as lucky as Amanda? The policeman didn't actually say this, but Amanda could read his body language. He was beginning to form a theory. Granted, it only partially explained the events, but it was a piece of a much larger jigsaw that was forming in his mind. Maybe when they found Bernard's prints on the knife that had killed her then this would add more pieces to the jigsaw. The theory with a picture, was very different to the real one that was hidden under the surface.

"How was Gill killed?" Gemma asked. She'd been quiet for some time whilst Amanda was answering his questions. "I'm afraid I can't say." The policeman replied. Gemma just looked at the floor. "I'm afraid that the British police are also on their way over – they're expected later this afternoon. You'll have to answer their questions as well." Gemma just looked at him, her eyes filling up once again. "I'm sorry, we know this is a very difficult time for you. You've lost a friend and a colleague. All we want to do is find out what happened and who did this awful thing. Time is of the essence as the ship will depart on Sunday evening as planned. So, it might mean you will be spending a lot of the weekend answering questions. All I can do is apologise." Gemma nodded at him. "We know you'll catch whoever did this." Amanda said. "Do you think it was someone we know?" Gemma asked. This seemed a strange question to ask. Maybe she had a jigsaw of her own. "I can't say at present, but we have several lines of enquiry. Please return to your cabins now and we'll be in touch. Please remain in your cabin. Food will be sent over to you. I stress, please remain there." They agreed to do so and quietly headed back to Amanda's cabin. They both went inside, and Amanda switched the kettle on. "You're welcome to stay as long as you like." she said to Gemma. Gemma just looked at her. Half a smile appeared at the same time as a tear. It had hit her very hard indeed. It was probably the first time she'd had to deal with death. Amanda washed the two mugs and made two cups of tea. She'd have to get more tea bags if Gemma stayed put.

CHAPTER 63

The girls had continued talking about the situation, and it was getting late in the afternoon when Gemma's phone rang. It was James. Apparently, they'd all been interviewed now, by both internal security and the Maltese police. The Brits hadn't yet arrived. Food had been delivered to their cabins on a tray but none of them had much of an appetite. Except Amanda, but only Gemma was party to that information and she hadn't really noticed. By 5pm Gemma had nodded off lying on Amanda's bed. Amanda sat at her desk with a mug of water pondering over the day's events, the questions she'd been asked, and the sheer number of police involved. She felt like Andre Previn conducting a series of musicians, each playing from a manuscript of her writing. All the right notes but not necessarily in the right order. Her order: that was all that mattered. But this was a piece she had only partially written.

Sure enough, the British police arrived just after 6pm. Amanda had just finished her burger and chips, they had been delivered around half an hour previously. Gemma's lay on table, with only a few chips consumed by her. Amanda didn't mind cold burgers, maybe she'd finish it off later, when Gemma was back in her own cabin. Another knock came at their door and it was the security guy again, he had come to take them to be interviewed by the British police. This time they wanted to interview all the band, and other witnesses, separately. It could run in to the early hours apparently. Amanda commented that Gemma was exhausted after the day's activities and the security man said he'd try and see if he could get them done sooner rather than later. He had probably said the same thing to each and every person he'd escorted up and down the decks.

Amanda was shown into one room with one policeman, Gemma into another with a policeman and a policewoman. Amanda wondered why Gemma had twice as many interviewers. Amanda sat down at the table as requested. The policeman identified himself as Detective Inspector Yeadon of Scotland Yard. Call me Andy he told Amanda. She was asked all the usual questions, with a few additional ones. The one of note was this: "Did you see anyone else on board that you didn't recognise in connection with Gemma or The Traynors? Speaking to them for example." Amanda considered her response to this question thoughtfully. "No, I don't think so. Most of the time I spent with any of them was when I was performing. With the lights and everything, and being focussed on the performance, you don't really see much of anything." she said. She wondered if the police knew of Vincenzo's arrival on board. Should she have told of her encounter? She decided not to as it could only open up more questions. She needed to preserve her identity; she didn't want anyone digging into her past because she didn't have one. Her interview lasted around twenty minutes; after which she was asked to return to her cabin. As she walked back, she saw the room where Gemma had been led and it was still occupied. She thought she could hear crying coming from inside. She wondered if it was Gemma, or the policewoman having spent twenty minutes in Gemma's company.

She went back into her cabin and eyed up the burger. She assumed Gemma would be back fairly shortly. She put the TV on and went to the BBC World Service as always, and there it was. Live on TV. Cameras were pointing at the boat, from onshore. There was the anchor guy talking about a cruise liner, with several hundred British tourists on board, three dead, one couple celebrating a retirement and a band member. All stabbed. So far, no suspects. More later... blah blah blah. The only good thing about the news, was hearing about your own exploits third hand. It gave her a kick to know that her actions had caused international repercussions. But what about Vincenzo? No-one had mentioned any Italian connection, or mysterious snappy dresser, who had arrived late via helicopter. She decided the best policy there was to keep quiet, no mention of knowing him or having seen him or any other Italian guy. The only time she was with him was after that show and that was only for a few minutes. Only the bar man could recall this, and she doubted he'd be interviewed. There were too many staff to interview them all. After every show she, and some of the other band members, were accosted by guests telling them how they enjoyed the show. It was the norm. Only the snappy suit could lead to this encounter sticking in the bar man's mind. She decided not to worry about it.

Just then she had yet another knock on the door – a familiar feeble one; not the hard knock of an assertive security guy. She opened the door. Gemma was there once again, following her well-trodden steps, eyes red. "Thank you for your support, Amanda. I think I'll go back to my own cabin and get some rest." Amanda smiled. "No problem. Give me a knock if you need me." she added and with that Gemma managed a brief smile of her own and headed down the corridor to her cabin. Further down the corridor she could see a security guard stationed outside Gill's cabin. And also a policeman, probably British, going in all suited up. Must be forensics she thought. Won't be long before they start to put the pieces together. Then, there would be more questions about Gill and The Traynors. No doubt they'd want her back to ask her more about her meeting with Bernard. She'd say the exact same story as before.

And it wasn't long either. By 7pm she had another assertive knock on the door. She answered straight away. "Have you found him yet? The murderer?" she said in a childlike way, feigning the victim, but one that was still alive. "I'm afraid the police need to speak to you once again." "No problem, I'll get my coat." She collected her coat and headed back to police central. A policewoman awaited her, the same one that had spoken to Gemma earlier. Gemma had told her that, in her interview, this policewoman hadn't said much but she seemed to have lots of empathy, a good cop so to speak." Empathy wasn't really something Amanda needed or really understood.

She followed the policewoman into the room and sat at the same desk she had sat at earlier. "My name is Janet Spangler. I'll try and be as brief as possible. I appreciate that you are upset and have spent a lot of time answering questions for us." Amanda smiled, in a tired but I understand sort of way. "I'm happy to stay here all night if it means you catch the person responsible and we can all sleep safely in our beds once again." Amanda replied. Janet nodded and started on with her questions. Same old, but, as she suspected, a little more detailed regarding her meeting with Bernard. She asked if Bernard had shown a similar interest with any of the other band members. She said not that she knew of. Gemma had told her she hadn't spoken to him, and Gill hadn't said anything. She forced a couple more tears at this point. Janet continued with more questions. Then, towards the end, she asked if she could think of any reason the Traynors might have wished any harm to the band, or any other members of staff. A strange question.

She looked at Janet genuinely confused. If they had recovered the knife and had time to do blood and fingerprint analysis already, and ascertained it was full of Traynor's dabs, then this was a weird, leading type of question. Her genuine confusion must have shown in her face because, before she had time to answer, Janet said "Sorry, it's OK, I know none of you knew the Traynors well. You seem to have spent more time with them than anyone else, apart from their party of four, who have been interviewed at length this afternoon." Amanda just nodded. She got the impression that the interview was coming to an end.

"One last thing, if I may. Were you aware of any intimate relationship between Gill and Gemma?" This really took Amanda by surprise. She stared at Janet, open-mouthed. "No. No. But I never saw them together, on their own as such. And I never saw either of them with a man on their own. I have absolutely no idea, I'm sorry." Janet looked into her eyes. She must have known she was telling the truth, the confusion apparent.
Amanda then added "Gemma has been in my cabin all afternoon. She never said a thing. I'm totally gobsmacked you suggested such a thing. Is it true? Were they, intimate?" Amanda asked, taking the front foot. This knocked Janet off guard a little. "Oh, no, please don't take it, that was the case. I was merely asking the question. I have to ask these questions I'm afraid, we get the short straw when it comes to asking the sorts of questions you'd rather not. Please don't infer anything from what I've said. I think we can call it a night now. Thanks again for your time."

After a brief pause, she added "The ship will be leaving on Sunday as normal, but the rooms may be sealed off for a week or so just in case we need to go back for any reason. Other than that, you can return to doing what you usually do. If you choose to leave the ship, please check in with us first so we can contact you if need be. Thank you for your cooperation. We'll be in touch if we need anything else."

Amanda stood up to leave. She was still a little shocked by the final question. Was that why Gemma had been so upset? Had Gill been her lover? She'd have to broach the subject with the other band members – maybe Ben. He could hide nothing in his body language. If she asked the question, she'd know the answer before he even spoke. Still, that would wait until tomorrow. Now she badly needed a drink but decided it would be seen as insensitive if she went to the bar and proceeded to drink it dry.

She returned to her cabin. She knew it would be foolish to do a runner at this point. No-one suspected her of any involvement in any of this. Gemma was getting more attention than she was. She'd ride it out and then review things in a week or two. After all, she liked this gig. She'd come on board, wanting to make money and within two weeks she'd managed to kill three people and she hadn't even received her first pay packet. It was fun. And she was being paid for the privilege. Happy days.

CHAPTER 64

She received no more knocks at the door and by 10pm she had finished off Gemma's burger. She put the dirty plates outside by her cabin door and looked down the corridor towards Gill's cabin. There was still a guard outside. No doubt he'd be there all night. She wondered if they thought the murderer was still onboard and somehow wanted to get back in there for some reason. By now it must have been apparent to everyone which cabins were involved. There may be gory hunters who would like to get in there and take pictures or something. There were some strange people out there and the cabins needed to be guarded for now.

She called room service and ordered three bottles of beer. They arrived about ten minutes later. She opened one and sat on the bed, switching the TV back on. The BBC World Service had moved on from the ship to other political news. After ten minutes or so she got bored and found one of the film channels showing a film in English. She watched the film until the end, at which point she'd run out of beers. Rather than order more she decided to call it a night. She could catch up on some of the sleep she had missed out on the previous evening. She was now aching everywhere. It added to her apparent distressed appearance.

CHAPTER 65

Davo and JJ were sat in a bar. "Where the fuck is he?" Davo asked. JJ shrugged. "He should have called back yesterday. His phone doesn't ring." "Maybe there is no service?" JJ replied. "I don't like it. It's not like him. The fucking ship has docked. He should have been off it last night. Something is wrong." "And we don't even know what the fuck was so urgent about getting on that fucking ship in the first place." JJ added.

Davo was a little smarter. He knew that Vincenzo was looking for a girl singer who had something of his but that was it. He didn't know what. All he knew was that, in several years of working for Vincenzo, he'd never seen him either this worked up about something or this willing to take things into his own hands. "Maybe he fancied a cruise? Pick up some girls?" JJ said with a wink. Tosser thought Davo. "If we hear nothing from him by tomorrow morning, I'm calling Rimmer." Davo said. JJ just looked at him. None of them liked Rimmer, everyone was afraid of him, even Vincenzo. "He'll not be pleased." Was all JJ said. With that he got up to get them more beers.

CHAPTER 66

The following morning Amanda got up around 10am. She thought about knocking on Gemma's door but decided against it, she'd let her sleep. Besides she'd had enough of her crying and whinging for one lifetime, even if it was her lesbian lover. She went to grab breakfast.

As she got there, she saw James, Ben, Ian, Nick and Howard sat at a table for six. She went over and joined them. "We were discussing about next week, we are a backing singer down, maybe two if Gemma doesn't get her act together. You have any pretty friends who can sing?" Ben asked Amanda. "Well one of my bandmates from my previous band, she can sing and play guitar. I don't think she's doing anything, at the moment. I could call her and ask her." This all seemed a bit matter of fact but suited Amanda more than being miserable. James spoke next: "James is due here today to speak to the band. He's bringing Gill's family apparently, they wanted to visit the place she died and speak to her band mates. They'd threatened to come to see her but hadn't made it." "Shame." said Ben.

Amanda was a little thrilled at the thought of James coming back on board. She knew he liked her, and he was nice too, and rich, or at the very least well off. It was funny how whenever the name James was mentioned, everyone automatically knew which James was being referred to. "Anyone heard from Gemma this morning?" Ian asked whilst looking at Amanda. "Not me. She left last night after our last interview and went back to her cabin as far as I know." Amanda said. Then she added. "I assume you were all questioned last night by the Brits and the Maltese?". They all nodded. Amanda went on to say "Well in my final interview, the woman police officer asked me if I thought that Gemma and Gill were.... an item.... or having an intimate relationship – I can't remember the words she used." James and Ben looked at each other. Then Ian said "She never said as much, but we did wonder. Neither of them seemed to have any boyfriends that we knew of. No one night stands or anything. I have to admit we did wonder." James then added "They never asked me that question."

Amanda now knew that it was indeed possible that Gemma had lost more than the rest of them. Maybe she wouldn't be able to face continuing on the ship after all. Time would tell, she didn't really care either way. They ordered their breakfasts, and their talk always ended back on the subject of who killed who and why. No-one mentioned Gemma and Gill again, Amanda decided they'd all accepted they were probably an item and it made things all the sadder.

After they had all finished eating, they decided to order a round of beers, a sort of toast to Gill. As they arrived at their table - James arrived. "I'll get those." he said to the barman, who obviously knew him. He nodded and returned with another one for James. James took a seat and squeezed in beside Amanda. "I can't believe it. It's shocking, simply shocking. But the show must go on as they say." He smiled and lifted his bottle in a toast. They all toasted a silent toast to Gill.

After reminiscing a little about Gill, James cut to the point. "As you know our contract requires two female backing singers. At present we only have one. And we must consider it a possibility that Gemma, under the circumstances, may choose a different career moving forward. The contract, of course, allows for unforeseen circumstances but with only a window of a week. So, we need one, maybe two backing singers appointed and joining us by the time we dock next weekend. Would any of you have any recommendations?"

The expressions on the rest of the band members' faces made it apparent that this type of talk, so soon, was a little uncomfortable. But they were all professionals, and the band meant a great deal to all of them. All the guys shook their heads in unison. James then moved his attention to Amanda.

She looked at James and then said "I wonder if Mandy might be interested? Rach was going back to Texas and Animal wouldn't move and she couldn't sing. Rach might be interested. Would there be an option for her to play some guitar as well?" "The position is for a backing singer. If you think she may be interested, and has a strong enough voice, then go call her now." James said. "Here's my phone, Animals' house phone number is stored in there under Animal. I don't have any other numbers I'm afraid." James passed Amanda his cell phone. She looked up Animal's house number and called it. She received the disconnected tone. She tried again a couple of times – same thing. "I can't get through." she said. "That's funny. It can't have been disconnected, all her bills were paid by her father and he was rich." "Don't worry yourself, I'll make some calls later and I'll get hold of her one way or another. For now, just try and get over this thing. Remember, come Sunday evening, it must be like nothing ever happened. "We know, the show must go on." Nick said, a little dryly. James then went away to meet some people and make some calls. He said he'd be back in an hour or so. They drank their beers and ordered another round on James' tab.

By the time James returned they were on their third. "Amanda, I have some rather bad news I'm afraid. There's been a terrible accident. The reason you couldn't get through to Animal is that, well there's no easy way of putting this, the house burned down, and Animal is dead."

The band just stared at him. Three deaths were something but now a fourth? "It's purely coincidence of course. Something to do with the gas cooker I believe, possibly related to drink; but it's too early to say." They just looked at him. "On the plus side

I did get a number for Mandy's cell. She is still there and staying with a friend. You might want to call her now on this number." James took his phone, looked up the number in question, and passed the phone to Amanda. "Take as long as you like. It must be hard learning you've lost another friend." Amanda just looked at the other band members, she felt like she was the kiss of death.

Her head was reeling. A gas accident? Vincenzo had paid her a visit no doubt whilst tracking her. But he was gone, she'd be safe now. "Thanks." She said and took his phone and clicked the green send button. She instinctively got up and walked out of the bar onto the deck. Mandy answered immediately. "It's Jacey, or Amanda, my real name – I'm using that now." Mandy started to cry. After a few moments she composed herself and said "Even when you lose a total bitch like Animal it's still a shock. All our stuff went up in smoke, all my equipment. I've got nothing. I just don't know what to do."

Amanda briefly explained the situation onboard and how they needed a backing singer. She never mentioned playing any guitar as Mandy now didn't have a guitar. "It'll mean you have money coming in, a roof over your head, a change of scenery and you'll be surrounded by friends. These guys are great, no ego's, no tantrums, they're professional. It's fun working with these guys, you'll love it. "But Jacey, I'm a guitarist first and foremost." "I know but you'll need to save up, or get your insurance cheque, before you can go buy a new guitar and all that." Mandy replied "And apparently, given the weird circumstances of the fire, they are investigating it and the insurance won't pay out until it's all cleared up. It could be weeks or months. All I have is the clothes on my back." "Well, there you have it. This is fate. What other choice do you have?" She finished by saying that they needed to know quickly. If she agreed James would arrange her travel. Luckily, she had her passport and some cash in her purse so was able travel. Mandy said she'd sleep on it and call her back on

James' number tomorrow.

Amanda went back to the gang and took her seat. She passed the phone back to James. She'll let us know tomorrow she told the guys. They nodded. After a pause Amanda said "Should I go check on Gemma? Maybe she'll come up for a bite to eat. She ate hardly anything yesterday." They all nodded, and James said "Yes that is a splendid idea. Off you go."

Amanda took a gulp of her beer, finishing off the bottle, and headed down towards Gemma's cabin. All the while thinking about how they had tracked her to Animal's house. Animal didn't know anything so, even if they worked on her, she couldn't have revealed anything. Her stuff had been locked in the safe so even if Animal had searched her room when she was out, she wouldn't have found anything. Why had she been killed? For fun?

When she arrived at Gemma's cabin, she knocked on the door, quietly initially. No answer. So, she knocked a little harder. "Coming." she heard a sad, little voice say. When she opened the door, Gemma's eyes were red from crying. "Come in." she said so Amanda went in. The cabin was a mess.
"James is here, we're all up top having a drink. We already ate breakfast. Come on up and get something to eat.". Gemma nodded. "I'll be there in a bit." she said and stared into Amanda's eyes; her eyes were full of loss. Amanda made her excuses and left before Gemma had chance to empty her heart again. Amanda couldn't face that again.

She went back to the band where a new bottle was waiting for her. "She'll be up in a bit." she said as she sat down. "Mandy called back whilst you were with Gemma. She's in. I've arranged for her to fly out tomorrow afternoon. I can get her transport to the ship by boat or something. You'll need to fit a rehearsal in at some point on Monday afternoon. Hopefully she'll be good to go after a couple of rehearsals." It was a tight squeeze but, so long as the flight was reasonably on time, she'd make it. Tomorrow's show had been cancelled; they had the day off. There was plenty of other entertainment on board for the customers.

And that was it. Mandy was heading out. Amanda would have to train her to call her Amanda not Jacey. She thought she'd head things off with the band. They were asking about Mandy, what she was like, what stuff she played etc. Amanda mentioned that, in her last band, they called her JC. They all had nick names. JC, or Jacey stuck. That's how everyone called her. Weird but there you have it." Now, if Mandy called her Jacey they'd know why.

Just then Ben piped up "Well now we have two Mandy's, maybe we should call you Jacey too!" The rest of the band smiled but the mood was still a little sombre despite the beers they had consumed. "Whatever." Amanda said and they laughed, funny how the slightest comment can break the ice. "All we need now is a Judas." Ben piped up, but quickly realising the awkwardness of his comment he added "And our James should be Jimbo."

Amanda wasn't keen on reverting back to Jacey as it was a link to her past incarnation. But there was nothing she could do about it now. The cat was out of the bag. She could insist on being Amanda but, knowing the guys, that would only make things worse. She would have to go with the flow. James didn't say anything but seemed a little amused by the whole thing. To him it was business, not personal. He was very good at what he did. He's only been in the bar a few hours and he had already sorted one big problem. Amanda, or Jacey, was pleased he hadn't chosen a career as a policeman.

Not long afterwards Gemma surfaced. She walked over to them with a half-smile. She looked a lot better than before. She'd showered and applied some light makeup. Her eyes were a lot less puffy and red. She still looked bereaved though. James pulled a seat over and sat her between Amanda and himself. The barman was prepared, he brought over a beer without being asked. Luckily the bar was quiet. The band updated Gemma on the new arrival. Gemma didn't say anything about what her plans were. They all hoped she'd get over it and things would return to normal in a few days.

CHAPTER 67

"What the fuck? Chasing after some two-bit singer?" was Rimmer's response. He didn't like that Davo, a junior in the grand hierarchy, had called him directly instead of going through Vincenzo, as was the protocol. However, when he heard the news, his tone changed. "You did the right thing to contact me. I'll make some enquiries." was all he said, and the call ended. He'd also told Davo and JJ to sit tight for now. They might be heading back to London tomorrow, who knows. But they'd make the most of what was possibly their last night in the sun. They had chosen not to share the comment that Vincenzo had made about the girl having something of his. Either it would stir up a shit storm or it was nothing in the first place. Better leave well along. Now for a beer or twelve.

Rimmer put the phone down. Vincenzo had been getting too big for his boots. He was already thinking of getting rid of him before all this. He wasn't keen on letting Vincenzo chase the girl as he was sure it would come to nothing. Just a few of the notes entering circulation – that was all. It was inevitable at some point. And the dumb fuck had took the helicopter and flown out to a cruise liner on a whim, without telling him, or anyone else, what the fuck he was thinking? And now he had disappeared.

Could it be that it was all a ruse? Vincenzo had done a runner. He'd fucked off. He immediately called his assistant, Mark, and asked him to bring up the account records for the bank accounts Vincenzo had access to. He saw that he had spent money on travelling in the last few days. But Rimmer made sure that none of the accounts had enough in to fund a decent getaway. And there were still funds left in there? What the fuck had Vincenzo done? Where was he? He could certainly look after himself. No-one stood a chance against Vincenzo either with a knife or hand to hand combat. And he was a crack shot but preferred the direct approach. Guns were for assassins, not killers he had once told Rimmer.

Rimmer himself was a businessman. He'd never gotten his hands dirty - ever. He was squeaky clean, and he kept it that way. And he couldn't afford for any loose ends lower in his organisation to lead back to him. Vincenzo had to be found. Unbeknown to his people, Rimmer had a tech team that installed tracking codes onto all the phones he issued to his staff. He called the tech guy and asked him to send him over the tracks for Vincenzo's phone from now, back a couple of days and do it pronto. Fifteen minutes later there was a knock on his door. It was Mark again; he had the printouts from the tech guy.

So, Vincenzo had been in Albufeira, and had flown directly to the boat by helicopter as he already knew. The signal had been lost during transit but had returned when he arrived onboard as they had a cellular network for the passengers use. So, he had definitely arrived on the ship. But then, shortly afterwards, the phone had been switched off and nothing since. Rimmer didn't like it when his operatives went to ground. Could Vincenzo be working on some kind of takeover? It wasn't possible. He had set things up so tightly that if he were to disappear then Vincenzo wouldn't have access to the things he needed most. He'd also left sealed instructions with a mandate to kill Vincenzo and others should anything untoward happen to himself. But why would Vincenzo choose to disappear on a ship? Mark had checked and the helicopter hadn't returned to the ship to collect him.

The ship had docked in Malta where Vincenzo could have departed. He would need to pull a few police strings to ascertain if Vincenzo had been spotted at the airport. He'd also do likewise at Heathrow. He'd track down Vincenzo at some point, and soon.

CHAPTER 68

The Maltese police had shared all the files with the British police. The four senior officers, two from each force, were now sat in their conference room. Their work would continue for the next week whilst the ship sailed. They had the results back and now knew that the prints found on the knife that killed Gill, were definitely those of Bernard Traynor, the retired police chief and victim. All the police had their fingerprints on file for elimination purposes if nothing else. It was confirmed. They also knew that Gill had been killed a little earlier than the Traynors. One line of enquiry was that Traynor had killed Gill, then returned to his cabin, where an altercation with his wife had ensued, resulting in him killing her and then himself. The wounds on all three victims were consistent in that a knife was used. They had two knives, one from each crime scene. One of the problems with a ship was how easy it is to dispose of weapons etc. over the edge and into the sea where they were lost forever. They weren't looking for any further weapons, they had all they needed. They'd searched the cabins and routes between extensively. They'd questioned everyone they were able to, but many of the passengers had left completely oblivious to what was happening. They may have missed vital witnesses but there was nothing they could do about this now. The cruise line wanted to keep this as low key as possible on board.

Meanwhile the Maltese and British news services were lapping it up!! Some of the officers had been stopped by new guests asking about the murders so the word was well and truly out. It would spread like wildfire and by tomorrow the whole ship would know. Still there was nothing the police could do about that. They needed to understand the series of events that lead to these three killings. It seemed all but certain that Traynor had killed Gill. It was logical he had then killed his wife and himself, albeit in a non-standard suicidal manner. If that were indeed the case, it would make their lives easier as they wouldn't be looking for any other murderers who were either long gone, on the island, or still on the ship which would be even worse.

The ship's crew would be remaining on the ship. There were also a further thirty-eight passengers who were staying on for a second week and four who were staying on for another three weeks. All these people would be interviewed in the next day or two. They needed to get a clear picture of the events that lead to these deaths. Then they could close the case and go back to their lives at home. It was no fun being stuck on a ship, in a dark cabin, working all the hours and being away from home. Every single one of them wanted nothing more than to get this case wrapped up and get the hell out. But they were there for the next week as there was no easy way to get off the ship now. They were all stuck there until they docked back at Malta the following weekend.

CHAPTER 69

Amanda had spent some time with James and Ben going through the set lists. They now knew which tracks Mandy knew. Amanda said that she thought that Mandy knew the words to all of them. She indicated the ones she may not know, and they put together a folder with the lyrics ready for their rehearsal on Monday afternoon. It was now only an hour before the ship was due to depart and no sign of Mandy. Jimbo was on shore – he hated his new name - he was to bring her on board, and then leave for other engagements. The band were sat up top in the bar. It was almost empty. The new guests were arriving, unpacking, and settling in. By the time Malta disappeared the bars would be full once again.

They were discussing tomorrow's rehearsal when a voice rang out across the deck. "Ahoy!" It was Mandy. One of the pursers carried her one, small bag. She ran over to Amanda and hugged her. "I never thought I'd see you again hon, let alone so soon." she said. "Terrible news about Animal." Amanda said. So, this is your new crew is it Jacey?" she asked. Amanda pulled a face. "Come on Jacey, introduce us then." Howard said with a wry smile. Jacey introduced the band one by one explaining their role and having a dig at each one. Mandy's arrival had lightened the mood somewhat. Gemma was still a little quiet but appeared to be in better form. The band had already had a couple of drinks whilst awaiting the new arrival. Ben went to the bar to order another round.

Mandy told them about the fire, how all her stuff had gone up in flames. She told Ben and James about her guitars and amps and the rest of her gear. Ben offered to let her come around to his cabin to play one of his guitars. Mandy knew how to deal with guys of all shapes and sizes. She brushed him off with a witty comment and they all laughed. She would fit in nicely. Even Gemma seemed to like her. They told her of the rehearsal and then discussed the songs. It turned out Mandy knew all the songs in the set but would need to brush up on the lyrics. James went to his cabin to retrieve the folder. Jacey told Mandy where all the clothes shops were. She volunteered Gemma to go with her to choose a couple of outfits that fitted in with the band. As one chapter closed, another opened in the world of show business.

CHAPTER 70

The rehearsal went well. Gemma had met with Mandy before lunch and they'd spent a couple of hours in the shops choosing two outfits for Mandy to wear. For the rehearsal they were all casual. Mandy wore one of her outfits though, partly to see what the rest of them thought and to get into the part. She brought the other outfit as well and when they had a break, she changed into that one. Jacey went with her. "They're great. Really good musicians." Mandy commented whilst getting changed. "But you'll miss playing the guitar." Jacey added. "I'll be back!" she said and smiled. Her second outfit looked great too. It hugged her figure. The guys wolf whistled her, then they went back to continue rehearsing.

Gemma had been showing Mandy the moves. They weren't complex but there were a couple of songs that required a short, choreographed sequence that fitted the music, such as when Proud Mary speeded up, or when Rock 'n' Roll stopped for the drum solo. She soon got the hang of the steps. By the end of the rehearsal Gemma was all smiles. She'd been laughing and Mandy and Gemma seemed to be getting on like a house on fire despite the fact they were both recently bereaved. The band agreed Mandy was all set for the first gig tomorrow evening. There were no private parties this week thank God. That would have been too much. None of them had been sleeping particularly well and they'd been drinking a lot more than usual. They agreed that tonight, they wouldn't be too late, then have a lie in so they would be refreshed for their Monday gig. Mandy have been given a cabin a couple of doors down from Jacey – it was between

Jacey's and Gemma's. Gill's and the Traynor's cabins were still locked up with sign on the door saying 'OUT OF ORDER'. Strange sign for a cabin door she thought.

CHAPTER 71

Scotland Yard was buzzing with stories of their old chief Traynor being murdered. Or had he gone and killed his wife and then himself? His loyal followers swore that he must have been murdered as you didn't get to his level without treading on a few toes and pissing a few people off and Traynor had excelled at this. Still there were many police who maintained he was always a bit funny and he could have done the murders. But the one thing they all agreed on was that none of them thought he would then kill himself. Especially not with a knife. But it wasn't their case. Nonetheless there were more than a few of them who would have liked to have knifed him in the neck, or the back.

Traynor's replacement was a tall guy, aged around fifty. His name was Harry Shafter. They all called him Shafter or 'The Shafter' on occasion. He had trodden on a good many toes to get where he was today. He wasn't as well liked as Traynor, and most of them didn't like Traynor. But it was tough at the top. No room for sentimentality. And Shafter had none. He was divorced with no kids. His marriage hadn't lasted long. He was nearly forty when he got married. She thought she could change him, and within a couple of years she learned that she never would. He was always at work. She met someone else. This went on for a further six months, Shafter oblivious. Then she left. He now lived in a small, two-bedroom house close to the station. Nothing fancy, but it was convenient for work, and that's all he did.

The case files on Vincenzo Dente and Shirley Rimmer were on

Shafter's desk. He was christened Shirley, but Shafter thought that none of his associates knew him by his real first name. They just called him Rimmer, or worse. Lots of files, lots of tenuous links to various dodgy business dealings, disappearances, drug smuggling and several gangland style murders. Lots of tenuous links, lots of circumstantial stuff but absolutely nothing that would even get them a warrant to search their offices.

These two were Teflon, nothing stuck. They couldn't even justify shadowing these guys. But even if they tried, Shafter suspected they'd lose their tails in minutes. These two were slippery. Half the force wanted to get them, but the other half seemed to feel they were untouchable. Shafter knew that these two had likely got a few cops in their pockets too. He even suspected that Traynor was one of them, but again he couldn't prove anything, Just hunches, his gut. He had never shared this thought with anyone. But his gut feel had served him well over the years. Personally, he thought Traynor had been murdered and set up. His money was on Dente or Rimmer or one of their cohorts. He didn't have a clue why though. Not a single clue. Just his gut. He had dispatched senior officers out there the minute the news broke. They were on the ship now interviewing. The last of the two-hourly updates he had received, indicated that the evidence at the scene pointed to Traynor having murdered a young woman. They had the weapon with his prints all over it, then returned to his cabin to dispatch his wife and then himself, again using a knife. Shafter knew Traynor well. Traynor hadn't exactly mentored him but he had recommended him for this role as his own replacement. This had gone in his favour and possibly tipped the job in his direction. He had quite a lot to thank Traynor for in that respect. He and his team owed it to Traynor to find out what had happened and bring the killer or killers to justice. Or hang Traynor out to dry if the facts pointed in his direction, as they seemed to do. The one thing that seemed strange to Shafter was the way Traynor had apparently elected to kill himself – with a knife, and to the neck. He hadn't come across this particular method of dispatching oneself before and he wondered where Traynor had come across this method had he indeed killed himself. It wasn't the quickest or least painful way to go about things. But as he knew only too well, people on the brink of suicide didn't think straight.

Right now, Shafter's team were reviewing everything they had on Rimmer and Dente. It was funny how everyone referred to Dente as Vincenzo. Maybe Dente reminded them of tooth ache. He himself preferred sticking to surnames. But the more they dug into Dente and Rimmer, the less they knew.

The word on the street was that Dente hadn't been seen for a few days. What was he up to? If Traynor was in his pocket then it was possible that Dente was involved, but why kill him now? He'd retired. It made no sense. But sometimes crimes outwardly made no sense. Things sometimes happened in the spur of the moment. People killed their partners. It was entirely possible that this was what had happened here. Time would tell. It was also possible it was nothing to do with Dente or Rimmer. Was Shafter allowing his personal vendettas to cloud his thinking? Again, time would tell.

CHAPTER 72

They were all sat together backstage, all dressed in their gig gear. Jacey in her first set outfit, Gemma and Mandy in their new outfits. Gemma had also bought a couple of new outfits. Maybe wearing something different would help give her closure. She had taken a real shine to Mandy and Mandy to her. Jacey wondered if Mandy also went for women. This thought had never crossed her mind before. But the more the thought of it, the more it seemed possible. Still, it didn't matter to her, each to their own. If it made them happy then go for it. Life knew no boundaries.

Jacey felt like she'd been part of this band for ages, but the reality was that, in a few short weeks, the band line-up had changed quite a bit. Their image had also changed – it was now a bit sexier and rockier than it used to be, and they seemed even more popular. Each show was full or very nearly full. The management were pleased with Jacey and the choice of backing singer didn't matter quite so much. The first couple of numbers went really smoothly. They didn't feature too much in terms of backing vocals, but the girls moved together well, their looks seemed to complement each other in the overall look of the band, and they seemed to be having a good time. If the band were happy then the punters were happy. Everyone had been worried, but unable to mention it, that Gemma's sadness could affect the band's performance. But there she was, singing away and smiling, having a great time, all her sorrows gone for the moment. This made everyone feel better. There were a couple of backing parts where Gemma sang on her own – Mandy having forgotten to sing. But it mattered not, the band carried on and Gemma just smiled at Mandy in a girlish manner. No recriminations just part of the fun. When they went backstage between sets Mandy was apologising about missing her parts, but the band assured her it didn't matter. Mandy said she'd prompt her for the tricky ones in the second set, and she did. The second set went smoothly. The harmonies Gemma and Mandy had worked out together, worked really well. Their voices complemented each other, sitting in different parts of the frequency spectrum. Even though they were relatively low in the mix, both voices could be heard. After their two planned encores the band returned backstage and downed the traditional post gig beer. Mandy was buzzing and Gemma was too, like a little girl with a new puppy. Everyone's spirits were high. Things were good once again. Jacey knew that the show was indeed going on. Onwards and upwards.

After finishing their beer and discussions, they changed into their normal clothes and left their outfits hung in the dressing room. Given the fun and games they'd had the previous week, Jacey, or Mandy as she was then, had arranged for laundry to visit the backstage area after each gig and collect any outfits left there and get them laundered and returned for the following show, be it in the afternoon or evening. It made their lives a lot easier. It didn't make much difference to the guys. They just had three of four shirts that they alternated. But the girls had two three or four outfits. Mandy said this was civilisation; no chores, no laundry, no cooking, it was bliss. She thanked Jacey for thinking of her. At no point was Animal's name mentioned.

Once changed they all went down to their preferred watering hole and sank a few more beers. They had two shows the following day, but it didn't deter them from celebrating. The closing of old doors and the opening of new. The show must always go on.

CHAPTER 73

Rimmer's operatives hadn't turned up a thing. Not a sign of Vincenzo. Both Vincenzo and Rimmer had enemies. Rimmer spent most of his time in his new penthouse pad located in his new office building that housed his legitimate, or mostly legitimate, business interests; a cover for some of his other interests. Vincenzo mixed with his mafioso family members and other low lifes. Rimmer didn't intend becoming a victim. Maybe Vincenzo had gotten complacent.

One thing that had come to Rimmer's attention, had related to the girl Vincenzo was chasing. She was a singer. The news was full of reports about three murders onboard that very same ship. Three murders, one a singer, plus an old couple. His sources told him this was in fact his old confidante Traynor and his wife. This stank of Vincenzo's doing. He'd found the girl and killed her. Maybe she had the rest of the money and he took it from her – who knows. What he did know was that, if he didn't surface in another couple of days, he'd have to appoint someone to replace him. By then it was too late. He was either dead, or off the radar and needing to be punished – fatally. Either way, Vincenzo had a couple of days to retrieve himself or that was that, Rimmer didn't have much patience. He'd put a hit out on him. His behaviour was completely unacceptable. Even his family hadn't heard anything from him. Rimmer wouldn't put it past Vincenzo to do a runner, fuck their business, fuck his own family, fuck the lot of them. Well, if he had done this, then it was he who was fucked. Well and truly.

CHAPTER 74

Another day had passed for the police team onboard the cruise ship and now only five or six more days to wrap things up. So far, they had their number one dialogue, and they hadn't found anything to offer an opposing story that fitted the facts better. All the forensics were back in. No other prints or items of interest had been found in either cabin. The party of friends the Traynors had brought along with them, were holed up in a hotel in Malta for further questioning. Every one of them was gobsmacked. They had told of how happy they were, happy to have a good few years left to enjoy their retirement together, then this.

Whilst it was by no means a cut and dried case, they had nothing to indicate the involvement of anyone else. They even had the murder weapons. The only thing that jarred with the team was why he had killed Gill, left the knife, then returned to his cabin only to use a different knife. Most spree killers kept the same weapon. But it was seeming like this was a spur of the moment thing. They suspected Traynor had tried it on with Gill and somehow, he'd gotten into her cabin, been refused or insulted or something, and he'd snapped and stabbed her. He then fled back to his own cabin to be confronted by his wife. Maybe he told her what had happened, who knows. Then it all ended with him snapping once again, this time beyond breaking point.

One thing familiar to all coppers was that, should you end up inside yourself, life was infinitely worse than for a normal criminal. Traynor knew this. Maybe that influenced his decision to die rather than risk being caught. It was a big ship, but they would have found him. You couldn't kill someone on a ship like this, a captive audience, and get away with it. Traynor knew this and took the easy way out. Still stabbing yourself in the throat like that – that was a suicide first to all the team members. But it was quick, adrenalin would have hidden much of the pain before he bled out or choked – whichever came first. Maybe it was no worse than hanging. That was his choice and he'd made it. Maybe he was expressing guilt in killing himself in the same way as his other two victims. A psychologist could work that one out. They followed the evidence.

By now all the team were pretty convinced that they had the true story of events leading to two murders and a suicide. The other elephant in the room was that, whilst they had found Traynor's fingerprints on the knife that killed Gill, they hadn't found a trace of her blood on his clothing. Had he changed? If so where were his dirty clothes? No-one dared ask this question. They had already started on their reports. Maybe they would get a few hours to spend sunbathing after all.

CHAPTER 75

It was noon and Mandy and Jacey were sat eating breakfast. Mandy was still buzzing about being onboard the ship. She'd had a long walk earlier that morning and gotten lost a couple of times. She commented on how friendly the staff were and eager to show her around. She'd found more shops and bars and a curry house! Jacey liked the sound of that. They decided to eat there early this evening before the show. Many performers wouldn't eat before a show, but it never bothered them. Maybe the rest of the band would come along too? Then they talked about the songs. Mandy had a few ideas of her own for moves during some of the songs. Jacey told her to take it easy on Gemma as she was still grieving. "Could have fooled me." commented Mandy. "You two are getting along really well aren't you?" Jacey asked, with a twinkle in her eye. Mandy didn't take the bait. "We'll see." She replied and smiled. Was she playing a game with Jacey? She'd slipped back into being Jacey now, but didn't want to slip back into character as a rock chick. She was more elegant, she'd moved on. Elegant singer chick. With a bit of rock chick.

"Jacey!" The guys had arrived together – James, Ben, Howard, Nick and Ian. They were liking her new name! She just smiled as they took their seats. They asked the girls if they'd ordered yet – they said no, they were waiting for Gemma. They agreed to wait but it was only a few more minutes before she arrived and squeezed in between Jacey and Mandy. "Hi Jacey!" she said. They all laughed. The name had well and truly stuck. "Maybe we all need nicknames." Jacey said and raised an eyebrow.

After discussing nicknames for a few minutes their breakfasts arrived. They continued to chat whilst they ate. Today they were on soft drinks, it was a workday. Well after a couple of beers that was. Jacey was surprised that Mandy hadn't talked more about Animal and the fire. She had lost everything in that fire. Jacey desperately wanted to know more about the fire. She decided to broach the subject later on when she could be alone with Mandy. She didn't want Gemma in on that conversation, or anyone else. It would have to wait.

CHAPTER 76

The police team were working on their reports. Every detail of every witness statement corroborating every event had to be written up. Every piece of evidence supporting each assumption had to be written up and photographs were included within the file. It was laborious work. There would be no trial for this crime though. Still, everything needed to be neat and tidy. The sooner they finished up, the sooner they could enjoy some free time, or so they thought.

In the incident room the phone rang. It was one of the detectives in New Scotland Yard. He'd heard on the grapevine that Vincenzo Dente had dropped off the radar. His cohorts were looking for him now. Strange. Still, not their problem. The two detectives shared a few of the interesting points regarding cases and rang off. None of the team on the ship were in the slightest bit interested in Dente or any of the many other cases. They just wanted to nail their own case and then get some free time. After all, they deserved it.

CHAPTER 77

After breakfast everyone had returned to their own cabin, but Gemma said she'd see them later, and walked on to her cabin, Mandy stayed behind and looked at Jacey. She knew something was wrong. "Come in." she said. They both sat on Jacey's bed. Jacey just looked at her waiting for her to spill. After a few seconds Mandy said "It's about Animal. There is another reason I bit your hand off when you called and it's about Animal and I." Jacey hadn't expected this – they were an item? How had she not noticed this? And why did it matter now, Animal was dead and gone. After a few more seconds, Mandy was obviously trying to think of the best way of putting things, she continued. "We had a good thing going on, just the two of us." When she saw Jacey's face she quickly corrected "No not that, not that. Something else. Something that may have gotten Animal killed. She was in Albufeira long before the rest of us. And she already had that house. I never bought her story of its ownership. I once saw a bill and all the details were in Animal's real name. It was her house!!!"

Jacey was taken aback at this news. She'd believed everything Animal had told her. "But where did she get the house? How did she afford it?" Jacey replied. "I confronted her about it, a few months ago. She came clean. She said her parents were dead, left her some money and she'd bought the house. I believed that bit. But she hadn't bargained on how much it cost to run a house like that. Drumming in a band didn't make enough to run a tiny place, let alone that one. So, she turned to other forms of income." Jacey immediately thought of prostitution, her face must have given this away though, but Mandy soon corrected her. "No not that either. As if. It was drugs. They're rife over there. Holiday makers pay top dollar and there are plenty of locals who regularly use. Animal was a user – not heavy or anything, but she liked to go to her room and chill if you know what I mean. She had contacts. She never sold at gigs, but just did deliveries during the day or in the morning – that's why she was sometimes up and out very early. When I joined the band, I too needed money. She asked me to run a few errands, deliver a couple of things here and there and that's how it started. One guy got a little rough with me – I had no idea what he was talking about until he told me. And then I knew what she was up to. But I couldn't do anything about it. I was living in her house playing in her band. So, it was a case of 'if you can't beat them then join them. Animal and I shared the work from then on. I didn't ask for money – it was kinda my keep. She also gave me a cut when she got paid, nothing formal. But anyway, it wasn't the people she shipped to, it was the guy she received from."

Jacey was watching her face, trying to verify the truth of what Mandy was saying. So far, she believed every single word. Mandy went on;" The guy she got it from gave her a bundle. She split it into maybe twenty smaller ones that she distributed for a set fee – cash naturally. She then went back to him with the cash for the one she'd sold, and he gave her another. Initially it was cash up front but as she got better, and he came to trust her, as far as anyone can trust a drug dealer, it went to paying him afterwards and the block became bigger and bigger over time. Anyway, when the band split up, Animal lost it. She'd just collected a big block and she went on a personal bender – jut smoked and smoked, for a whole week. She was that gone that she never noticed someone break into the house and take the rest of her stash. Even at her rate of consumption she'd only used around 5 percent of it or less. As you can imaging one block of that stuff was worth a lot. When she went for her next fix, she realised it was gone. The first person she went to was me. I think she knew me well enough to know I wouldn't steal from her, but she was still high. Then she suspected you and Rach, but I told her that neither of you had ever used drugs and probably couldn't recognise it if they saw it. And anyway, you'd been gone too long." "That's true." Jacey added. She went on to ask, "Did you find out who did it then?" "That's the thing, we didn't. When Animal didn't have the cash to pay her own dealer guy she asked for more time, always a bad move, he immediately sensed something bad. He could tell from looking at her that she'd had a rough week. He gave her forty-eight hours to come up with the cash or he would 'sort her out'." "Did she find the dope or the cash? Or did he sort her out?" Jacey asked, getting straight to the point. "I don't believe she found the stuff or raised the cash. And it was a couple of days after this altercation that the house went up with Animal in it." "So that was that then?" Jacey said in a matter-of-fact way.

Mandy just looked at her, her, did she not care? "Well.... yeah. I went to the house, saw the police and fire engines and headed out of town and checked into a hostel. I thought that maybe they knew I'd been helping her and that they would now come after me. I spent a few nights, holed up in my room, lying low and wondering what the hell to do when James called me. He'd tried the house and then when he got no answer made a few calls and one of the owners of one of the bars we played had my number. He called me, told me about your band wanting a singer. Fuck, I'm no backing singer, I'm a guitarist, you know that. But it offered me a way out. And I took it – with both hands. And I'm here now."

It was a lot for Jacey to take in. "Fuck. Do they know who you are? Do they know you were working with Animal? Will they follow you here?" Mandy's tough exterior was cracking. She now had tears in her eyes. "I don't know, I just don't know." She replied.

After a few moments of silence Jacey said "Look, they caught up with Animal in forty-eight hours. If they had known about you, they'd have gone straight for you. They didn't. They probably assumed she worked alone and left it at that. They may have found enough cash stashed somewhere to cover it and more for all we know." Jacey said, trying to make Mandy feel better. "But you don't understand." replied Mandy. "They never stop until they get what they want. If they speak to Animal's customers, they'll describe me as well as her. We looked nothing like each other. They'll know she was in a band, put two and two together, and bingo. It's the girl from the band." Another pause. Jacey then said, "How much was one of these blocks that Animal distributed worth?" "I have no idea. Each collection I made was for between two fifty and five hundred Euros. I don't know how many deliveries were made. Jacey was getting a little ratty now. "Think, how many trips per batch between the two of you. We can multiply it up. When we know how much she owed them then we'll know how far they'd go to get it back."

Mandy tried to hold back the tears. "I don't know." She was now sobbing. "Twenty, I guess. Maybe more." And the tears came flooding. Jacey comforted her for a while. "OK, assume twenty batches of two-fifty to five hundred. Averaging it out that's around, what, five to ten thousand Euros – call it 10k for a round number and the worst case. I can understand they possibly killed Animal, probably more as an example to others. I can't see how they'd come after you. Not here anyway. But I wouldn't go back there again in case they recognise you." Mandy thought about this for a few minutes, then looked at Jacey and said "How do you keep so cool? We're talking about life and death. I could have roped you into my shit, but you still have a cool head. I wish I was more like you, Jacey." No, you don't, she thought to herself. Again, they sat in silence for a few moments. "So, here is the big question, who the fuck was she getting the stuff from? Was he a player? A big guy? Or a little guy. If he was a little guy, he'll have had his arse whooped as well and might not be in any position to come after you, and that's assuming he even knows about you in the first place." Mandy thought for a long time. "I think he was called Joey, but I'm not sure. I never saw him of course. I don't even know where he lived or operated from. But it can't have been far. Animal was never out of the house more than a couple of hours when she was collecting; she went straight there and back. She didn't particularly like carrying the big block back. She was always worried someone would find out and rob her on the street or even kill her. I think she was in too deep but couldn't see a way out. The band kept her going. When the first singer left, she wobbled. When you and Rach left, she collapsed." Jacey had always thought of Animal as a moody cow and didn't really have much time for her. But she didn't understand the landscape as well as she thought. She still had a lot to learn about this cruel life and how to survive and thrive.

They talked a little longer and Mandy seemed to lighten up a little. Their talk had made her less uneasy. She had agreed that it was unlikely they'd follow her here even if they worked out that she had been helping Animal. The debt was on Animal's shoulders and she must have had a stash of cash in her room somewhere. They'd burned her house down as a sign to others. If they had any brains, they'd have extorted it from her and sold it. By now Jacey was pretty sure that the fish that Animal swam with were not in the same league as the ones she caught and ate. Nevertheless, this was yet another bit of clutter in her life that was unexpected and unwelcomed. A loose end that could cause complications. If the police found drugs in the house, maybe Animal had hidden them in a drugged-up stupor and forgotten where she put them, then they'd find traces. But only if they were looking for drugs. They had no cause to think Animal was connected with drugs or organised crime, after all she was just a drummer. But she owned a big house that was beyond her means, surely that would prompt questions at the very least? She'd been insured but who was her next of kin? Had she made a will? No-one makes a will at their age. What would happen to the insurance money for the house? All these questions.

Jacey said she needed to rest before the show. Mandy agreed that she did too. She said she felt much better after their talk and headed back to her cabin for a rest. But Jacey couldn't rest. She had too many things flying around her head. Drugs, a house, yet another bad guy, this time a faceless, nameless, and one who no-one would see coming. Better to worry about the problems around you rather than the ones that might never happen she mused. After all she'd found out about Mandy, she still didn't know if she was falling for Gemma and vice versa. Still, what did it matter?

CHAPTER 78

Rimmer had assigned a team of four to seek and destroy Vincenzo. None of the four guys were keen on this mission. They were hard and bad but not in Vincenzo's league. But it would bode them well, give then credibility, maybe help move them up the order of villainy. The team were Davo and JJ, who had had the most recent dealings with Vincenzo, and David and Ginger – Dumb and Dumber as referred to by everyone else. Dumb but hard. Sometimes not thinking got the job done better. The four of them would make a good team – brains and brawn.

He had told them of the killings on the ship, that Vincenzo had committed, namely the girl singer he was after plus two other people. The news would report this as murder suicide but Rimmer was certain that Vincenzo had killed the three of them for some reason. Traynor had served them well over the years. Vincenzo's reasons for killing the pair of them must have been personal. Did he know the Traynors were on the ship or did he meet them by accident? Maybe he asked Traynor to do something, like kill the girl for him, and he refused, or they got into a struggle. Who knows and who cares? The three of them are dead and Vincenzo was as good as dead. On borrowed time. Soon to be dead.

Vincenzo's last known location was on the cruise ship and it had docked at Malta. They knew he'd been dropped off but never picked up. The ship had docked in Malta then set off again. He wouldn't be fool enough to stay on a floating prison cell, so he must have gotten off at Malta and either holed up somewhere or gotten a flight or ship out to somewhere else. None of them knew what had triggered Vincenzo's sudden transformation. He wasn't one to flee and he wasn't one to back down. To them, it made no sense. They had to get to him before the police did. If he slipped up in his haste to get away, he might get caught. Then he might squeal. That was the biggest concern all round. He knew so much. Shut him up, no-one wanted him back but every one of them wanted him dead.

The team got the first flight they could to Malta. They got a direct flight from Faro to Luqa in Malta. The following day they would be there. Now they had a strategy to plan. What they did, how they divided the labour, who did what. They were told to pair up – Davo and Ginger and JJ and David. They had been provided a list of people on the island known to their bosses. First they met with them and found out what they knew. Then they fed the intel back before they got their next set of orders. None of the four of them expected to actually find Vincenzo – they all thought he was far too clever to leave any clues. They were in awe of how he had disappeared in style from a cruise ship! That was class. He hadn't driven off at warp speed or jumped on a train. He'd taken a helicopter to a cruise ship and then disappeared. Davo had asked if they would be required to follow up on Vincenzo's search for that girl but he'd been told firmly that that was Vincenzo's personal thing and nothing to do with business. And she was now dead. So, they'd left it. But Davo wasn't stupid. Vincenzo must have had a really good reason to up and go like that after some chick. He felt sure it was something to do with Vincenzo's disappearance and warranted further attention. But he did what he was told. He'd forget about this and follow orders.

They had booked into a modest, two-star hotel in town, in good proximity of the location of their contacts. As they travelled Davo had done a little research. None of them had been to Malta before. He looked on google maps and found that Malta actually comprised three islands – Malta itself where Luqa was,

Gozo at the top and a small island between. There was only a kilometre or so separating these three islands. The island had a rich history and even had grottos. Maybe Vincenzo had a hide-away planned and used the cruise as an elaborate excuse to conceal the fact he was going to Malta. But even then, it was their first thought to look there, so it wasn't elaborate. Again, Davo couldn't see the picture here. No narrative. It didn't make sense. Still, in a couple of days, after speaking to their contacts, they'd know more.

They were told they had three days to come up with enough information to decide if a more detailed search of Malta was required or to find something to indicate he'd travelled on to somewhere else. They didn't have any time to drink in bars or walk along the beach. They knew they had to come up with something or they'd all be in the shit. Vincenzo's shit.

CHAPTER 79

The show was over, the audience were very appreciative. Mandy had seemingly recovered from her afternoon's tribulations and performed really well with Gemma. They made a good team. When Jacey wasn't singing, during a solo for example, she turned around, or walked over to them as they danced side by side or shook a tambourine or a shaker or whatever. They were all loving it. Mandy made a good backing singer.

After the set they all went down to the bar and had a few drinks. Gill's name wasn't mentioned once. None of them wanted to disturb their fragile happiness; not tonight as it was part of the healing. Mandy had all the lyrics now, so she could catch up with Jacey in terms of their repertoire. Mandy also had ideas of new songs to learn and not just ones from their old set. She picked a couple with really good backing vocal parts. The three girls said they'd get together in one of their cabins to work out the vocal arrangements ready for sound checking a couple of new ones before the next gig. The bandwagon was rolling once again.

CHAPTER 80

Davo and Ginger did the brain work and JJ and David did the legwork. Davos' team carried out research, visiting and speaking to people, asking questions, finding things out. JJ's team tracked people down in readiness for Davos' visit. It took three days to track down and speak with the people on their list. Whilst learning a lot of useful intel about Malta and the various goings on, they hadn't learned anything relating directly to Vincenzo. No-one had seen him or anyone fitting his description. They now knew the security processes relating to such a boat. They also learned that some ships had thermal camera systems that monitored the decks and could highlight jumpers or fallers. Such footage had been used on evidence in courts apparently. Still, it was no use to them as Vincenzo wouldn't have jumped and if another ship was waiting for him it would be seen by the crew. He had to have gotten off at Malta somehow.

When they reported back to Rimmer that evening he said the search was over for now. Too much time had passed, and he could be anywhere. But he'd put feelers out with international contacts. If anyone heard from him or saw him, they'd find out. For now, they had other things to focus on. Were they to see him at any point then their orders were simple – kill him. Their trip was over, back to London tomorrow. That evening, in the bar, the four of them were planning their retirement to Malta, discussing all the ways they could leverage their combined experience to organise something interesting.

CHAPTER 81

Jacey was still on guard for any visitors relating to Vincenzo, whom she had dispatched. But nothing had happened. She still didn't know how he had found her. If he could find her then others possibly could. But he'd come alone, maybe no one else knew he was here? Maybe she was indeed safe. She'd put the word out that, should any helicopters land whilst at sea, to tell her immediately. She hinted that it was about possible celebrities coming on board for their private performances. She felt reasonably safe whilst the ship was at sea and no passengers were dropping in from the skies. But she still had to make longer term plans. This business of Gill's murder – well she could use it as an excuse to leave the band should she chose to. It would sound perfectly normal that she couldn't face things anymore. That card was up her sleeve should she need it.

She still had a huge amount of Sterling to deal with somehow. The best way to get rid of that would be back in the UK naturally. People bought large items for cash, cars, jewellery, even homes. Maybe she should put it into a private pension. That made her smile. Getting rid of hot cash wasn't as easy as it was made out to be in the movies. She would need to choose a city that was vibrant, not squeaky clean, and used to dealing in cash. She could open several accounts and deposit a fair chunk in each. None of them large enough to raise any alarms. She could say she was paid in cash or received tips onboard the ship. She'd think of something. Once she had the accounts set up, she could transfer between them, close a few and hopefully not set off any warning bells anywhere. She needed to learn more about the banking system and its foibles. So much to learn. She could have a massive city shopping blast, blow a few thousand at a time. A trip back to England would also let her conduct more research into her father's estate. But she would have to be careful. The more time elapsed, the more different her appearance would be as she grew older. There was no rush. For now, she should focus on now.

CHAPTER 82

It was a miserable day in London. Grey skies, drizzle, and a wind that both chilled you to the bone and ensured the rain seeped into your every pore. The traffic down below moved in small fits and starts, twinkling with the rain. Pedestrians walked with inside out umbrellas; cyclists were being blown all over the road. Rimmer was looking out of the window of his top floor office, come living area, at the scene below. He had poured over all the information available to him. He still hadn't got the first clue as to Vincenzo's whereabouts. When someone as high up and well connected as Vincenzo disappeared it was all the more difficult to stay underground. When someone succeeded, it often meant that they were in fact dead. Vincenzo had gone on that ship specifically for the Little Weasel. She was dead, as were the Traynors. Why had the Traynors died and had Traynor himself really killed The Little Weasel, his wife and then himself. From his sources he knew this is what the police now believed. They must have had evidence to back this up. Could it be that Vincenzo had actually killed the three of them and framed Traynor? To Rimmer this seemed equally plausible. Maybe it was punishment to Traynor for something in the past that Rimmer was unaware of. This whole matter had been distracting him from his other, more legitimate, duties. He couldn't afford to be distracted and not at his best. He should put this aside and leave the guys to pursue it. For now, he had other fish to fry.

CHAPTER 83

It was a good hour before their evening performance and Jacey was snoozing on the bed, resting up. She was roused by a loud rapping on her door. She assumed it was Gemma or Mandy but upon opening the door she was a little surprised to find Ian, the drummer standing there. He looked down at her and said "May I come in." She opened the door and showed him in. She assumed his cabin was exactly the same has hers, but she'd never visited any of the guy's cabins just the girls. "I've not slept well since Gill's death. The thing is, I'm not the most outgoing guy or the most sociable guy. I don't know about you, but I've got a past. Everyone I meet on these ships seems to be running away from something and I'm no exception. But if I tell you something, can I trust you to keep it to yourself? You see I believe you and I have more in common than you think.

She sat on the bed, Ian towering over her. She just looked at him. He was very serious. He obviously had something he considered of great importance to tell her. "Go on." she said. He sat down on her chair facing her. "Me for one, I'm running away from something. When I was younger, I got mixed up with the wrong crowd, usual thing, nicking cars, joyriding and some petty theft, then onto drugs. A couple of my mates started dealing on a small scale. It was in the Kings Cross area. I stopped short of drugs as, being so tall, I stood out like a sore thumb. Anyone wanted to find me, I couldn't escape. This was, what, ten years ago? Maybe eleven, I lose track. Anyway, my two friends got taken for a ride from some punter. They were dumb enough to extend credit. At first, he paid up the next day, but the amounts

grew. When the amount was large, he just fucked off. Left them with a big hole they couldn't cover. They were both in debt to the people they were distributing for, nasty people, well they always are, but these lot were particularly nasty. They decided to come clean about being ripped off. Trouble is that's the oldest scam in the book. In their business you cover your costs and your losses, but they hadn't learned that yet. They both got severely done over, broken bones, the lot. One of my mates, Denny, never recovered. He had a stroke caused by a clot and it turned him into a vegetable. His parents were gutted. The thing I never told anyone was, that I saw them that night, and I saw the guy that did them over, I don't know his name and I tried to forget the whole thing. But when I realised that debts were transferrable, and my other friend then lent on me, I saw no other choice than going to the cops. I identified the guy who had done them over using police photos. I then identified him from a line-up. The whole thing seemed to snowball and the next thing I couldn't go out anywhere. The police told me to lay low before the trial. Anyway, someone came to my house and attacked me. Luckily, I was prepared, and I frightened him off. I was still battered and bruised from the struggle. After that they moved me into a safe house. My girlfriend was long gone by then. I stayed there until the trial. After that I got a new identity and was helped to find work on a cruise liner. That's how I ended up here." He stopped for air.
Jacey then spoke. "But I don't understand, what has all that got to do with now, or with me?" Ian looked into her eyes, even more serious than before. "The guy I testified against got off on a technicality. I saw him in court. Fancy lawyers, brown envelopes who knows. He walked. And I never saw him again until recently and on this ship."

Now this got Jacey's attention. Who was he referring to? "I'm sure it was completely innocent, but I saw you talking to him, after Gill's last gig. It was at the back of the room. I know it didn't last long, and you had no idea of who he was, but I wanted to warn you. That guy is real bad news. He was on our ship and he might be looking for me. Then the next thing three people were killed. It might be coincidence, but until the police tell us what happened I'm scared – for both you and myself."

Jacey just looked at him. What could she say? She gathered her thoughts and then replied "That guy came over to me after the gig and offered to buy me a drink. It was just small talk, nothing more. I left and that was that. I never thought about him again until now. He was a real snappy dresser though, looked Italian." "He is Italian. He's part of some massive mob gang that manages thousands and thousands of pounds worth of drugs in London and all over. He's as bad as they get. Did he ask anything about Gill? He could have been pumping you for information before he killed Gill. I don't even know that he did, but, like I said, none of it makes sense."

She thought about how to answer this question. "I think he mentioned the other band members, I might have said something about Gill but, to be honest I didn't know much about Gill or any of the others – then or even now. I don't know what I could have said to him." Ian was looking at the floor, his hands fidgeting. "Shouldn't we tell the police what you know?" she said "Fuck no. I'm not going back to court ever again. I just want peace and quiet. This life suits me. He never saw me and probably wouldn't recognise me even if he did see me. Plus, if he had seen me, I'd probably be dead too. So, I'm not going to any cops and neither are you. This stays between you and me."

Jacey looked at him and, after a few seconds, replied "Sure – I understand. That's the way I want it too. The sooner this whole mess is cleared up and the police are gone the better." and she meant every word.

Ian seemed a little happier. He looked around the cabin as though trying to think of something else to say but it eluded him. Jacey then spoke again. "So, no one here on the ship knows about your past, not even James and the agency or the staff on-board?" "No-one. Only you. And now I'm not even sure why I mentioned it to you. I should have just kept quiet. He'll be long gone by now." "Well, that's OK then. That's how it should stay. We won't mention it again. The guy you saw, whatever he did or didn't do, must have left at Malta and is long gone by now. He won't bother us again. We're safe so long as we get on with things as normal." Jacey said. Ian nodded and smiled. He looked a little more comfortable. "OK, I'd better be going, we need to get moving in half an hour or so." He stood up. Jacey stood up and followed him to the door. "See you in a bit." She said and off he went. This was getting too much.

Backstage Ian was quiet, but then again, he was always a bit quiet, so no one noticed anything. The outfits were freshly laundered and hung up nicely. They all got changed and out they went – once more onto the stage. By then end of the show the whole band seemed a little tired. James and Ben were discussing the police and why they were still on the ship. "That's easy, they can't get off until we dock." Mandy had said to them. They both looked at her and Ben started to laugh. "I know that. I meant..." "I know." Mandy said. Gemma was sat beside Mandy and listening but not saying much. Mandy and Gemma had performed well, they were becoming a great duo.

Talk then went on to music shops. Mandy was hankering after buying a guitar and small practise amp when they were able. James and Ben offered to take her to a shop they knew at their next port of call. Mandy seemed excited at the prospect of playing again. Though whether there was scope for another guitarist in this band was questionable and Mandy didn't yet have the money she needed for her purchases.

Jacey's thoughts kept going back to Ian – what a small world it was. She now knew that she could never be too careful – whatever she did, wherever she was, someone could be there and crop up one day to haunt her. Ian wasn't a threat. But he was a little unstable or appeared to be at least. She'd keep an eye on him. No-one needed to know about Vincenzo's mini cruise, no-one. Unless he had told anyone – like the helicopter pilot, or one of is sidekicks. It's possible he worked alone. The helicopter pilot was just a glorified taxi driver. It was entirely possible no-one else knew Vincenzo had been on board. The pilot may not have even known who he was in the first place. If someone else was after her they'd have gotten on at Malta and found her by now. Unless, like her, they were waiting for the last night of the cruise to strike, just before the ship docked once again. Could it be? She'd already made too many mistakes. One more could lead to her death. Or prison. Maybe she should work out a plan B to disappear at the next port. But where could she go and hide and stay low for days or weeks. Most of her money was Sterling, the UK would be her best bet. And then it hit her. Dom's terraced house up North!! The very same place he'd kept her his prisoner. That room, a great prison cell and a great hiding place. He'd had a camera in the cellar to watch her. She could set up cameras by the front and back doors so she could watch from her hiding place. She was by no means sure that she was being pursued, but she had a feeling in her gut. A feeling that said 'Run.'

That night she lay awake thinking about the pros and cons of going back to England. She knew it better than anywhere. She spoke the language and had lots of cash to see her through. She had several identities so far as documents went. She even had Dom's keys to the place. She also remembered that he had said he left the place totally empty between uses - no one looked in or cleaned or visited. It would make a great hideout so long as it was still empty, no squatters, and hadn't been repossessed or something. He had plenty of money in his account – standing orders should get paid for months to come. She believed that his body wouldn't have been identified by the French, and he was supposed to have already died in prison he had told her, escaping using someone else's identity. The only documents he was carrying at his death were the false ones. The police would either realise and he would remain unidentified or, if they were lazy, they'd assume the fake ID was him. But there would be no family or relatives to contact to make arrangements. Maybe they just buried him somewhere – who cared. It was a shame she didn't have any close police friends who might gain access to the police records to see what they had on Dominic Devizes, his last known whereabouts, place of death if known and such like. It would also be useful to know more about what they knew about her own disappearance. How could she make this happen?

CHAPTER 84

The following day they had two gigs. They'd discussed Mandy's new song suggestions and the three girls had worked out vocal parts. The guys said they needed a day or two to learn their parts. They pencilled in Friday's sound check to try them out. No more news had come from the police team. No more revelations or disclosures were revealed. All seemed normal on board. Both gigs went well and were enjoyed by the band and audience. More beers were consumed. Things were settling down. Meanwhile Jacey was still making plans.

If she ran for it when they docked, should she tell the band? Tell them she couldn't face it after Gill's death and so on? If she just ran the police may become suspicious and possibly involved and that would be bad, very bad. She would have to officially leave the band and then the ship. The next stop was Barcelona. Lots of ways to disappear in Barcelona, lots of ways to travel North and back to the UK. Much better than Malta. She had two days to plan and affect her departure. She had made up her mind, it was too hot on board. Too easy to become someone's prey. And her role in the band made her too easy a target. She had decided to return to England.

When the band were all together backstage before the gig, she pretended to be a little preoccupied. Instead of chatting to the other band members she moped on her own. Eventually Mandy asked her what was wrong. After a few seconds she said "Nothing." In a very unconvincing manner. "Tell me." Mandy replied. "OK but after the show, I don't want to spoil it." Mandy looked even more concerned at this remark but respected Jacey's wishes. The gig went smoothly even though Jacey's mind wasn't quite as fully on the job in hand. Her brain was still in planning mode. All the more focussed, given her recent slip ups.

Sure enough, after the gig, and when they had changed clothes and were heading down to the bar for the after-gig drinks, Mandy pulled Jacey to one side. "Get our drinks will you Ben. We'll be down in a few minutes." Ben nodded, Mandy and Jacey watched the rest of the band head down to the bar. "OK, hon, what is it that's eating at you." "I know I appear cool and hard and unaffected by what goes on but I'm not. Gill's death has hit me hard. I don't think I can do this anymore. I'm going to leave at Barcelona and go home." Mandy just looked at her. She must have thought it was some trivial thing that was getting to Jacey, nothing quite as serious as this. "You're quitting your job? Walking out on me and the band – again?" Jacey feigned tears and Mandy hugged her and held her close. "I can't do it. I need a break. Maybe I'll get over it and come back." "If you go, James will replace you. You know how persuasive he is at getting new band members. If you go that'll be it." Jacey just looked at her. "I just don't know; my life is a mess. I ran away from my home, tried to find a place where I fitted and all that follows me is death and destruction." A little dramatic but Mandy didn't seem to think so. "Hon, it's not your fault – Gill, Animal. It's just life. Shit happens, bad shit sometimes. None of it is any of our faults." "Bad things come in threes." Jacey said. Mandy looked at her. Let's go get a few drinks, everything will seem better tomorrow. It did.

CHAPTER 85

Jacey awoke with a thumping head. Nothing more was said about Jacey's departure. She thought that Mandy thought she had calmed her down and it was all over. Today was Friday, the ship docked in Barcelona in the morning. Today's task was to pack her clothes and the cash and documents into two bags that she could carry. She chose her father's holdall and her newly acquired Italian hand luggage bag. She ordered breakfast in her cabin and ate as she packed. She left clothes for tomorrow and a change of clothes in her small bag. That way the large bag wouldn't need to be touched until later. She hadn't decided on the best mode of transport. She knew that planes were the riskiest given all the security and CCTV cameras.

The day before she had purchased a phone and pay as you go UK SIM card from the shop on the ship. She pre-paid for enough data to see her through the start of her journey. On the ship she had Wi-Fi. She took the phone and researched ferries from Barcelona to the UK. She found that she could get a ferry from Bilbao to Portsmouth. Barcelona to Bilbao was a long trip by road. But this seemed safer than flying.

She found a coach company and noted the details. She would buy the ticket with cash – she couldn't afford to leave any electronic money tracks for anyone to trace. She would do the safe option when paying for the ferry ticket. She could probably pay in Sterling. If not, she could exchange some. She put aside twenty fifty-pound notes to use for this purpose. That should be more than enough. She also put her remaining Euros in the same purse. She would collect her gig outfits and then dump them somewhere along the way, in a bin or clothes bank or something. If she left them then it was possible that a DNA test might be done on them. She felt sure the police would have her DNA from her kidnapping. She couldn't afford any more loose ends.

All this time, her mind kept returning to how Vincenzo had tracked her to the boat. This eluded her. Had she made a mistake? If so, what was it? And did it matter? Vincenzo was dead. She didn't even know if anyone else was still after her. But better to be safe. She needed to learn from her mistakes if she were to learn and grow.

The band had arranged to meet up for lunch at 1pm in the bar on top. It was here that she made her announcement that she was leaving. She explained that, with Gill's death, she had realised that she needed to be back home on familiar ground. Everyone was disappointed naturally. Ian just looked at her, he knew more than the rest of them. Next, she called James and told him of her decision. He remained calm and professional but advised her that it would be better to tender four weeks' notice, as per her contract, to give him time to replace her. If she didn't, she may not get paid. She suggested that they give Mandy a try out for lead singer - she had a great voice. James asked her once again to stay for two weeks but she said she couldn't. She had family meeting her in Barcelona and it was too late to back out now. With that the call was over.

When she returned to the band, Ian was gone. She assumed he had gone to the toilet. She couldn't see him over by the bar. Howard told her that, if she had a change of heart, the band would put in a good word with James to get her back, or at least in a different band. She thanked him but said she'd made up her mind. She knew it was the right thing to do.
She was feeling a little sad herself, now that it was definite that she only had one more gig with the band. James had said that he would try and fly someone in for tomorrow. Jacey told Mandy that if she fancied stepping up then to call James. Mandy said she

wasn't confident enough in her own voice. Gemma didn't fancy it either.

The final gig went smoothly. No clangers dropped; no words forgotten. She really enjoyed it, knowing that she wouldn't be doing this any time soon, if ever again. Whilst she felt a little sad, she had to move on to survive. After the gig, they all went down to the bar and drank heavily. She had to help Mandy to her cabin. Gemma helped. Gemma wasn't a big drinker and was in better shape than any of the others. Mandy found her key card and they left her lying on her bed. Gemma went back to her own cabin and Jacey went back to hers. They would all see her off when the boat docked in the morning.

PART 4

CHAPTER 86

Jacey slept like a log and she awoke with a clear head. Strange, given all the alcohol consumed. But she had a lot to do. She wrote a note saying goodbye to the band and slipped it under Gemma's door. She then went up on deck and left as soon as the boat docked. She didn't want them seeing her off. She wanted to disappear without any trace and before anyone asked her for contact details to stay in touch. Whilst her two bags were quite heavy; she could manage them. She disembarked and headed straight for the bus company's ticket office and bought a ticket to Bilbao. The journey was billed as lasting some nine hours, with a few stops on the way but that was fine. It was scheduled to depart at 8pm. She had her headphones but no music on her new phone. It had an FM radio that worked using the headphones as an aerial so that sufficed for the journey. She didn't want to waste her data on music streaming, and she slept part of the way. She would use her most recent ID, Amanda Macey, for the journey. When she arrived in England she could dump or hide these old ID's and look at getting a new one. She found the idea of murdering a similar girl and acquiring her identity more appealing than mixing with trash to get a false ID made up. And she had managed this quite easily already.

When she arrived in Bilbao it was approaching 7am. The journey had taken longer than they had indicated. No matter. She hailed a taxi and went straight to the ferry ticket office. She was there before 8am and it wasn't yet open. She found a coffee shop and ordered a double espresso and a sandwich. At 9am she was outside the ticket office as it opened. She purchased a ticket to

Portsmouth that left at noon. She paid in Euros and now had a couple of hours to kill before boarding. The journey would take around eight hours.

She looked around the shops and bought a coat. Something she'd need in England, that she hadn't really needed thus far. It was dark with a fluffy hood. Stylish but also something that could make her disappear in a crowd. Stealth. She was one of the first people to board the ferry. There were a great many cars. She seemed in the minority being on foot. She would also need a car at some point. But she would first need to learn to drive properly. Driving was something she had never done officially. She had liked the TT that Dom had purchased. It was quick and seemed easy to drive. All in good time. During the voyage she would need to make more plans about what to do when she returned to England. She decided that she would go by train from Portsmouth to London then up to Preston. From there she could get a train to Horwich Parkway and then get a cab to Horwich town centre. By the time she arrived in London it would be late at night. She would endeavour to travel up to Preston that evening. Arriving under cover of darkness was ideal given she was effectively breaking into someone else's house. Also, she had to make sure it was empty and hadn't been used since her and Dom had left the place weeks ago.

When she arrived at Euston, she found that she had missed the last train to Preston but there was one to Manchester Piccadilly. She bought a first-class ticket for that train. She could get some sleep and she hoped that first class would be much quieter and have less people than standard. She paid in Sterling cash. The ticket seemed very expensive compared to travel in Europe - welcome back to Blighty. Manchester was a big city; she could hail a cab from there, she had plenty of cash.

At the station she purchased a large coffee and a sandwich and a cake. It was a struggle to carry them all onto the train. The platform was very long. When she was seated, she placed her smaller bag, containing the valuables, on the seat beside her by the window. The larger bag in the overhead space. She put her coat over her like a blanket and settled down to sleep. She dreamt about ships and killers and she was running away from someone, but she couldn't see their face. She knew it was a man and he wanted to kill her. She awoke with a start. The train was moving still, and it was pitch dark. There was still an hour before they arrived at Piccadilly. She had promised to call Mandy to let her know that she had arrived safely, but she had no intention of contacting any of them again, ever. She needed to disappear. If anyone came looking for her on the boat, then the less anyone knew the less likely they were to track her down. No-one would expect her to return to England. After all she'd fled England and Vincenzo knew this. And she still had the letter. She knew it would come in handy at some point – when it did, she would know. For now, it was up her sleeve, hidden in the hand luggage with the rest of the cash and valuables.

CHAPTER 87

The hunt for Vincenzo was over. Now they had the wider team on alert to watch for him or any sign of him anywhere. He would surface at some point. If he didn't then that was fine. Rimmer didn't like loose ends but he knew Vincenzo couldn't get into the building let alone get up to his penthouse apartment. He had very tight security in place and all access codes and key cards had been replaced. And Vincenzo had no cause to want to do Rimmer harm. If anything, he would be coming to Rimmer for help should he be in need of it. If he asked for help, he'd get it – in the form of an execution squad. Rimmer would need to appoint a new deputy and soon. By the appointment of a new deputy, he would have someone who wanted Vincenzo to not turn up even more than he did. He would appoint someone who would have no problem whatsoever dispatching Vincenzo at the first opportunity. He knew who that man would be. He would call a meeting of his family to make the announcement.

CHAPTER 88

It was dark and damp in Manchester. She followed the sign for taxis and found a long road ramping downwards towards the main road. There were a few taxis waiting even at this time. She got in the nearest one, heaving her bags onto the back seat beside her. “Horwich please.” The driver nodded and replied “It’ll take us around half an hour at this time. “ And without further ado he set off. She watched the sparse pedestrians on the rain-soaked pavements. Red reflections of brake lights in the road and in the widows of the shops. She looked up the address on google maps as she wasn’t that familiar with Horwich. Before long they were on a motorway. She recognised the exit as they passed a football stadium on the left-hand side. “Where abouts in Horwich?” asked the driver. “In the centre – that road that crosses the other two main roads – I can’t remember the name.” “I know the one - Winter Hey Lane.” The taxi driver said. Before long he made a right turn, and she knew she was in the town centre. He parked up outside Wright Reads bookshop. “Here OK for you?” the driver asked. “Fine.” She replied and paid him with a fifty-pound note, telling him to keep the change. He seemed pleased with the arrangement. She got out with her bags and he headed off back to Manchester. She looked at Google Maps on her phone and headed off in the direction of Dominic’s house, it wasn’t far at all. As she approached it she was glad to see that there were no lights on. Good, as she expected, the place seemed to be empty. There were no lights on at either side either – in fact hardly any lights on in Robinson Street at all. She took the keys from her coat pocket and strode up to the front door like she owned the place – purely for the benefit of anyone who may be watching from afar of from a window.

She put the key in the door, and it opened, not even a squeak. She knew there was no alarm – Dom didn't want an alarm going off causing the police to be called. He wanted his place empty until his return. That's how he kept it. Now she had returned. She shut the door and locked it. There were a few letters at the back of the door, nothing official like bills, just junk that had likely been delivered by hand. She wondered where the bills went to. She walked to the kitchen and turned on the lights. She then closed the blinds. Everything looked exactly as they had left it a few weeks ago. So much had happened in that brief time. She had grown wings and flown the nest, only to return once again.

Next, she went to the basement door, removed the rug and pulled up the hatch. She half expected to find someone down there, either waiting to jump her or mummified. The room was empty and had a stale smell. She switched on the light. Old sandwich wrappers were still on the floor from her stay down there. She placed her bag with the money, letter and documents under the bed where it couldn't be seen from the hatch. She then went upstairs, secured the safe room and looked in the fridge. Dom had left a few beers in the fridge, nice. She took one out, a Corona, found the bottle opener and drank the cold bottle.

So far so good. The electric was on, no one had been in the place so far as she could tell, and there was beer in the fridge. She took some cash, put on her coat and walked back to the petrol station they'd passed on the way in. She didn't like walking in cold, wet weather – it was a shock after so long. By the time she got there her feet were wet. She picked three sandwiches and a couple of pies, a small bottle of milk, some chocolate bars and four bottles of beer and walked back carrying them in two carrier bags. She needed to choose an ID and find out what she needed to book a course of intense driving lessons. She needed wheels but couldn't drive. She knew how to drive naturally but needed to be legal, in case she was stopped.

She went back into the house, sat by Dom's computer and switched it on. She opened one of the sandwiches and got herself another bottle of beer. She researched the requirements for driving legally. She needed an identity document – a passport, £34 pounds, and an NI number. She'd also have to pay online so she'd need a bank account. To open a bank account, she'd need bills with an address on. She had none of these, only passports. She either had to obtain documents in order to make a proper application and pass the test or acquire the documents and learn to drive herself. She couldn't even buy a car at auction without documents. She'd need a license and insurance. She needed documents so she could produce them in the event of being stopped. Could she steal some? Maybe she could find a homeless person who had documents and buy or steal them. Fat chance of finding a homeless person with a driving license on them she thought. It was becoming more complicated than she had imagined.

But first she had to make plans. When she knew what her plans were then she could better understand her requirements in terms of travel. Then, she could make plans to sort out transport. She would also keep an eye out for someone who was physically similar to herself with a view to stealing their identify and possibly bumping them off aka Stiff Steph. Maybe a Stiff Stella or a Stiff Sheena.

But there was also another way. She needed to think long and hard about the pros and cons of this other way. She could go back to her true identify – turn up after being kidnapped. She could also then inherit her father's estate. But how could she effect the transition? Would anyone believe she'd been held hostage for so many weeks? She knew the answer to this one at least was yes, particularly in America. Girls had been held for longer periods than that, but these abductions usually involved being held for sex, not ransom money. Maybe she could say the kidnapper went to collect the money and her father hadn't shown up – she had no idea why, but the kidnapper was pissed off and kept her thereafter. She certainly had the right location for such a story. She even had evidence of her being held down there for the period – DNA, sandwich wrappers, and probably more. She could dirty up some clothes, and tell how her captor took her upstairs, blindfolded her to shower once or twice a week. If she were to pull that one off, she'd have to get a very tight story and be able to evidence it. If they saw through it she'd be in deep shit. That was one risky way forward. But nevertheless, it was an option to her. She even thought she'd lost some weight in recent weeks. Although she'd been drinking more, she'd been eating quite well – hardly any fast food. She lay out on the settee to consider her options and was soon asleep.

When she awoke it was fully daylight outside. These old terraced houses had a front room and a back room. She would stay in the back room and not use the front room so the house remained untouched in appearance to any neighbours who walked past every day and who may be inclined to notice even the slightest change. No doubt they were all curious about the neighbour who was hardly ever here. He wouldn't have spoken to any of them she was sure of that. If she did meet anyone and couldn't avoid contact, she could claim the house was hers and she travelled a lot. She'd keep the door closed so no light seeped from back to front to become visible from the outside. She wanted the front of the house to remain as it was, empty.

Today she needed to hone her plans and get more beer - in that order. She also needed some new, scruffier clothes so she could blend in. She also needed a new SIM card for her phone. She should dispose of the current one in case anyone was tracking it. Maybe she was being paranoid, but she had money and SIM cards were cheap. She ate a sandwich and one of the pies that she had bought from the petrol station the previous evening. The pie was dry and greasy - British food at its best. But nevertheless, she ate it. During the afternoon she searched the internet and made plans.

When it became dark, she put her wastepaper into one of the carrier bags she had bought the previous evening and set off into town. She went out of the back door where she was less likely to be noticed. Then got the bus to Asda, only a couple of miles away and back towards the football stadium. She wore her cap to cover her face slightly. After buying two pairs of jeans, a couple of tee shirts, another cheap coat and a pair of trainers. She got the bus back into Horwich and stopped by the late shop and bought six bottles of beer and some crisps. When she returned to the house, she went in through the back door, not having come across anyone in close proximity to the house. She put the beers in the fridge and then got back to her plan, taking with her the last of the original, cold beers. She continued to go over all her options in her mind in order to work out her next step. This time she wouldn't make any mistakes. She would focus on her planning for however long it took – possibly days? But this time it would be perfect.

PART 5

CHAPTER 89

The weather in London was depressing. Grey skies, black clouds and fine drizzle. It had been like this for a couple of days now and didn't bode well for the weekend. It was Friday night and most people had finished work for the week. DI Cable was clearing his stuff in readiness for leaving the office until Monday when his phone rang. "Bob, you'll never believe it. She's turned up, she's only gone and fucking turned up!" Bob had no idea what Bill was talking about. "Who?" replied Bob. "Who's fucking turned up?" His patience had worn thinner and thinner during the course of the week. He was about to leave and the only thing between him and the weekend was Bill on the other end of the phone. "The Montgomery girl! It turns out that she was being held captive in a house somewhere in Greater Manchester, Bolton in fact." Bob was both elated and highly pissed off, both at the same time. "Bolton? Bolton! Fuck. Where is she now?" he said, his mind spinning. He knew his weekend was now completely trashed. He couldn't just leave as his mind would be on this case once again. He had to work it through. "In an ambulance on the way to hospital to get checked over. She wasn't too bad by all accounts, but the medics thought she'd been used for sex and treated a little rough and she hadn't eaten or drunk for a while, but she'll be fine in a few days. She seemed understandably traumatised by the whole affair – weeks of being incarcerated in some psycho's cellar - apparently, he'd turned it into a sound proofed prison cell. And she didn't know anything about her father. When they found her, the first thing she asked for was Daddy, poor kid. They had to tell her there and then that he wasn't for coming any time soon, or indeed at all. She was in bits, just like her father... sorry. Well, she knew nothing about the terrorist attacks or anything with her being locked down in that cellar. She said that the guy had blindfolded her and taken her upstairs for a shower occasionally and this is where he sometimes raped her, then showered her to remove any evidence she assumed. Apparently, he'd told her that he would be away for a day or two and left her some bottled water and sandwiches, apparently this was quite usual, but one of the neighbours must have seen something funny that aroused their attention as an anonymous call came in that someone suspected a girl was being held at that address. The caller hadn't as yet been traced, must be a neighbour, they're being questioned now."

Bill needed a big breather after all that talking. Bob's ears were buzzing. After a brief pause Bob said, "It is still technically our case, I guess we should get over to the hospital now then.". "No need Bob, the doctors have said she won't be talking until tomorrow at the earliest. So, I suggest we meet at the hospital at 10am and take it from there." Bob agreed and with that hung up. All the way home he thought about this poor girl. What an unusual case – you wouldn't believe her story if you read it in a book. Kidnapped, dad blown up, locked in a cellar for weeks, used as a sex toy. Shit really does happen.

CHAPTER 90

The girl was still very shaken up. She'd had a lot to deal with, being kidnapped, repeatedly raped, held hostage, finding out about terrorist the attacks and then that her father had been blown up in one of these attacks. After their first, fairly brief interview, the doctors would only allow them ten minutes, they had pushed initially for a description of the man. This would be given without ever having seen him as she was wearing a blindfold. She told how he had broken into her home, knocked her out, broken her nose and chained her in the cellar. After a period of grooming her, he had then latterly left her unchained as, by now, he'd broken her down and she couldn't see any means of escape. She described his accent as sounding possibly Italian – he certainly had an accent but tried to disguise it.

The local police were searching the house from top to bottom. They found old sandwich boxes dating back to her initial capture. The cellar was a stinking mess, shit and piss everywhere, poor kid. The only things of interest they'd found upstairs were a small, Italian, expensive travel bag and, hidden in the kitchen, a letter. The letter disclosed details of certain crimes that were never made public. It looked like the letter implicated a certain half Italian businessman known to the police. In fact, his whole organisation was known to police but, so far, untouchable.

They long suspected this organisation was behind several organised crime rackets including drug smuggling and small-time protection rackets probably for fun or even to uphold family traditions. The guy implicated in the letter was a senior figure in this organisation. After legitimate enquiries into his whereabouts, it transpired that none of his business associates could claim to have seen him for a couple of weeks.Damn convenient that, Bob thought. They knew they would only get cursory information from his supposedly straight up colleagues; they couldn't even tell Bob what the guy actually did as his job – all jargon. Find him and they might be on to something.

There was also a webcam installed in the basement. It could be viewed remotely. This was how her captor monitored her. The techies would be trying to see if there was a way to track any device that had connected to the camera, but they didn't hold out much hope. For now, there would be a news blackout. It was possible the guy would return and, if he did, the police would be waiting for him. The letter would need to be studied and verified. If it were usable as evidence, it would go a long way towards putting the bastard in the dock. The organisation had plenty of money and expensive lawyers so the police would need a watertight case to get a conviction. This letter was a coup for them, if it turned out to be real. A street which was once a sea of black windows was now a sea of twitching curtains and lights.

CHAPTER 91

By the end of the week, they knew the guy wouldn't be coming back. If they hadn't rescued the girl, she'd be dead by now, dehydration. Whoever the mystery caller was they had certainly saved her life. He must have caught wind of the situation, or something had happened to him. By now they couldn't keep a lid on the news getting out any longer. The papers had agreed to wait for five days and this period was now up. It was front page news in all the papers. The girl, Annie, had been released from hospital and taken to a safe house and was under twenty-four-hour police protection until they found the guy who had taken her and they had the evidence they needed to bring a prosecution. She would be there for several months, maybe even longer.

They had succeeded in getting an injunction on the papers to prevent them from printing her picture. So far, no pictures of her had been released. They'd also pulled her social media accounts and anything with her picture on, the day they found her. But they simply didn't have enough to go on. They suspected her captor was part of the crime organisation headed up by Rimmer and Dente. Dente was still missing – it was entirely possible, and looking probable, that Dente was indeed the kidnapper himself. He could have had help from within his organisation. All the other Italian so-called colleagues had watertight alibis for key times, but this would always be the case and didn't really mean anything. They closed ranks.

Tracing and corroborating Dente's movements over the past few weeks would be near impossible. The police working the case all now thought it was Dente who had kidnapped her.

The trouble was, it was difficult proving it either way. No-one would say if and when they'd seen him or had dealings with him. They had no idea of his whereabouts over the past year let alone days or weeks.

They suspected that Vincenzo Dente might be holed up in Rimmer's building in London – in hiding. Rimmer strenuously denied this but the police couldn't get a warrant to search the place. In time, they would. Rimmer and his associates had friends in high places. The police suspected that Dente had left the girl to do some business in London, expecting to return in a couple of days. He'd left the letter secreted in the house, so he must have expected to return, or he would have destroyed it or taken it with him. Bob wondered why he hadn't destroyed it the second he got hold of it. The only explanation was that he hung on to it as a sort of trophy or leverage for something he had planned. If he went down maybe he could use it to help bring others down. Who knows! Either that, or it wasn't Dente who did the kidnapping, someone on the opposite side to him – whatever that was. Unfortunately, the author was no doubt dead, probably murdered. They knew Dente was the likeliest candidate to have organised this, or even done himself, hence the trophy. But Rimmer's people were careful and well connected. Nothing stuck. But it was in the news now. Bob was waiting to see what came out of the woodwork. When someone as big and bad as Dente leave town, the rats come up to fight to take his place. Forensics had found the Italian bag had been cleaned down, but minute traces of DNA had been recovered. They would compare this to Dente's. And whilst it wouldn't prove he was the kidnapper; it would go a long way to supporting this dialogue.

Bob would add the letter and the bag to his growing pile of circumstantial evidence relating to Rimmer's business empire which included this kidnapping case amongst many others. One day, with the favourable ear of a magistrate, he would get to see the inside of Rimmer's empire, and only then could they hope to make something stick. He was getting there, slowly. He was hoping that Dente would turn up, but in his heart of hearts, he knew that Dente was either hiding, or more likely dead as a result of his trip to London having indeed been the sole kidnapper as it now seemed likely. Hopefully the body would pop up at some point and tie up that loose end. But if it were one of his business associates that had bumped him off then Bob felt sure that Dente would disappear as sure as Jimmy Hoffa had done all those years ago.

CHAPTER 92

Annie was curled up in bed. She was 'coming to terms' with the shocking news that her father had died. Her mother, who had been living in South Africa, was coming over to look after her in the safe house. She couldn't go back to her old home to even visit. In fact, the police were talking about giving her a new identity to protect her. She was a potential witness in part of a long running battle with Rimmer's organisation. Witnesses seldom lived long when up against Rimmer, but they hadn't told her that.

So far, her plan had worked well. The anonymous tipoff didn't get the attention of the police as quick as she had thought it would though. She was beginning to think she would indeed die in that cellar by the time they arrived! This served her well however, in that the room was a mess – three days of toileting in the bucket and she was dehydrated and hungry. She would be OK in the long run. Her father's estate wasn't small, and she would be well looked after when it all went through. Her other documents and cash were secreted where she knew they'd be safe for several months.

At some point, when she had her new identity, she would retrieve them and then disappear on the next leg of her career – planning for this next, exciting phase was well underway. She needed to make sure her mother didn't complicate things. She wanted a legitimate, new identity and she wanted his cash. From then on, she could start a new life with no one coming after her and no loose ends, all legal and fully above board.

At her request, she'd been given a guitar and she was learning quickly, using videos from the internet. Sadie, her old best friend, had been allowed to visit her. Sadie said that everyone had thought that she was dead and, even though she'd had a rough ordeal, at least she was still alive. Her friends from school had all signed a card and Sadie had brought it, along with some flowers and chocolates. Funny how a few short months can change a person and change their life. Sadie was the closest thing she had to a friend at the start of this journey, now she seemed like a little girl, just as Annie had been, not that long ago. But no more. She had flown the nest, a cuckoo all along. And she would fly high, just as soon as she put all this behind her and started her next new life.

CHAPTER 93

Rimmer was watching the news – he couldn't believe what he was hearing. The Little Weasel had turned up – she'd been locked in a fucking cellar for weeks. So, who the fuck had Vincenzo been chasing after? And why? Something didn't add up. Vincenzo was absolutely certain that the girl he was after, was Little Weasel. Vincenzo didn't make mistakes on such a scale, it had to have been her. But he must have made mistakes, as she was still alive, and he likely wasn't. He'd met his match.

It would be some time before he understood the full picture and what it meant to him. But understand it he would. And when he did, there would be only one sure way to tie up this very big and potentially damaging loose end. But he had to be patient. When the case was finally dropped, like all the others, she'd be given a new identity and then he would be able to set about finding her. His team would do the rest. But for now, he had to be patient.

THE END... FOR NOW.

Acknowledgements

Thank you to everyone who bought my first book, the first of this trilogy. I hope you enjoy reading this one even more.

And a big thank you to Janet Yeadon and Sean Moore for proof-reading the first edition of this book.

If you would like to discover more about the author and his works please visit www.roberthpage.co.uk

Printed in Great Britain
by Amazon

55735422R00163